THE

PERFECT

ALIBI

THE

PERFECT

ALIBI

Phillip Margolin

Minotaur Books
New York

THE PERFECT ALIBI. Copyright © 2019 by Phillip Margolin. All rights reserved. Printed in the United States of America. For information, address St. Martin's Press, 175 Fifth Avenue, New York, N.Y. 10010.

www.minotaurbooks.com

Designed by Omar Chapa

The Library of Congress Cataloging-in-Publication Data is available upon request.

ISBN 978-1-250-11752-6 (hardcover)
ISBN 978-1-250-11753-3 (ebook)

Our books may be purchased in bulk for promotional, educational, or business use. Please contact your local bookseller or the Macmillan Corporate and Premium Sales Department at 1-800-221-7945, extension 5442, or by email at MacmillanSpecialMarkets@macmillan.com.

First Edition: March 2019

10 9 8 7 6 5 4 3 2 1

For Noelle, Brianna, Tess, Brent, Camille, Pat, Janelle, and George
—my new family. Thanks for your warm welcome.

PART ONE

THE GREEK GOD

CHAPTER ONE

At five thirty on a rainy Monday morning in October, Robin Lockwood ran the five miles from her apartment to McGill's gym in Portland's Pearl District. For decades, the Pearl had been home to dusty, decaying warehouses. Then the developers moved in. Overnight, most of the grimy, run-down buildings were replaced by gleaming high-end condos, trendy restaurants, and chic boutiques. McGill's was on the ground floor of one of the few old, brick buildings that had escaped gentrification. It was dimly lit and filled with the rank odor you never found in modern, air-conditioned workout emporiums.

Barry McGill, the gym's owner, was taciturn, monosyllabic, and profane. Rumor had it that he had mob connections, but people with any amount of common sense were too wise to ask him about it. Salt-and-pepper stubble sprouted on McGill's fleshy jowls and whiskey-reddened cheeks. He'd fought as a middleweight in the 1980s and had the broken nose and scar tissue to prove it, but his days as a 165-pounder were long past, and the weight he carried in his gut, butt, and thighs had elevated him to the heavyweight division.

"Lockwood," McGill called out when Robin walked in.

"Yeah?"

"See the kid slacking off at the heavy bag?"

A young man in his early twenties was hitting the bag with lackadaisical punches that barely made it move. Robin judged his weight at welter, around 147 pounds, slightly more than her 140, and she couldn't see an ounce of fat on him.

"That's Mitch Healy. He just won his first two MMA fights and his head is swelling. Want to take him down a peg?"

Robin was five feet eight inches, with a wiry build, blue eyes, high cheekbones, and short blond hair. She had earned some of her Yale Law School tuition fighting in mixed martial arts matches and had been ranked as high as ninth nationally. Her straight nose was a testament to her defensive skills as a cage fighter.

"In case you haven't noticed," Robin said, "that 'kid' is a man, and you just told me that he's in training."

"I never took Rockin' Robin for a pussy," McGill said, referring to Robin's ring nickname and the old rock-and-roll song Robin's fans would sing when she walked into the octagon.

"Fuck you, Barry," Robin snapped back.

"I wouldn't ask if I didn't think you could give him a hard time."

Robin gave McGill a hard stare. He raised an eyebrow. Robin sighed.

"Are you gonna cover my dental work?" she asked.

"Fuck no," McGill answered.

"You always were a cheap bastard."

McGill grinned.

Robin went to the locker room to change.

"Hey, Mitch!" McGill shouted when Robin returned.

"Yeah?"

"Come over here. I got you someone to spar with."

Healy looked around as he walked over. "Are they in the locker room?"

"Nah. She's right in front of you."

Healy looked at Robin. Then he laughed. "She's a girl, Barry."

"That's one brilliant deduction. You're a regular Sherlock Holmes."

"I'm not sparring with a girl."

"You see anyone else around? You been dancing with that bag for the past twenty minutes. Might as well dance with a flesh-and-blood female. Hell, maybe you can give her a few pointers."

Healy hesitated. Then he gave Robin the once-over and shrugged. "Okay, let's go."

Robin had stopped fighting professionally after suffering a brutal knockout on a pay-per-view card in Las Vegas in her first year in law school, but she was still in great shape. Robin could see that Healy had no respect for her, which meant he would underestimate her. When they got on the mat, Robin started moving like a beginner, flicking out slow, sloppy jabs. Healy looked bored and he pawed at her unenthusiastically. Robin moved a little closer. Healy threw another lazy jab. Robin slid past it, spun behind him, threw one arm through his crotch, and encircled his waist with her other arm. Then she grasped the encircling arm with the hand that was between Healy's legs and lifted him in the air. While Healy thrashed around, Robin aimed his head at the mat and drove him straight down. When he hit the mat, Robin wrapped her legs around him in a figure-four scissors and slapped on a choke hold. Healy struggled for a while, then tapped out.

Robin rolled off Healy and jumped to her feet. Healy sprang up. He looked furious. Robin circled and Healy charged. Robin counted on his anger clouding his judgment. She sidestepped the charge and landed a shot to Healy's jaw that would have unhinged it if she hadn't pulled the punch. Healy stumbled and Robin snapped a kick that landed on the side of Healy's head. She pulled the kick, too, but it still sent Healy sideways.

"Okay, that's enough!" McGill shouted.

Robin bounced out of range and Healy glared at her.

"I said, that's enough, Mitch. Now, why don't you start your workout again. And let's put some effort in this time."

McGill rarely complimented anyone, but he nodded at Robin. "Next month is a freebie," he said as she took off her headgear and walked to the weights.

"Who the fuck was that?" Healy asked.

"A girly girl who just kicked your ass," McGill answered.

Healy watched Robin for a second before turning back to McGill. "Is she single?"

Robin was still feeling pretty good an hour later, when she walked into the offices of Barrister, Berman & Lockwood. The firm took up one side of the tenth floor of a downtown high-rise, and the waiting room was decorated with glass coffee tables and comfortable sofas and armchairs.

After law school, Robin had gotten a clerkship with Stanley Cloud, the chief justice of the Oregon Supreme Court. When her clerkship ended, her boss had helped Robin get her dream job, a position as an associate with Regina Barrister, the queen of the Oregon criminal defense bar. Shortly after Robin was hired, Regina started showing signs of dementia while she was defending a complex death penalty case. When the case ended, Regina stopped practicing law and turned over her firm to Robin and Mark Berman, her other associate. Justice Cloud was Regina's lover, and he had retired from the supreme court so they could travel the world while Regina still had the capacity to enjoy the journey.

As soon as Robin walked in, Linda Garrett, the firm's receptionist, pointed at two women who were seated in the reception area. "They were waiting in the hall when I opened up," Linda said. "They don't have an appointment, but they want to see you."

Robin studied the women. The contrast between them was dramatic. The younger woman looked to be in her late teens or early twenties. She was slender—gaunt, actually—like someone with an eating disorder.

The older woman was so obese that she barely fit in her chair. Fat rolled over the top of her stretch pants, and her doughlike arms and face were rounded and undefined.

The contrast extended to their posture. The younger woman curled up in her chair, and she looked as if she'd rather be anywhere else. The older woman leaned forward aggressively, her anger energizing her to the point where stillness became impossible.

"Hi, I'm Robin Lockwood. I understand you'd like to see me."

The older woman struggled to her feet. "We most definitely do," she said.

"Why don't you come back to my office."

Robin walked slowly so the heavyset woman could keep up. She led the women down a long hall decorated with prints by Honoré Daumier that depicted lawyers and courts from the 1800s. On the way, they passed the office of Jeff Hodges, the firm's in-house investigator, and Mark Berman, Robin's partner.

Mark was thirty-two with long brown hair, brown eyes, and the rock-hard body he had developed while competing on the University of Washington's nationally ranked crew. Robin's partner was married, with a four-year-old daughter, and seemed immune to stress. When Regina retired to travel the world, he had graciously given Robin Regina's corner office, which had a spectacular view of the Willamette River, the foothills of the Cascade Range, and the snowcaps that crowned Mount Hood and Mount St. Helens.

"I'm Maxine Stark, and this is my daughter, Randi," the older woman said when they were seated with the door closed. "Randi's been raped, and we want you to help us set things right."

"When did this rape occur?" Robin asked.

"Three weeks ago. The cops already got the guy."

"What do you want me to do, Mrs. Stark?"

"We want you to make Blaine Hastings suffer the way he made my Randi suffer. He's an animal, and animals belong in cages."

"I can't help you there, Mrs. Stark. A district attorney will be prosecuting. That's the person who will try to send Mr. Hastings to prison."

"But you can take away the money that made him so high and mighty, can't you? You can sue for every penny he has."

"I can help you sue," Robin agreed.

"Good! That's why we're here."

Randi Stark's shoulders were hunched, and she seemed to be pulling into herself. Robin guessed that her mother's aggressive behavior was upsetting her.

"I'll need to talk to your daughter so I can find out the basis for her lawsuit."

"Go right ahead. She has nothing to hide."

"I assume you're aware of the attorney–client privilege that makes anything Randi says to me confidential."

"I watch a lot of lawyer shows on TV," Maxine assured her.

"Then you know that Randi will lose the privilege if a third party hears what she says to her lawyer."

A look of confusion clouded Maxine's features. "I'm her mother."

"Unfortunately, there is no mother–daughter privilege. So, I'm going to have to ask you to wait outside while we talk. My secretary can get you coffee or tea while you wait."

"Randi needs me," Maxine insisted.

"Of course, you're her mother. But you don't want to be the cause of losing her lawsuit, do you?"

"Well, no, but—"

"I knew you'd understand. And I'll call you back in as soon as we're done."

Maxine hesitated for a second, then slowly levered herself out of the chair. "I'll be outside if you need me, honey," she said before she waddled out of Robin's office.

Randi relaxed as soon as her mother left the room.

"This has to be a terrible ordeal for you," Robin said when her office door closed.

"She won't leave me alone," Randi answered, not realizing that Robin was talking about the rape. "All she wants is the money."

"And what do you want?"

For the first time since entering her lawyer's office, Randi came alive. She sat up and stared into Robin's eyes. "I want that bastard to pay. Money won't ever make up for what Blaine did to me. That's not why I'm here. But the Hastingses think they can get away with anything, and I want them to know that for once, they're not going to be Kings of the Universe."

Robin frowned. "Do you have a history with Blaine Hastings and his family?"

"We went to the same high school."

"Did you date?" she asked.

"Are you kidding? I don't live in a mansion, and I don't drive a fancy car or dress like the stuck-up princesses who gave him blow jobs at their sorority parties."

"You sound like you really hate Hastings. Did something specific happen to you before the rape?"

"There was a guy I was dating in high school, Ryan Tucker," Randi answered quietly. "Blaine baited him. Then he beat the hell out of him. But he didn't stop there. He called the cops and got his buddies to swear that Ryan started the fight.

"Mr. Hastings gives money to every politician's campaign. So, no charges for Mr. Perfect, and juvie for Ryan. I don't know what happened to him in there, but Ryan wasn't the same when he got out—and Blaine just kept moving toward silver spoon heaven."

Randi's outburst seemed to have exhausted her. Robin made some notes so Randi would have some quiet time to pull herself together.

"Are you still in contact with Ryan, in case we want to interview him?"

Randi choked up. "A month after he got out, he . . . he killed himself."

"I'm so sorry."

"Yeah, well . . ." Randi shrugged.

"Do you want some water?" Robin asked.

"No, I'm okay," Randi said, but she didn't sound okay.

"What does Blaine Hastings do now?" Robin asked when Randi had regained her composure. "Is he working or in school?"

"Blaine is a big football star at Oregon. I hear he's probably gonna go pro."

"What year is he in?"

"Senior."

"I take it you want me to sue Blaine Hastings for damages and pain and suffering because he raped you?"

"Yes."

"If Hastings is a student, he won't have much money. We might sue him, but you might not get anything."

Randi looked embarrassed. "My mom did some research on the Hastingses. There was a trust fund he'd get when he turned twenty-one, and he just had his birthday."

Robin studied her client. Randi seemed convincing. She probably did want a measure of justice. But Robin thought that her mother was probably motivated by money.

"Why don't you tell me a little about yourself."

Randi shrugged. "Not much to tell. I'm twenty, I graduated

high school, and I'm in community college, studying to be a nurse. Still living with my mother."

"Where's your home?"

"We used to live in a housing project, but Mom got this insurance settlement and she used some of it to buy a place in Northeast Portland."

"Is your mom married?"

"Divorced. He walked out on us when I was two, and we haven't seen him since. Good riddance, like Mom says."

"So, you two live alone?"

Randi nodded.

"Does your mom work?"

"She used to, but she was in a car crash and she's been on disability ever since. I work. School's part-time."

"What do you do?"

"I'm a waitress."

"Okay. Now, where did the rape occur?"

"At a frat party. Annie Roche, my girlfriend, found out about it. We weren't doing anything, so we went."

"Did Annie see what happened?"

"Not all of it, but some."

"Have the police interviewed Annie?"

Randi nodded.

"Is she going to be a witness for the State?"

Randi nodded again.

"You're going to be the star witness at Blaine Hastings's trial, and in your lawsuit, so I have to ask you some personal questions."

"I told the cops. I got probation for shoplifting once."

"Is there anything else Hastings's lawyer can dig up?"

"Not on me."

"Have you been sexually active?"

"I'm not a virgin, if that's what you mean."

"Exactly," Robin said as she flashed a kindly smile. "But let me ask you this. Hastings is going to say that you're making up the rape so you can get his money. Have you ever accused another boy of rape?"

"No. I wouldn't do that."

"Why don't you tell me what happened at the frat party."

"Annie and me went to the PSU–Oregon game. We knew some of the guys on both teams from high school. Annie found out that there was a party that night at one of the PSU frat houses, and we decided to go.

"When we got to the party, Blaine was in a group of people I knew. I started talking to someone. Then, at some point, Blaine started talking to me, and a little later, he asked me to dance."

"Why did you talk to him if you hated him because of what happened to Ryan?"

Randi flushed. "You're right. I should have walked away. But I'd been drinking more than I should have, and, well, I'm not proud of what I did, but, like I said, he didn't pay any attention to me in high school and he's a big football star, so I was flattered by the attention."

"Okay. What happened after you started talking?"

"There was this slow dance and he started touching me and I got a little hot. The lights were low and he kissed me just before the dance ended."

"Did you resist when he kissed you?"

Randi blushed. "No. I kissed him back. And that's when he whispered in my ear that we should go someplace private."

"What did you do?"

"He headed for a bedroom in the back of the house and I followed him."

"So, this was consensual?"

"Right then, yeah."

"You said that you'd been drinking at the party?"

"I had a few."

"Were you drunk when you followed Blaine to the bedroom?"

"I was tipsy, but I knew what I was doing."

"What about drugs?"

"No. The cops asked me the same thing at the hospital. They took some blood. The DA said the tests showed the booze but I was clean, no drugs."

"You went to the hospital after the incident?"

"Right away." Randi became animated again. "And they did a rape kit. The stupid fuck didn't use a condom, so they have some of his DNA—and the DA says it's what they need to put that prick away."

"In many of these cases, the man will say he had sex but it was consensual."

"Well, this wasn't. My guard was down because of the booze, and I did let Blaine make out. But I told him to stop when he started feeling between my legs."

"How clear were you?"

"Pretty fucking clear. First, I said no, but he kept jabbing his finger between my legs and telling me how much he liked me. I told him I wanted to stop and I tried to sit up, but he pushed me down."

"Did you fight him?"

Randi barked out a humorless laugh. "Miss Lockwood, Blaine is a linebacker at the U of O. He's a solid muscle. Look at me. He could bench-press me with one hand."

"So, you didn't resist?"

"I did. I tried to push him off. That's when he slapped me and told me to be a good girl if I didn't want to get hurt."

"What did you do?"

"I shut up and shut my eyes and he pulled up my skirt and ripped off my panties."

"Do you have the ripped panties?"

"I gave them to the cops."

"Okay, that's good. Now I need to know, did he enter you? Was there penetration? That's important in a rape case."

Randi choked up. "It hurt. I was dry, and he . . ."

"Do you want to stop? Do you want some water?"

Randi shook her head.

"Who did you tell about what happened, and when did you tell them?"

"I didn't have to tell. Annie came in right after he finished. I was crying and saying, 'Get off me.' She'd seen me go to the bedroom with Blaine, and she knew his reputation."

"What is Blaine's reputation?"

"I've heard I'm not his first victim."

"He's raped other women?"

Randi hesitated. "That I can't say for sure. I mean, no one ever told me that specifically. But I've heard that he doesn't always take no for an answer."

"Okay. What did Annie do when she saw you go into the bedroom with Blaine?"

"She followed me down the hall, and she opened the door when she heard me yell."

"What did Blaine do?"

"When the door opened, he told Annie to get out, but she's got guts. She told Blaine to get off me or she'd call the cops. Blaine started for her and she threatened to scream. That's when he looked worried for the first time. Then he zipped up his pants and stormed out. Annie and me waited until we thought it was safe. Then she drove me to the hospital. I said I didn't want to go; I just wanted to forget the whole thing. But she convinced me I shouldn't let him get away with it."

"She was right."

"When are you going to sue Blaine?" Randi asked.

"We have plenty of time to file a complaint, so I'm going to wait until we see how the trial comes out. I'll sit through it. If he's con-victed, we should be in good shape."

Half an hour later, Robin showed the Starks out. Then she walked into Jeff Hodges's office. Robin's investigator was six-two with shaggy, reddish-blond hair that almost touched his broad shoulders. He had green eyes, pale, freckled skin, walked with a limp, and had a faint tracery of scars on his face. The scars and the limp were the result of injuries suffered in an explosion in a meth lab Jeff had raided when he was a police officer.

Robin had been attracted to Jeff since she joined Regina's firm. There was a moment during a recent case when she'd asked him to go to bed with her. It was in Atlanta, right after someone had tried to kill her. Jeff was enough of a gentleman to avoid taking advan-tage of the situation. Wary of an office romance, neither had ever mentioned what had happened. That didn't stop Robin from find-ing Jeff attractive, and she was certain that he felt the same way but was as gun-shy as she was.

"We just got an interesting new case," Robin said as she took a seat across the desk from Jeff.

"What do you want me to do?" Jeff asked when Robin finished filling him in.

"Find out who's prosecuting and see if they'll share, but it wouldn't hurt to get some background on Blaine Hastings. See if you can find any other women who say that he molested them. And interview Annie Roche if you can do it quietly. We don't want to give Hastings's lawyer ammunition to argue that Randi is setting him up to make money with a lawsuit."

"Gotcha, boss."

Robin liked spending time with Jeff, and she was tempted to ask if he wanted to go to lunch, but Jeff's intercom buzzed and Linda asked if Robin was with him.

"I'm here," Robin said.

"Judge Wright phoned while you were in with your clients. He wants you to call him."

"I'll go back to my office. Get him on the line for me, will you?"

Robin liked Harold Wright and considered him to be one of the sharpest jurists on the Multnomah County Circuit Court, but she didn't have any cases in the judge's court right now. She wondered what he wanted to talk about. Moments after she was back in her office, she found out.

"Robin, I have a favor to ask," the judge said when they were connected.

"Shoot."

"A police officer was killed last night, and the DA has charged a man named Everett Henderson with aggravated murder. It's going to be a controversial case. You're next up on the capital murder court-appointment list. Do you have the time to handle it?"

"Yeah. My caseload isn't too demanding right now."

"Okay. Thanks, Robin."

"Who's the DA?"

"Rex Kellerman."

Robin stifled the urge to swear. Rex Kellerman was a handsome runner of marathons, who dyed the gray strands mixed into his wavy black hair. He sported a well-groomed mustache, a year-round tan, and looked great smiling at juries with pearly white teeth and laughing blue eyes. Anyone who didn't know him would take him for a gentleman. Within the bar, Kellerman had a reputation as a dishonest little shit who could never be trusted.

"I assume you waited until I agreed to take the case to tell me that Rex was prosecuting."

Wright chuckled. "No backsies."

"Yeah, well, you just lost my vote when you run for reelection."

The judge laughed; then he said, "See you in court, Counselor."

CHAPTER TWO

English majors were expected to read highbrow literature, and law school students were supposed to spend all their time slogging through legal minutiae, but Douglas Armstrong had a dirty little secret. As an undergraduate and a law student, he had spent an inordinate amount of time reading mystery novels. Agatha Christie's Hercule Poirot was his favorite detective. That's why the lawyer had fallen into the habit of using his "little grey cells" to deduce facts about potential clients as soon as they were ushered into his law office.

Blaine Hastings Sr. pushed his way past Armstrong's secretary, and Armstrong decided Hastings was a take-charge type who was used to having his way. Hastings's thinning blond hair was combed across his scalp to hide his bald spot, which the lawyer took for a sign of vanity. The broken corpuscles that crisscrossed his puffy nose, and the beefy man's beet-red complexion, screamed *alcoholic*. His six-foot-plus size, thick chest and shoulders, and the paunch that strained the fabric of his buttoned suit coat were the physique of an athlete gone to seed. And he kept sucking his gut in, another indication that the man was vain. Armstrong also noted that Blaine's suit was expensive—possibly hand-tailored—so the Hastingses had money.

These deductions were strengthened by a quick scan of Hastings's wife. Gloria followed her husband into Armstrong's office, her hands gripping her purse tightly and her shoulders bowed from tension. The expensively dressed bottle blonde looked like an aging cheerleader who had suffered through too many plastic surgeries and undergone way too many tanning studio appointments in a losing battle with Father Time. Cheerleaders dated football players, and people with money could afford plastic surgery and spa treatments.

Armstrong indicated the client chairs on the other side of his granite-topped desk and said, "Please, have a seat."

Blaine accepted the offer grudgingly, which told the attorney that he was not in the habit of following orders even when they were benign. Gloria sat stiffly. Her stress radiated toward Armstrong like a laser.

"How can I help you?" Armstrong asked.

"It's our son," Gloria answered. "He was arrested this morning."

"What is he charged with?"

"He said he was arrested for rape," Gloria answered. She sounded bewildered.

"What's your son's name?"

"Blaine Hastings Jr.," Senior answered proudly.

"And how old is he?"

"He's just turned twenty-one," Gloria said.

"Do you know where he's being held?"

"He's in the jail across the park from the courthouse," Mrs. Hastings answered.

"And they won't let us see him," Blaine added indignantly.

"Yes, well, there are visiting hours," Armstrong explained. "But a lawyer can talk to him anytime. Can you tell me a little about your son?"

"Blaine is unique, a shooting star," his father said forcefully. "He's a senior at Oregon, an honor student, and a preseason All-American linebacker. The pros are looking at him."

"Did you play football, Mr. Hastings?" the lawyer asked in an attempt to stroke Hastings's ego.

Blaine pushed out his chest. "Offensive line. I was a second-team All-American at Oregon, and I was drafted by the Steelers." Hastings frowned and tapped his left knee. "Blew this sucker out during training camp, and that was that." Then he brightened. "I always wondered how I would have done in the pros, but the bum knee turned out to be a blessing in disguise. I went into insurance and made more money than I ever would have playing football."

"So you were your son's inspiration?"

"Blaine inspires us," Gloria said. "He's an angel. He could never have done what they're saying."

"Has he ever been in trouble before?" the attorney asked.

"Of course not," Senior answered indignantly. "Not real trouble." Senior laughed nervously. "Boys will be boys. That type of thing."

"Were there ever problems with his relationship with a girl?" Armstrong asked diplomatically.

"Blaine can get any girl he wants," Senior answered, sidestepping the question. "They fall all over themselves when he's in a room. He would never have to resort to rape to get laid!"

Gloria reached out and covered her husband's balled fists. "Please, there's no need to talk like that."

Blaine's head snapped around, and he glared at his wife. "You're worried about my language when our son is caged up like an animal?"

For the time being, Armstrong decided not to pursue the possibility that Blaine Junior was not always an angel.

"Do you have any information about what's behind the charges?"

"No. Blaine just called us from the jail," Gloria said. "He was arrested in his apartment in Eugene by detectives from Portland. We didn't have a chance to find out any facts."

Senior leaned forward and jutted his jaw toward Armstrong. "We want our son out of jail and his name cleared. Can you assure us you can do that?"

Armstrong had dealt with A types like Hastings, and he knew Senior wouldn't be satisfied if he said he could guarantee only that he would do his best.

"I've handled several cases where an innocent person has been accused of a crime, Mr. Hastings, and my track record speaks for itself. But I won't be able to tell you much until I've talked to Blaine, read the police reports, and finished my own investigation. I can tell you that seeing Blaine as quickly as possible is my first priority. The longer I wait, the higher the possibility that he'll say something to the detectives or a cellmate that could doom him at trial. So, I suggest that we get the business aspects of my representation out of the way so I can go over to the jail."

"What do you charge?" Blaine asked bluntly.

Armstrong quoted his hourly fee and the retainer he would require.

When Hastings hesitated, Gloria touched him on the arm. "Please, don't haggle," she said, taking the initiative for the first time—a lioness protecting her cub.

Senior wrote a check for the amount Armstrong requested. The lawyer took down the Hastingses' contact information, then saw them out. Thirty minutes later, after making a few calls, Armstrong headed across town to the Multnomah County jail.

The Justice Center is a eighteen-story, concrete-and-glass edifice in downtown Portland that is separated from the Multnomah County Courthouse by a park. The building is home to the Central Precinct of the Portland Police Bureau, a branch of the Multnomah County District Attorney's Office, several courtrooms, state parole and probation, and the Multnomah County jail.

The jail occupies the fourth through tenth floors, but the reception area is on the second floor. To reach it, Doug Armstrong walked through the center's vaulted lobby, past the curving stairs that led up to the courtrooms, and through a pair of glass doors. Armstrong showed his ID to the duty officer and went through a metal detector before taking an elevator to the floor where attorneys met their clients.

A few seconds later, Doug stepped out of the elevator into a narrow, concrete hall with walls painted pastel yellow. There was a thick metal door at one end. Armstrong pressed the button on the intercom that was affixed to the wall next to the door and announced his presence. Moments later, electronic locks snapped. A guard opened the door and ushered the lawyer into another narrow hallway, which ran in front of three contact visiting rooms. Armstrong could see into the rooms through large windows outfitted with shatterproof glass. The guard stopped in front of the solid steel door that opened into the second visiting room. Two molded plastic chairs stood on either side of a table secured to the floor by metal bolts. Moments after Armstrong sat down, a second door on the room's other wall opened and a guard escorted Armstrong's newest client into the visiting room.

Blaine Hastings Jr.'s mere presence made Doug Armstrong feel inadequate. The fifty-two-year-old lawyer was five feet six inches, balding and pudgy, and always had his nose in a book. He had tried jogging for a while but gave up on his physical fitness regime as soon as Portland's rainy season began. Other than his failed attempt at jogging, an occasional game of golf was the closest he came to physical exertion.

Blaine Hastings Jr. radiated physical perfection. Even clad in an ill-fitting orange jumpsuit, unshaven, his wavy blond hair un-combed, and his steel blue eyes bloodshot, he looked like a Greek god.

Doug estimated his client's height at six-three and his weight at 220 pounds. The jumpsuit had short sleeves, and every muscle in Hastings's cannonball biceps and corded forearms was clearly defined. Doug thought that Senior might have been right when he swore that Blaine Junior would never have to resort to force to get a woman in his bed.

"I'm Doug Armstrong," the attorney said as soon as the guard left. "Your folks hired me to represent you."

Hastings looked anxious. "Can you get me out of here?" he blurted out.

"I'm having an associate work on bail as we speak. Your folks will be posting it later today, and you should be out sometime today or tomorrow at the latest."

"Thank you, Mr. Armstrong. This is a nightmare, being ac-cused of something so serious when you know you're completely innocent."

"Blaine . . . Can I call you Blaine?"

Hastings nodded.

"Before we go into details about your case, I need to tell you a few things about the relationship a client has with his attorney."

Hastings leaned forward and listened attentively.

"First, it's important that a client trust his attorney and be com-pletely open and honest. To ensure that you can speak freely, lawyers and clients have a special privilege that ensures that anything you say to me is confidential. That means I can't disclose anything you say to me to anyone without your permission—not to the DA, my wife, your parents, anyone."

"I get that," Hastings said with a quick nod.

"Good. Now, I made a few calls before I came over. Rex Keller-man is the DA assigned to your case. He told me that a woman named Randi Stark told the police that she met you at a party and you had intercourse with her against her will."

Hastings's features morphed into a terrifying mask. He lurched forward and his jaw jutted out. Doug had to fight to keep from recoiling. He imagined he was feeling something similar to what a running back would feel if he saw Hastings barreling toward him.

"Stark is a lying bitch," Hastings spat out. "I did meet her at a party and we did make out in one of the bedrooms, but I never screwed her. That's just not true."

"Why would she lie? That's what a jury will want to know."

"Two reasons. Revenge is one. When we were in high school, Randi's boyfriend attacked me. I beat the shit out of him. When I told the cops what happened, they arrested the little prick and he served some time in juvie. So, this could be payback."

"Why did he attack you?"

The question caught Hastings off guard. "What do you mean?" he asked. Doug thought he was stalling for time.

"People don't usually attack other people for no reason."

Hastings shrugged. "I insulted Stark, and he came to her rescue."

"What was the insult?"

"The bitch told her boyfriend, Ryan, I came on to her. I called her a slut."

"Did you come on to her?"

Hastings looked appalled. "No! Jesus. She's cleaned up a lot, but back then, she was into this Goth thing. Rings in her nose, a stud in her tongue. She looked disgusting."

"If nothing happened, why did she accuse you?"

Hastings's temper flared. "Why are you cross-examining me?"

"If we go to trial, the district attorney is going to come at you a lot harder than I am, so you've got to be prepared. Getting defensive on the stand could sink you."

Hastings calmed down. "Okay, I get it. Sorry I went off on you."

"So, why do you think she accused you that time?"

"I have no idea." Hastings shrugged. "I was pretty popular in high school, and she was anything but. Maybe she wanted everyone to think I was into her." He shrugged again. "Maybe she wanted to make Ryan jealous. But it was all bullshit."

"You said there was another reason for Miss Stark's false accusation. What is it?"

"Money. I just turned twenty-one. I have a trust fund that's worth a lot, and it vested on my birthday. You can bet your ass that little bitch is planning to sue me."

"This is very good to know, Blaine. We can use this to cast doubt on Stark's accusation. If you get any other ideas, don't keep them to yourself."

"I won't."

"Okay. Now, you did know Miss Stark in high school. What kind of relationship did you have?"

"None. I hardly saw her. We didn't run in the same circles. My family is pretty well off. We're members of the Westmont Country Club, we have a really big house in the best part of town. When Randi was in high school, she lived in this housing project that is just barely in my high school's district. Not that I look down on someone because they're poor. Several guys on my teams were from the same project. But I didn't bump into Randi outside of school, and not even in school much.

"Part of that was because I was in the AP classes, and she isn't that swift. Also, I hung with the athletes and she hung out with the class losers. You know, tattoos, piercings, and pride in their D's and F's."

"If you weren't attracted to her, why did you make out with her at the party?"

"Like I said, she cleaned up since high school. No piercings or Goth shit. She's still no knockout, but I was drunk. A lot of women look great when you're drunk."

"Why don't you tell me what happened."

"Okay, well, we—Oregon—came up to Portland and played Portland State that afternoon. I knew some of the guys on the PSU team from high school, and they invited me and some of the other guys from the team to this frat party.

"We're a top twenty-five team and PSU isn't in our class, so we pretty much ran over them, and I had three sacks. I was feeling good and I had too much to drink."

"Were there any drugs involved?"

Hastings gave a vigorous shake of his head. "There's a good chance that I'm going to get drafted by an NFL team, so I'm very careful about what I put in my body."

"Okay, go on."

"Anyway, sometime after I'd started feeling a buzz, Randi and I got to talking. She'd been drinking, too, and one thing led to another and we ended up in one of the bedrooms."

"Who initiated the move to the bedroom?"

Hastings thought for a moment. He looked concerned when he answered. "Now that I think about it, I'd say that she was the one who took the initiative."

"But you went along with her."

"Like I said, I was a little wasted."

"Okay, so you're in the bedroom. Can I assume it's just the two of you?"

Hastings nodded.

"What happened?"

"We closed the door and we started making out on the bed."

"How far did that go?"

"When we got on the bed, we started kissing. Then she unzipped my fly."

"This is very important, Blaine. Did you put your penis inside Miss Stark's vagina? The State has to prove penetration in a rape case."

"Look, Mr. Armstrong, I'm not some dumb jock. I'm premed, and I know all about the way babies are made. I didn't have a condom with me, so there's no way I was going to risk getting Randi pregnant. But it didn't matter, because the minute she got my penis out of my pants, she gave me a very fast hand job and I came right away. Then, as soon as I came, Randi yelled at me to get off her."

"Did you honor her request?"

"Definitely. My folks brought me up to respect women, and I know that 'no means no.'"

"So that was the end of it?"

"Most definitely. She sat up and yelled something like 'Get off me.'"

"Did that surprise you?"

"Yeah, it did, because I got up as soon as she asked me."

"Okay, what happened then?"

"The door opened and her friend, Annie Roche, came in and I left."

"Did you talk to anyone on the way out?"

"When Annie came in, I might have said something to her, but, like I said, I was a little drunk, so my memory is hazy."

"What did you do after you left the bedroom?"

"It was getting late and I'd gotten banged up in the game, so I went home."

Armstrong made some notes. Then he looked up. "So, you're saying that you never forced yourself on Miss Stark in any way?"

"Absolutely."

"Your father hinted that you may have been in some trouble before this. He was vague and I didn't want to push him. Can you tell me what he might have been talking about?"

Hastings looked chagrined. "I have a temper, Mr. Armstrong. I'm not proud of it. It comes out when I play, and I try to keep it under wraps when I'm not on the playing field, but I had a few fights in high school, like the one I told you about. I can take care of myself, and I sent one boy to the hospital."

"Were you prosecuted?"

"No. I was the victim. I had witnesses. It was a kid from the housing project, and he had it in for me because I'm rich and a jock and I do well in school. Once the school and the police learned the truth about what happened, I wasn't in any trouble."

"Let me ask you something else," Doug said. "Have you ever had problems with women before this? And remember, the prosecutors have investigators. If there's anything out there, they'll find it. And there is nothing that leads to a conviction quicker than a surprise at trial."

"What do you mean by *problems*?"

"Let me be blunt, Blaine. Are any women going to go to the DA and say you sexually assaulted them?"

Blaine hesitated.

"This is very important," Armstrong emphasized. "If the DA puts on witnesses who swear you sexually assaulted them, it will have a huge impact on the jury."

"Okay. There was this one time in eighth grade when this girl— Julie Angstrom—said I forced her to have sex, but it wasn't true and there were never any charges."

"Was the situation similar to what allegedly happened at the party: drinking, a bedroom, et cetera?"

"No. She said I followed her into Forest Park and pulled her into the woods."

Forest Park was the largest urban forest in the United States and had many isolated areas.

"Were you in the park when she was?"

"Yeah, but I had three witnesses who told the police that I was with them all the time we were in the park. Plus, there was no forensic evidence like hair, DNA. I mean the whole accusation was complete bullshit."

Armstrong made a note to find out more about the Angstrom girl's complaint.

"We may have a serious problem that we need to discuss," Doug said. "The DA told me that Miss Stark went to the hospital after the party and they did the tests they always do when a woman says she's been raped. They found semen in Miss Stark's vagina and tested it for DNA. I assume you know what that is if you're premed."

Hastings nodded.

"Okay. Well, the lab says the DNA is a match for your DNA."

"What!"

"Do you have an explanation for that?"

"No, I . . . It's impossible."

"It's definitely a problem if you insist that you never penetrated Miss Stark and never ejaculated inside her."

"Well, I didn't."

Hastings was lost in thought for a moment, and Armstrong gave him time to think. "I do have a possible explanation for the sperm. Randi had a reputation in high school, if you know what I mean."

Armstrong nodded.

"She could have had sex with someone else that evening. She was pretty drunk."

"That wouldn't explain the match."

Hastings looked genuinely puzzled. "I don't know what to say. That can't be mine."

"Okay. Let's leave this for the time being," Doug said. "I'll hire an expert on DNA, and we'll see if we can get to the bottom of this. So, do you have any questions?"

"Not right now."

Doug stood. "I'm going to check on how much progress we've made with the bail as soon as I get back to my office. Meanwhile, do not—under any circumstances—discuss your case with anyone, no matter how sympathetic they may seem. I am the only person—and that includes your parents—that you can talk to. A fellow prisoner will run to the DA with anything you tell them. Remember, I am your only friend until the jury says *not guilty*."

CHAPTER THREE

If ever a man looked like a criminal, that man was Everett Henderson. His massive head was shaved, his bulging biceps and thick neck were evidence of hours spent pumping iron in a prison yard, a knife scar crawled down his pockmarked cheek, teardrop tattoos under his right eye announced to the world that he was an ex-con and more tattoos attested to his membership in a racist prison gang.

As soon as she'd been court-appointed to represent Henderson, Robin looked up her new client's rap sheet. It read like a list of all the possible ways one man could violate the criminal statutes of the State of Oregon.

"Mr. Henderson, the Court has asked me to represent you," Robin said when her client was seated across from her in the contact visiting room at the jail.

Henderson studied Robin and he didn't look pleased. "You're awfully young to handle a case like mine."

"I am young, but I'm very good. Have you heard of Regina Barrister?" Robin asked.

"Sure, who hasn't?"

"I'm Regina's partner, and this is not the first death penalty case I've defended."

Henderson relaxed a little, but Robin could see that he was still skeptical.

"Look, Mr. Henderson, I can see why you might not trust me. You didn't choose me to be your lawyer and you don't know a thing about me. So, let me give you a little background: I graduated from Yale Law School, which is one of America's best, and I clerked for the chief justice of the Oregon Supreme Court before Regina hired me."

Robin was about to continue, when Henderson suddenly leaned forward and stared at her.

"Are you Rockin' Robin Lockwood?"

Robin smiled. "I am."

Henderson broke into a grin. "I seen you fight. You were pretty good."

"I was okay."

Henderson nodded. "That Kerrigan broad did put a hurt on you."

Robin nodded in agreement. "That she did, which is why I decided it was safer to duke it out with DAs and judges."

Henderson laughed.

"So, Everett . . . Can I call you Everett?"

"Sure thing."

"I read the police reports before I came over. The DA is saying you killed Greg Schaefer, an off-duty cop, in a bar fight."

Henderson stopped smiling. "I did kill that motherfucker, but he started it."

"Why don't you tell me what happened."

"My lady and I was in the Shamrock and we were dancing. The asshole I killed was in civilian clothes, and there's no way I could tell he was a cop. He'd been drinking with his buddies, and he'd had way more than one too many—or he would have known better than to come on to Felicia."

"Felicia is your girlfriend?"

Henderson nodded. "And she'll tell you she told him real polite that she did not want to dance with him. She'll also tell you that he wouldn't take no for an answer. That's when I suggested that he fuck off or get hurt. Which is when he took a swing at me."

Henderson shook his head. "Dumb move. I done a little fighting of my own. Tough-guy competitions and plenty of street stuff. Plus, I was sober and he wasn't. I decked him pretty quick and Felicia pulled me off of him. We was walking back to our table when he grabbed a bottle and smashed me on the head."

Henderson bent his head down to show Robin his stitches.

"Fucker hit me from behind and was jabbing at me with the jagged end after the bottle broke. That's when I knifed him. But he started the whole thing. I was just defending myself."

"His friends tell a different story."

"Yeah, well, they're lying motherfuckers. Hell, I doubt they saw what happened. Their table was way on the other side of the bar."

"Other than Felicia, were there any other witnesses who can back up your story?"

"Anyone in the bar who saw what happened."

"My firm has an excellent investigator named Jeff Hodges. Give me the names, addresses, and phone numbers of your witnesses, and I'll have Jeff talk to them. Then he'll talk to the State's witnesses. I'm also going to get a doctor to look at your head wound, and I may have Jeff take some pictures."

"What about getting me out of here?"

"I'll try, but I'm not optimistic. There's no automatic bail in a murder case, and you are charged with killing a cop. Proving that the charge is bullshit may take a while. I may change my mind about the chances for bail when I've read all of the reports."

"Take your time. I'm okay in here."

"I figured that this wasn't your first rodeo," Robin said.

Henderson grinned.

"I'm still going to warn you about discussing this case with anyone except me and Jeff."

"I know all about jailhouse snitches. I've had to explain why that activity is unhealthy to a few of them."

Robin held up her hands. "Too much information, Everett."

Henderson laughed and Robin stood up.

"Get me that witness list as fast as you can. Call when it's ready, and I'll send Jeff over to talk to you."

"Thanks for coming over so quickly."

Robin rang for the guard. It was a little after four when she left the jail, and she decided to go home instead of returning to the office. During her walk, Robin thought about Henderson's case. She didn't like to predict how she would do, because she knew that clients weren't always truthful, but she felt pretty good about Henderson's chances. If he was telling the truth.

CHAPTER FOUR

The phone was ringing. Robin sat up and stared at the clock. It was two in the morning.

"Miss Lockwood," a frightened voice whispered.

"Yes."

"This is Randi Stark. They're after me."

Robin was still groggy. "Who's after you?"

"Blaine."

"The boy who raped you?"

"Yes."

"Is he there?"

"Not him. One of his friends. He followed me from the club."

"Why do you think he's a friend of Hastings's?"

"Because he's a giant. He's gotta play football."

Robin suddenly realized that Randi was slurring her words. "Have you been drinking?"

"Yeah, at the Blue Unicorn. That's where he was."

"Where are you now?"

"I didn't think I could make it home, so I hid around back of this gas station between two Dumpsters."

"Okay. Give me the address, and I'll come over right away."

Last year, Robin had purchased a .38 Special after someone involved in one of her cases had tried to kill her. After pulling on jeans, a T-shirt, and a sweatshirt, Robin put the gun in its holster and headed out.

The gas station was fifteen minutes from Robin's apartment by car. It was deserted, and the lights on its two islands and those that had been left on in the office provided the only illumination. Robin switched off her headlights and parked in the shadows at the far edge of the lot. She closed her car door quietly, then headed for the back of the station. Halfway there, she heard voices.

Robin pulled out her .38, jogged along the side of the building, and looked around the corner. There were no lights in the back of the station, and the Dumpsters were at the end of the building farthest from her. Robin squinted into the shadow and saw Randi Stark cowering in front of a man who was the size of two normal humans. The neck of Randi's T-shirt was clamped in a hand the size of a catcher's mitt.

Robin walked toward the Dumpsters and raised her gun. "Stop right there," Robin commanded.

The man spun around and released Randi, who fell hard onto the asphalt. The man's face was in shadow, but she heard the disdain in his voice when he said, "You're in the wrong place at the wrong time, bitch. Get smart and leave fast."

"I'm going to make this very simple," Robin answered, "since anyone who is unarmed and insults someone with a gun has to be very stupid. This .38 Special is loaded with hollow-point bullets. Anywhere I shoot you will fuck you up big-time, and I'd have to be a horrible shot to miss someone the size of a rhinoceros. Leave now and live, or stay here and die. Your choice."

The man hesitated, and Robin could see he was fighting the urge to charge. Then he backed away, his eyes never leaving Robin's, until he disappeared into the shadows.

Randi began to sob. Robin waited a few seconds to make sure that the behemoth didn't decide to sneak back. Then she placed the gun on the asphalt, where she could get to it quickly, and knelt next to Randi.

"You're safe," she said, but Randi continued to cry and shake. "It's okay, I scared him off. Can you stand up? I want to get you out of here."

Randi struggled to her feet. Robin picked up the gun, led her to her car, sweeping the lot in case Randi's attacker was hiding in the shadows. Robin didn't relax until they were locked in the car and driving out of the lot. And even then, she kept looking in her mirrors to make sure they weren't being followed. Eventually, she parked at a fast-food restaurant and put Randi in a booth near the back.

"Stay here while I get you some coffee. Do you want something to eat?"

"Just coffee," Randi said.

Robin returned with two take-out cups and put one of them in front of her client. "Tell me what happened," Robin said.

"I went to the club. It was crowded and I danced with a couple of guys. Then the door opened. I was facing it. When he came in, you couldn't miss him. I wasn't worried until he made eye contact and started wading through the crowd toward me.

"I go to the club a lot, and I know there's a back door by the ladies'. I went through it and down the alley. Then I started to run. I thought I was safe, but he found me just before you showed up." Randi lost it for a moment.

Robin covered her hand. "It's okay. He can't hurt you now. Take some deep breaths."

Randi did as she was told. Then she sipped some more coffee. "I never heard him. You'd think someone that big, you'd hear him." She shook her head. "One minute I was huddled between the Dumpsters, and the next he had me by my shirt and he was shaking me like a rat."

"Did he say anything?"

"Yeah. He said I was pretty, but I wouldn't stay pretty long if I kept telling lies that got nice people in trouble."

"Did he name the 'nice person'?" Robin asked.

Randi shook her head once more. "But I'm not stupid. He's got to be one of Blaine's teammates."

"I can find that out pretty easily. There will be team photos. I'll check it out in the morning. Did he say anything else?"

"He asked me if I understood him, but I was too frightened to answer. And that's when you scared him off."

"Okay. If you can ID this guy, we'll go to the police and tell them what happened. Hastings is out on bail, but this might be enough to get his bail revoked."

Randi started to sob again. "He'll just deny he was involved."

"If we can find the man who threatened you, the police might get him to talk."

"Blaine will buy him an alibi. He has all the money in the world." Randi stared into her coffee cup. "Maybe I should just drop it."

"What do you mean?"

"Not testify. Then Blaine would let me alone."

Robin cupped Randi's chin and lifted it until they were eye to eye. "That would be a mistake. My investigator has been working up background on Blaine Hastings. He's got a reputation as a violent bully and an egotist. A person like that won't forget what you've done. Hastings is premed and a preseason All-American. Getting accused of rape is going to cost him when he tries to get drafted or go to medical school. If that happens, he'll want revenge.

"And there's something else. A guy like Blaine, if he raped you, you can bet you're not his only victim. If he's locked away, you'll be protecting a lot of innocent women."

"He'll never be locked up."

"Do you remember what you told me in my office—how you wanted to bring the Hastings family down? If your testimony puts Blaine in prison, we will kill him when you sue."

"All that money won't do me any good if I'm dead."

Robin was tempted to pursue her argument, but one look at Randi convinced her that this wasn't the time.

"Look, you're scared and exhausted. You shouldn't be making serious decisions in your condition. What's important now is that you get some rest. Where do you want me to take you?"

"Not home. They'll be watching."

"Is there a friend you can stay with?"

"Annie, maybe."

"Do you want to call her?"

"It's so late."

Robin hesitated. Then she said, "You can stay at my place tonight. I can make up the couch."

Randi looked up. "That would be good. They wouldn't guess I was there."

"It would just be for the night."

"I get that. Thank you."

They finished their coffee in silence, which Robin thought was good because it gave Randi time to calm down. Randi was a mess, but Robin understood why. Blaine Hastings was desperate, and he was coming after the only person who could take away his freedom. The man he'd sent was only interested in scaring Randi; otherwise, he wouldn't have threatened her—he'd have beaten or killed her. Now that plan A had failed, Robin wondered if Hastings would escalate.

CHAPTER FIVE

Robin lived in a corner apartment in a four-story, brick walk-up in a funky part of town populated by homegrown shops, a movie theater that showed indie films and second-run features at reduced prices, and so many good, reasonably priced restaurants that choosing where to eat was often a problem.

The front door of Robin's apartment opened into a kitchen and small dining area. Between work and the gym, Robin wasn't home much, so she let dishes pile up in the sink and old newspapers accumulate on the coffee table and the couch in the open area in front of the television until she couldn't stand the way the apartment looked and went on a cleaning spree.

As soon as they were in Robin's apartment, Robin cleared the couch of debris and threw a sheet, blanket, and pillow on it. A combination of exhaustion and alcohol sent Randi into a deep sleep as soon as she lay down on Robin's couch. Robin was too wound up to sleep, so she booted up her laptop and searched for pictures of the University of Oregon football team.

When Randi woke up a little after nine, Robin cooked her

breakfast, then showed her the team photos. "Does anyone look like the guy who attacked you?" Robin asked.

Randi leaned forward and scanned the team photograph slowly, stopping to look closely at a few of the linemen. Then she sat up and pointed at one of the players. She looked scared.

"That's him."

"Are you sure?"

Randi nodded.

Robin picked up her cell phone and dialed Detective Carrie Anders.

Half an hour later, Robin and her client were seated in front of the detective who had arrested Blaine Hastings. Carrie Anders was six-two, thick bodied, and as strong as some men. She had sad brown eyes; a large, lumpish nose; and short, shaggy black hair. Her lumbering appearance and slow drawl often led people to conclude that she was slow-witted, but she had majored in math in college and was one of the smartest detectives in the Portland Police Bureau.

"That's Marlon Guest," Robin said as she handed the detective a photograph. "He's a six-foot-six and three-hundred-forty-pound offensive lineman for the Ducks and a teammate of Blaine Hastings. Around two in the morning, Guest attacked Randi in back of a gas station and threatened to hurt her if she didn't, and I quote, 'stop telling lies about nice people.' I saw Guest threaten Randi before I scared him off."

Anders gave Robin a hard look. "Just how did you do that?"

"I bought a gun after what happened in Atlanta, and I have a permit."

Anders smiled. "Just asking. So, you got a good look at Miss Stark's assailant?"

Robin started to answer. Then she hesitated as she tried to recall exactly what she had seen.

"Guest and Randi were standing at the far end of the back of the gas station. There aren't any lights there, so his face was in shadow. But this has to be him. Randi made an ID from the photo, and there aren't many people who are that big."

Anders turned to Randi. "How certain are you that this is the man who attacked you?"

Now it was Randi's turn to hesitate. "I did see his face."

"Yes?"

Randi blushed. "I was a little drunk, but I'm sure it's him."

"How drunk?"

"I don't know. I was feeling woozy before he started chasing me. I sobered up a little while I was running."

"Randi, this is important. Are you sure this is the man who attacked you? You don't want to accuse an innocent man."

"I . . . It was him."

"Okay. I'll question Guest. Maybe he'll admit he attacked you."

"Thanks, Carrie," Robin said.

"Hastings is an arrogant bastard, and I want him off the street. If I can get Guest to say Hastings asked him to threaten Miss Stark, I might be able to get his bail revoked."

CHAPTER SIX

Rex Kellerman's secretary led Doug Armstrong to the assistant district attorney's office. Kellerman was reading a case when Doug walked in.

"Have a seat," Kellerman said without bothering to look up.

Doug sat down and waited patiently. Kellerman always treated Doug with disdain, and Doug had dreaded the meeting. After three minutes of the silent treatment, he started to get angry, but he suppressed his emotions. He was hoping to get a decent plea offer in Blaine Hastings's case, and he didn't want to antagonize the man who could make it.

Finally, Kellerman looked up from his laptop. "To what do I owe the pleasure, Doug?"

"Blaine Hastings."

Doug waited for Kellerman to say something, but he just leaned back in his chair.

"I was hoping we could discuss the case," Doug continued, trying not to seem too anxious.

"What's to discuss?" Kellerman asked. "Your guy is guilty as sin, and I'm going to see he spends a long time down at OSP."

"Come on, Rex. He's a kid, an honor student, and a top athlete. And he says he didn't rape Miss Stark."

Kellerman shrugged. "She says he did, and we have DNA test results that back her up."

"Yeah, but the DNA just means they had sex. The allegation of force is uncorroborated."

"How does he explain the ripped panties, Doug?"

"This will ruin Blaine's life. He's planning on going to medical school or the pros. We should be able to work something out. He's never been in trouble over something like this before."

Kellerman raised an eyebrow and flashed a smug smile. "Really, Doug. Is that what Mr. Hastings said? Julie Angstrom says he should have been. Has your client mentioned her? She sure remembers him."

Kellerman fished through a file that was sitting on his desk. After a moment, he grabbed a police report and handed it to Doug.

"We found this old complaint two days ago. I sent Carrie Anders over to talk to Julie. You'll get Anders's report as soon as she writes it up."

Doug didn't want Kellerman to know that he knew about Angstrom, so he kept his head down as he read Angstrom's account of the rape in Forest Park.

"I'll ask Blaine about this."

"I wonder if he'll remember what happened as well as Julie does."

"I don't think you can get this testimony into evidence."

"Maybe, maybe not. I'll certainly try. Not that I need it."

"This happened years ago, and there were never any charges."

"If it did happen, doesn't it make you wonder what your boy's been up to in the intervening years?"

"I'm guessing you don't have anything else like this or I'd have gotten the reports in discovery. And this case still boils down to

Stark's word against Blaine's. I don't see your case being that strong. Is there some way to settle it out of court?"

"Sure. Have Mr. Hastings plead guilty to the charges. You can ask the Court for mercy. If he gets it, it will be more than he showed Randi Stark."

Kellerman waited until the door closed before breaking into a grin. The *Hastings* case would be a walk in the park with Doug Armstrong as his adversary. With a good lawyer, he'd have to work for a guilty verdict, but Armstrong was second-rate.

Kellerman took a moment to think about what a win in Hastings would do for his career. It was common knowledge that Paul Getty, the Multnomah County district attorney, was not going to run for another term. Vanessa Cole, the chief criminal deputy, was rumored to be a candidate, but Rex thought he could beat her at the polls. A few headlines trumpeting victories in big cases would certainly help, and prosecuting a privileged brat like Blaine Hastings would score a lot of points with blue-collar voters.

Kellerman's smile widened. Life was good.

CHAPTER SEVEN

Robin had spent the past two days sitting in on Blaine Hastings's trial. It had been a disaster for the defendant, which was great for her client. Maxine Stark made certain that everyone who had a connection to the internet knew that her daughter had been raped by a star athlete who was a child of privilege. To get into the Multnomah County Courthouse, Robin was forced to fight her way through pickets from feminist organizations who were parading outside, demanding Blaine Hastings's head.

The judge had ruled that Julie Angstrom could not testify, but that hadn't mattered. The testimony of the expert from the police crime lab had been devastating. She'd told the jury that the DNA in the semen sample that had been found inside Randi Stark matched Blaine Hastings's DNA. All the jurors watched crime shows on television, and they knew that a DNA match was infallible proof of guilt.

Annie Roche had been the last witness for the prosecution that afternoon. She was a short, heavyset brunette with a pug nose and wide brown eyes, who had dressed conservatively in a white, long-sleeve blouse and ankle-length dress.

Rex Kellerman established that Roche was working in a nail salon and checking in a grocery store to pay for community college and planned to become a physical therapist. Robin thought that Roche was very nervous when the DA's direct examination started but had calmed down when Kellerman was through with his preliminary questions.

"Miss Roche, did you attend a Portland State–Oregon football game in late September?" Kellerman asked.

"Yes."

"After the game, did you talk to some PSU students who had attended high school with you?"

"Yes."

"Did you learn about a fraternity party that was going to be held that night?"

"Yes."

"Did you tell Randi Stark about the party?"

"Yes."

"And did you and Randi go to the party?"

"We did."

"Was the defendant at the party?"

"Yes."

"Tell the jury what you saw happening between your friend Randi Stark and the defendant."

"The defendant," Roche said, referring to Blaine Hastings the way she had been instructed to by Rex Kellerman, "was talking to another boy in a group of people we knew. At some point, I noticed Randi talking to him. Later, I saw them dancing."

"Did they stop dancing?"

"Yes."

"What happened after they stopped?"

"I saw the defendant lead Randi down a hall."

"What did you do?"

"I followed them."

"Why?"

"I was worried about Randi being alone with the defendant."

"Why?"

"He had a bad reputation in school. He did things to girls."

"Objection!" Doug Armstrong said.

"Sustained. Jurors, you will ignore that last comment."

"What happened next?"

"The defendant and Randi went into a room at the end of the hall, and I waited outside. It was quiet for a short time. Then Randi screamed, 'Get off me.'"

"What did you do when you heard the scream?"

"I opened the door."

"What did you see?"

"Randi was on the bed. Her panties were on the floor. . . ."

"Did you get a chance to see the panties up close?"

"Yes, when I picked them up."

"What was their condition?"

"They'd been torn like someone had ripped them off her."

"Go on."

"So, Randi was on the bed. She was crying and pushing against the defendant, who was on top of her."

"Was there anything unusual about the defendant?"

Roche blushed and looked down. "His . . . his penis was exposed."

"It was out of his pants?"

"Yes."

"What did you do?"

"I yelled at the defendant to get off Randi. He threatened me and told me to get out. I said I would scream if he didn't leave Randi alone."

"What happened then?"

"The defendant started toward me. I backed into the hall and

told him again that I would scream. He stopped. Then he pushed
past me and ran away."

"What did you do after the defendant ran away?"

"I took Randi to the hospital."

"No further questions."

"Mr. Armstrong?" the judge said.

"Miss Roche, was Blaine at the football game?"

"Yes."

"Did you and Miss Stark see him there?"

"Yes. He plays for Oregon."

"Did Miss Stark talk to Blaine at the game?"

"No."

"Was he talking to the same boys who told you about the
party?"

"Yes."

"You learned that Blaine was going to be at the party, didn't
you?"

"No."

"So, you didn't know he would be at the party until you saw
him there?"

"Yes."

"Randi wanted to go to the party, didn't she?"

"Yes."

"Randi talked to Blaine and danced with him at the party,
didn't she?"

"Yes."

"So, they were friendly?"

"I guess."

"And she went into the bedroom with Blaine willingly, didn't
she?"

"I guess."

"You testified under oath that you saw them go in, didn't you?"

"Yes."

"Did she scream in the hall?"

"No."

"Did Blaine drag her inside?"

"No."

"After they were inside, the door closed, didn't it?"

"Yes."

"So, you couldn't see what happened in the bedroom, could you?"

"No."

"For all you know, Randi Stark was a willing partner?"

"She screamed."

"You can't tell this jury from what you know personally whether she screamed after having consensual sex, can you?"

"I . . . No."

"No further questions."

Robin didn't think that Doug had scored many points on cross. She wasn't surprised. She'd met Doug a few times and thought he was a nice guy, but he had a reputation as an unspectacular litigator. Nothing she'd seen during the trial changed Robin's opinion.

Randi was scheduled to testify in the morning. She was not allowed to be in court while the witnesses were testifying. When court adjourned, Robin returned to her office and called her to give her moral support for her upcoming ordeal.

"Annie was great," Robin said. "Hastings's attorney tried to trip her up, but he didn't do a thing."

"Is he any good? Is he, you know, gonna make me look bad?"

"Not if you tell the truth. I'll be in court and so will your mom, and the DA will object if Armstrong tries anything that's improper. Stay strong."

"I'll try, but I'm scared."

"It would be weird if you weren't scared, but Hastings will be in prison where he belongs if you just tell the jurors what he did to you, and you won't have to worry about him anymore."

They talked for a while longer. As soon as Robin hung up, her receptionist told her that Portland detective Carrie Anders was calling.

"What's up?" Robin asked.

"Nothing you're going to like."

"Oh?"

"I drove down to Eugene and tried to talk to Marlon Guest."

"And?"

"I'm not going to arrest him," the detective said.

"Why?"

"Guest refused to talk to me, and he lawyered up right away. This morning, Guest's lawyer sent me statements from three witnesses who swear they were with him in Eugene when Randi was assaulted in Portland."

"That's bullshit. Randi and I will swear he was there."

"Randi admits she was drunk and terrified. A good defense attorney would be able to make mincemeat of her on the stand."

"I wasn't drunk."

"True, but you told me that there's no light in the back of the gas station, Randi's assailant was at the end of the building farthest from you, and his face was in shadow."

"I didn't see his face, but how many people are the size of a *T. rex*, Carrie?"

"Every offensive lineman on a Division One football squad."

"So, you're just going to let him go?"

"For now. And Marlon Guest isn't my main interest, anyway. I want Blaine Hastings Jr. in the state penitentiary. As long as Randi stays strong, that's where that asshole is going."

"She's scared to death, Carrie."

"Yeah, I would be, too. Look, I'll call her and tell her that I let

Guest know that I was watching him. I doubt he'll try anything again."

"Thanks, Carrie. I've tried to get her to calm down, but it will mean more coming from you."

When Robin hung up, she thought about going to the gym, but she was too tired, so she bought some sushi to go at a Japanese restaurant around the corner from her office and headed home.

Robin finished her dinner and picked up a book she had been reading, but she gave up after a chapter because she was too tired to read. There was a Trail Blazer game on TV. It wasn't going to start for twenty minutes. Robin remembered that she hadn't talked to her mother in a while.

Talking to her mother could be a trial. Before Robin's dad passed away, he had been her biggest supporter. When the school board of her high school district had tried to keep Robin from wrestling on the boys' team, her father had hired a lawyer who forced the board to let her participate. When she decided that she wanted to be the first person in her family to go to college and then law school, he'd been her champion. That was not always the case with her mother.

Robin's mom wanted Robin to stay in their small town, get married, and give her grandchildren. She'd never liked the idea of a girl going to law school—especially one that was on the liberal East Coast—and she had been upset when Robin chose to practice law in Oregon instead of coming back to the state where she had been born.

Her mom had gradually come to accept Robin's life choices, but her doubts about them surfaced on occasion during their phone calls. Robin phoned her anyway.

"Nice of you to call," her mother said.

"How are things at home?" Robin said, ignoring the icy tone her mother used when there were too many days between calls.

"The boys were over for dinner this weekend. It would have been nice if the whole family was together."

"I'm definitely coming home for Thanksgiving," Robin assured her.

"That will be good. Are you still enjoying your job?"

Robin knew that her mother would be thrilled if she said no, but the truth was that she loved her practice and couldn't imagine doing anything else.

"It's going very well."

"You're able to handle your cases without Miss Barrister there to help?"

"Yes. In fact, I have two new cases that are very interesting. The court appointed me to represent a defendant in a death penalty case."

"What did he do?" asked her mother, who had a hard time accepting the fact that her daughter tried to help guilty criminals escape punishment.

"Nothing, as far as I've been able to determine. He killed an off-duty policeman, but the policeman was out of uniform and drunk. He attacked my client from behind with a broken bottle. My client shouldn't be in jail, and I think I have a good chance of winning his case."

"What's the other case?"

"I'm going to sue a rapist on behalf of the woman he raped. I've been sitting through the criminal case, and I'm pretty sure that the rapist will be convicted. My client is a nice young woman. The money won't stop her suffering, but she's poor and it can give her a better life."

"Well, that's good. I'll pray for her."

"Thanks, Mom."

Robin and her mother talked until they ran out of things to say. Robin was glad she had called. Her mother had been lonely since Robin's dad passed and Robin did feel a little guilty because she wasn't there to help her. But Robin's three brothers lived nearby, and her mother kept busy sitting for her grandkids and working with her church groups, so Robin didn't feel too bad.

The game started shortly after Robin hung up. She watched a half, but was too tired to finish, so she went to bed early so she would be sharp when the *Hastings* case started up in the morning.

CHAPTER EIGHT

Doug Armstrong was failing so badly that he couldn't sleep, so he was exhausted when court started. Rex Kellerman called Randi Stark to the stand. Randi broke down twice during her direct testimony. Doug chanced a glance at the jurors. What he saw on their faces was not encouraging.

"Miss Stark," Kellerman asked as he continued his direct examination, "did you tell the defendant that you did not want to have sexual intercourse with him?"

Randi nodded.

"You have to answer the question so the court reporter can record it," Kellerman said gently.

"Sorry. Yes. I told him to stop."

"And did he stop?"

"No . . . no, sir."

"What did he do when you told him to stop?"

"He ripped my panties off. Then he slapped me and told me to be a good girl. Then . . . then he forced himself inside me."

"What were you feeling when he penetrated you?"

Randi started to cry. "It hurt. I told him but he wouldn't stop."

"Did the defendant ejaculate inside you?"

"Yes."

"What happened then?"

"I yell 'Get off me,' and Annie came into the room."

"Did he leave then?"

"Only after Annie threatened to scream."

"What did you do after the defendant left?"

"Annie took me to the hospital."

"Thank you, Randi. I have no further questions."

"Mr. Armstrong," Judge Mary Redding said.

"Thank you, Your Honor. Miss Stark, you don't like Blaine, do you?"

Randi looked stunned by the question. "He raped me. No, I don't like him."

"What about before the party? Isn't it true that you hated him because in high school, your boyfriend, Ryan, attacked Blaine and was sent to jail?"

Randi glared at Armstrong. "Blaine baited Ryan. He was much bigger and stronger, and he beat him up. Then he reported Ryan to the police and lied about what happened. Ryan was never the same after he got out of juvie," Randi said.

"You claim Blaine lied," Doug said, "but Ryan had his day in court and he was convicted, wasn't he?"

"That's because he got his friends to lie at the trial."

Blaine leaned over to his lawyer. "Object," he said. "Ask the judge to strike the answer."

Before Armstrong could say anything, Randi pointed at Blaine. "Because of him, Ryan killed himself. So, yeah, I hate him."

"Objection!" Doug shouted.

"Sustained. Miss Stark, you must not volunteer that type of statement. Confine yourself to answering the questions Mr. Armstrong asks."

The judge turned to the jury. "I am instructing you to ignore

Miss Stark's last two statements about what Mr. Hastings's friends and Ryan may have done. They are inadmissible guesses, and you may not use them in any way in deciding Mr. Hastings's case."

"A lot of good that's going to do me," Blaine whispered. "You're letting that little bitch say anything she wants."

"Mr. Armstrong," the judge asked, "do you have any more questions?"

"Yes, Your Honor. Miss Stark, I see Robin Lockwood in the spectator section. Is she an attorney?"

"Yes."

"Have you hired her?"

"Yes."

"And that's because you plan to sue Blaine if he is convicted, isn't it?"

"Yes."

"And isn't your motive for accusing my client of rape the money you hope to get in a civil suit?"

"No. I called the police because he raped me against my will. He's an animal, and I want to protect any other woman he can rape if he's not behind bars."

"Move to strike that answer, Your Honor?" Doug said.

"You asked the question, Mr. Armstrong, and you're stuck with the answer."

"The State rests," Rex Kellerman told the Court as soon as Randi was excused.

"All right. Let's recess and be back in twenty minutes," the judge said.

"Let's talk outside," Blaine said.

"Sure," Doug said.

Blaine and Doug passed Senior on their way up the aisle. He looked furious, but Junior waved him down. Blaine led Doug into a deserted stairwell at the back of the fifth-floor corridor.

"Do I go on next?" Blaine asked.

"I don't think you should testify."

"Oh yeah? Why is that?"

"Are you going to say that you never penetrated Stark?"

"That's the truth."

"Kellerman will crucify you. He'll ask you how your sperm got into Stark, and you won't have an answer."

"You should have given the jury an answer. I told you to hire a DNA expert who would tell the jury that isn't my DNA."

"I did hire an expert. I told you, he conducted his own test, but he agreed that the DNA in the rape kit was a match for your DNA."

Hastings's face flushed with anger and a pulse started throbbing in his temple. "Then you should have hired another expert, you fucking incompetent." Blaine's low growl was more frightening than if he had screamed in Doug's face. "I never fucked that halfwit. She lied on the stand, and you didn't do a goddamn thing."

They were alone in the stairwell, and Doug thought Blaine might attack him.

"I am not going to prison," Hastings said. "Do you understand me?"

"Calm down, Blaine—"

"I'll calm down when I hear 'not guilty.' And you better make sure that's what I hear, or you are going to be very sorry."

Armstrong's stomach turned. "What are you talking about?"

"Do your job," Hastings answered. Then he walked away.

"Do you have any witnesses, Mr. Armstrong?" the judge asked.

"Mr. Hastings is going to testify."

Doug spent the first part of his direct examination asking his client about his academic and athletic accomplishments.

"And are you planning to attend medical school?"

"Yes, sir, if I'm not drafted by an NFL team. But medical school is definitely in my plans for the future after a career in the NFL."

Blaine turned to the jurors. "I want to work with children in some capacity."

"Let's talk about the night of the party after the Portland State–Oregon game. Did you see Miss Stark at the party?"

"Yes, sir. She came up to me and started talking."

"Had you been drinking when Miss Stark approached you?"

"Yes, sir. I was tired from the game and I had a little more alcohol than I should have."

"How were you feeling?"

"A little tipsy."

"Did you dance with Miss Stark?"

"Yes."

"What happened while you were dancing?"

"She came on to me. She started kissing me and she started stroking my crotch."

"What happened next?"

"She led me down the hall to a bedroom."

"So, going to the bedroom was her idea?"

"Yes, sir."

"Mr. Hastings, please tell the jury what happened inside the bedroom."

"We started making out on the bed. And right away, she unzipped my fly and began stroking me. I was pretty excited and I came right away."

"Inside Miss Stark?"

"No, sir. In her hand."

"What happened next?"

"She screamed, 'Get off me.'"

"Did that startle you?"

"Yes, because she'd been really willing up until she screamed."

"She never said she didn't want to continue making out?"

"No."

"What happened next?"

"The door flew open and Annie Roche came in and started yelling at me."

"What did you do?"

"I was confused. Stark was hitting me on my chest and Roche was yelling at me. I was embarrassed, so I left."

"Did you force Miss Stark to have sex of any kind with you?"

"No, sir. She initiated everything, and she never said she didn't want to make out."

"No further questions," Doug said, relieved that his direct examination was over.

"Do you have any questions, Mr. Kellerman?" the judge asked when Doug returned to the defense counsel's table.

"Just a few," Kellerman said. "If you are convicted of rape, will that affect your ability to get into medical school?" Rex Kellerman asked.

"Yes, sir."

"How about your draft status with NFL teams?"

"I probably wouldn't get drafted."

"So, you have a lot to lose if this jury believes Miss Stark?"

"Yes."

"Which gives you a lot of reasons to lie about what you did to Miss Stark in that bedroom, doesn't it?"

Hastings's face flushed with anger just as it had in the stairwell. "I'm not lying—she is. She's made this whole thing up to get my money. She and her crowd always resented me, and now she wants to bring me down to her level."

"What level is that?"

"Stark always ran with losers. I worked hard to get good grades. I want to make something of myself. She can't stand that I'm rich. She wants my money. That's why she's lying."

Rex Kellerman smiled at Hastings. "You just accused Miss Stark of being a liar. Is she also a magician?"

Hastings looked confused. "What do you mean?"

"If what you say is true, you never penetrated Miss Stark."

"Yes."

"Well, then, in addition to crying and screaming at you to get off her, did Miss Stark say 'abracadabra' and make your sperm magically appear inside her?"

Hastings's mouth opened, and he stared at the DA. Then he stammered, "I . . . I didn't rape her."

"No further questions," Kellerman said.

CHAPTER NINE

"Madam Foreperson, have you reached a verdict?" Multnomah County Circuit Court judge Mary Ann Redding asked after telling Blaine Hastings to stand.

"We have, Your Honor," answered Juror Number Four, a fifty-year-old CPA.

"Is your verdict unanimous?"

"It is."

"How do you find the defendant on count one in the indictment, which charges that Mr. Hastings raped Randi Stark?"

"We find the defendant guilty."

Doug watched his client out of the corner of his eye as he learned that the jurors had found him guilty on all counts. He looked stunned. As soon as the verdicts were read, the judge dismissed the jury. When they were out of the room, Rex Kellerman asked the judge to revoke Blaine's bail.

"Mr. Armstrong?" the judge said when the DA finished.

"Yes, Your Honor," Armstrong said as he stood. "I would ask the Court to let Mr. Hastings remain on bail pending sentencing. Mr. Hastings has no criminal record and has always been a law-abiding citizen. He is an honor student studying to be a doctor. Mr. Hastings has surrendered his passport and has made all of his court appearances, and I have every reason to believe he will continue to do so."

Judge Redding looked at the defendant. "Do you have anything you wish to say to me regarding the question of bail, Mr. Hastings?"

Blaine stood up and straightened his suit jacket. "I do, Your Honor. I am completely innocent. I did not rape Randi Stark. I've been set up. Stark accused me so she could sue me for money. Everything she said is a lie, and I suspect that the police pressured her to lie. If I wasn't rich, this case would never have come to court. And if I'd had a decent lawyer, Stark's lies would have been exposed to the jury. I shouldn't go to prison for something I didn't do."

Hastings dropped into his seat and stared defiantly at the judge. Doug had to exercise great restraint to keep from edging away from his client.

Judge Redding tapped the pen she'd been holding on the dais for a moment before addressing Hastings. "I was uncertain about whether to let you continue on bail before you spoke. Then, in the space of a few minutes, you blamed your victim, the police, and your lawyer for your situation—never once accepting the blame for your actions. If you had shown one scintilla of remorse or one iota of compassion for your victim, I might have had some compassion for you. But you have convinced me to revoke your bail." The judge turned to the courtroom deputies. "Please see that Mr. Hastings is booked into the jail."

Randi Stark and her mother were sitting in the spectator section with Robin Lockwood.

Hastings leaped up and pointed at Randi. "You'll regret this, you lying bitch."

Maxine Stark leaped to her feet and balled her fist. "Don't you dare threaten my Randi, you animal."

The guards moved in. Robin took Randi's hand and stared fearlessly at Hastings.

"What are you looking at, cunt?" Hastings screamed at Robin.

"Not much," Robin replied evenly as the guards restrained Hastings.

"Take this piece of garbage out of here," Kellerman ordered the guards, acting bravely now that the prisoner couldn't hurt him.

"I'll settle with you, too," Hastings threatened as the guards led Blaine away.

Judge Redding shook her head. "It looks like I made the right decision. Court is adjourned."

As soon as court recessed, Carrie Anders walked up to Randi. "I'm proud of you. It took a lot of guts to stand up to Hastings."

"Thank you," Randi said. "I never really believed Blaine would get convicted."

"Well, he has been, and he's going to pay for what he did to you for a long time."

"You bet he's going to pay," Randi's mother said.

"You've raised a very brave young lady, Mrs. Stark," Carrie said.

While Carrie talked to Randi and her mother, Robin followed Rex Kellerman into the hall.

"Congratulations, Rex. You did a terrific job."

"You've got the civil suit, right?"

"I do."

"We should split the attorney fee," Kellerman said with a smile. "After all, I did your work for you."

Robin returned the smile. "Can I talk to you about the *Henderson* case when you're through talking to the reporters?" she asked.

"Does he want to plead?"

"No. I wanted to talk to you about dismissing. My investigation shows he was acting in self-defense. Henderson should never have been indicted."

"Hey, Robin, he killed a cop."

"An off-duty, drunk cop in civilian clothes who attacked him from behind. You've seen our reports."

"And you've seen ours. I don't deal with cop killers. And now, if you'll excuse me, the press awaits."

Robin watched Kellerman walk away. She'd hoped he would be reasonable, but she knew she was being naïve. Robin sighed. It looked like Henderson was going to trial, and she wasn't happy about that, even though she was certain she would win. Going to trial with Rex Kellerman was one of Robin's least favorite things. He was obnoxious and unethical, and she'd have to watch her back every second she was in court with him.

CHAPTER TEN

As soon as Judge Redding left the bench, Doug pushed his papers into his attaché case and started to flee the courtroom, but Blaine Hastings Sr. barred his way.

"You were pathetic, Armstrong. A first-year law student could have done a more competent job."

"I'm sorry you're upset, but—"

"Upset! You bet I'm upset. That slut railroaded my boy, and you didn't do a thing to stop her."

"There are some good points for an appeal," Armstrong said, anxious to get away.

"You think we're going to let you handle Blaine's appeal after the piss-poor job you just did? You're fired."

"You have to do what you think is best," Armstrong said before hurrying out of the courtroom. Several reporters waylaid him, but he fended off their questions with a repeated "No comment." Then he hurried down the steps to the lobby, too anxious to get away from the Hastings to wait for the elevator.

●　●　●

Frank Nylander, Armstrong's partner, was talking to their receptionist when Doug walked into the waiting room. Nylander was a head taller than his partner. Though he was ten years older, his trim figure and full head of black hair made him look as if they were the same age. Nylander turned when he heard the door open. Doug looked disheveled and unhappy. His tie was askew and his white shirt was rumpled and sweat stained.

"I take it that things did not go well," Nylander said.

"They went as badly as they could possibly go."

"As you predicted."

"I didn't predict that Hastings would go ballistic in court." Armstrong shook his head. "He made a complete ass of himself, and Judge Redding revoked his bail."

Nylander shrugged. "As ye sow so shall ye reap."

"The only good news is that Blaine Hastings is not my problem anymore. His father fired me."

"Is that why you look upset?"

"No. Actually, I've never been so glad to be fired. Hastings Senior and Junior were some of the most unpleasant clients I've ever represented."

"Then what's got you in a lather?" Nylander asked.

"Junior threatened me during the trial."

"You're not worried he'll get out, are you?"

"No. There are some arguments that can be made in an appeal, but I don't see them winning."

"Then relax. Hastings is locked up, and he'll have a lot more to worry about than getting revenge on you. A pretty boy like that in prison. I've heard that cons don't like child molesters and rapists."

"Anything he gets he deserves," Armstrong agreed.

Nylander studied his friend. "You look like shit, Doug. Slap some water on your face, comb what's left of your hair, and I'll take you out for a stiff drink."

"I should get home to Marsha."

"She'll be a lot happier to see you if you're not in a state. Come on. That's what friends and law partners are for."

Armstrong hesitated. Then he smiled. "You are a friend, Frank, a good friend. Let me call Marsha and get myself together. I can definitely use that drink."

CHAPTER ELEVEN

Ivar Gorski sat in the front seat of his rental car and took a sip from his thermos. Just a sip, because he did not want to have to relieve himself, thus creating the possibility that he would miss his subject.

Ivar was whip-thin with wiry muscles kept hard by hours in a Manhattan dojo. He began his study of the martial arts in the Ukraine, where he had served in the army, and he had continued his training after emigrating to the United States, where his job occasionally required violence.

Ivar focused his dark, deep-set eyes on a house halfway down the street. Those eyes were on either side of a narrow nose that bent like a hawk's beak. Ivar's wide, flat forehead, close-cropped blond hair, high cheekbones, and pale skin made his head look vaguely like a skull.

The door to the house opened and Ivar sat up. A woman in jeans and a Windbreaker pushed Leonard Voss's wheelchair outside before locking the door. Voss's head canted to one side and he slumped in the chair: a stroke victim, just as it said in the medical report Norcross Pharmaceuticals had received.

Ivar wrote down his observations in a notebook. He had been following Voss for a week, and he'd seen nothing to indicate that Voss was faking, which was bad news for his employer.

The woman pushing the wheelchair was Rita, Voss's wife. She opened the door of their van and helped her husband inside. They were probably on their way to a doctor's appointment. Mrs. Voss started to walk to the driver's door. Then she stopped and looked down the street at Ivar. After a moment's hesitation, she started walking toward his car. Ivar turned the car away from the Voss's van and sped away. He thought he'd been careful, but he'd been spotted. It didn't really matter. He had all the information he needed, but his pride as a professional was wounded.

Rita Voss got her husband in the van. Then she got in the driver's seat and locked the doors. She thought she had seen the red Honda Accord following them to two of Leonard's hospital appointments. Now that the driver had driven off so quickly, she was certain that Norcross was having Leonard followed.

Rita hesitated. Was she being paranoid? No, she was sure that someone was following them. She pulled out her phone and dialed 911.

"What's your emergency?" the operator asked.

"It's not an emergency, but I think my husband is being fol-lowed."

"Are you in immediate danger?"

"No. The . . . the person drove away."

"Nine-one-one is for emergencies, but if you'll hold on for a mo-ment, I'll give you the number for the nearest police station and you can ask how you can file a complaint."

Rita pulled a pen out of her pocket and wrote down the num-ber. She felt a little foolish, but she wouldn't put anything past Nor-cross. She decided to drive Leonard to his appointment and call the police while he was being examined.

PART TWO

THE *HENDERSON* CASE

CHAPTER TWELVE

The door to the coffee shop opened, and Robin looked up from the case she'd been reading. Jeff Hodges paused in the doorway. When Robin saw Jeff, she waved.

Jeff limped over to her table and uncapped the latte she'd ordered for him. "How's it going?" he asked.

"Great. I found a case from Florida that's on point concerning that jury instruction Kellerman wants."

"Kellerman is grasping at straws," Jeff said as he sat down.

"Remember what Regina says," Robin warned. "No case is over until it's over."

Jeff smiled. "Speaking of Regina, we got a postcard from Justice Cloud. They're in Venice, and he says Regina is having the time of her life."

"I'm so glad," Robin said, but she didn't look happy.

"Hey, cheer up. It's a beautiful thing they're doing."

"I know. It's just so sad."

"And out of anyone's control."

"I guess," Robin sighed.

"Think about how happy Regina must be and how happy you're going to be when you kick Kellerman's ass."

Robin smiled. "There is that. And no one deserves it more."

"Are you referring to your mentor or Mr. Unethical?"

"Both, I guess."

"I'll drink to that," Jeff said as he took a sip of the latte. "Now, let's head to court."

Rex Kellerman's case was a mess. The testimony of the police officers and lab techs who'd responded to the crime scene had not made a dent in Everett Henderson's claim of self-defense. Under cross-examination, the three men who'd been drinking with Greg Schaefer admitted that they and the dead off-duty policeman were heavily intoxicated. They also admitted that they never saw how the fight started and came around the bar only when Henderson and Schaefer were squaring off.

Robin had called her client to the stand—a risky move given Henderson's lengthy criminal record. But the defendant had been great. Henderson's girlfriend and drinking companions all swore that Henderson had been attacked from behind by the dead man. The bottle Schaefer used in the fight had been taken into evidence, and Robin was able to show it to the jury. The jagged edges were intimidating, and Henderson had shown the jurors the stitches in his skull. Some of them had grimaced when they saw photographs of the gaping, bleeding head wound before the gash had been stitched up.

On Wednesday afternoon, the defense rested its case, and the judge asked the prosecutor if he had any rebuttal witnesses. Kellerman had looked the judge in the eye and swore that he did not.

When Robin walked into Judge Harold Wright's courtroom on Thursday morning, the bailiff told her that she was wanted in chambers. Jeff and Robin found the judge in shirtsleeves. He did not look happy.

Kellerman was leaning back in a chair. When he saw Robin, he turned his head so the judge couldn't see him and smirked.

"Have a seat," the judge said.

"What's up?" Robin asked.

"We have a situation," Judge Wright replied. "Mr. Kellerman wants to put on a rebuttal witness."

"What witness?" Robin asked. "He's rested."

"A witness my investigator located last night," Kellerman said.

"What's he going to say?" Robin asked.

"Willis Goins will testify that he was in jail with the defendant. During a recreation period, Mr. Henderson confided that he had made up his claim of self-defense and had bribed his buddies to back him up."

"I assume Mr. Goins is a solid citizen who is testifying out of the goodness of his heart," Robin said, barely able to keep her anger in check.

"I haven't made him any promises," Kellerman said.

"Just out of curiosity, what's this paragon of virtue charged with?"

"Burglary and possession of heroin."

"I see. Can I assume that no one else heard this conversation?"

"It was just the two of them."

Robin turned to the judge. "The legal term for this is 'bullshit.' The Oregon discovery rules were passed to prevent this kind of trial by ambush. They're very clear. Mr. Goins wasn't on Mr. Kellerman's witness list, he's rested, and I move for an order barring Goins from testifying."

Kellerman spread his hands and tried to look angelic. "I would have notified counsel, but I didn't learn about the witness until after court recessed, and I didn't finish debriefing him until after ten last night."

"I gotta tell you, Rex, I'm leaning toward granting Robin's motion. This is awfully late in the game to spring this on the defense."

Kellerman handed a copy of a case to Robin and the judge. "I'm within my rights to put on a witness if I had no knowledge of the witness when the defense rested. Rocky Stiller, my investigator, got a call from the jail at five thirty Wednesday night and went right over to interview Goins. I'd never heard of him until Rocky called me at home late last night."

Judge Wright leaned his head back and closed his eyes. Robin waited, her heart beating fast.

Wright opened his eyes. "I'm going to send the jury home. We'll reconvene tomorrow morning with this issue briefed. That's all."

Kellerman walked out and Robin followed.

"This is a chickenshit move, Rex."

"I don't understand why you're so upset. Aren't we trying to discover the truth here?"

"Go fuck yourself."

Kellerman grinned. "See you tomorrow."

Robin's hands curled into fists, and Jeff put a restraining hand on her arm.

"He's not worth it."

"I don't know, Jeff. It might be a fair trade if I were disbarred for breaking Kellerman's nose."

"Yeah, well, wait until tomorrow. I have an idea. I'll let you know if it pans out."

Robin finished briefing the discovery issue at four thirty, then headed for McGill's to blow off steam. Julie Tapanoe, a young MMA fighter with a four-and-two record, was working the heavy bag when Robin walked in. Julie waved Robin over and asked her if she wanted to spar. Robin was still fuming when they started, and she dropped Tapanoe with a vicious kick to the head a few seconds into the sparring session. Barry McGill was watching, and he walked over when Robin landed another brutal shot soon after Tapanoe got up.

"Time!" he shouted.

Robin spun toward him.

"What's going on, Lockwood?"

"We're sparring," Robin snapped.

"Julie is, but you're not. It looks like you're trying to take her head off."

Robin started to argue. Then she dropped her hands to her sides and looked contrite. "I'm sorry, Julie. I had a rough day in court. There's this prick of a DA who's trying to sandbag me by calling a jailhouse snitch named Goins. I'm furious with the DA, but I shouldn't be taking it out on you."

"No, you shouldn't," McGill said. "Now, get your shit together."

Robin restrained herself during the rest of the workout. As she was walking to the locker room to shower and change, McGill intercepted her.

"The snitch, is his name Willis Goins?" McGill asked.

Robin looked surprised. "Yeah, why?"

"Meet me at the courthouse tomorrow morning at eight."

Robin was exhausted from her workout and still depressed and angry because of Kellerman's slimy trick. She didn't feel like eating out, so she stopped at a supermarket and bought a salad for dinner. Robin ate her salad out of its plastic container without really tasting it while she watched the news on TV. She had just finished eating when her phone rang.

"I struck pay dirt," Jeff said excitedly.

"Tell me."

Jeff explained what he'd discovered at the jail, and Robin had a big smile on her face when she hung up.

CHAPTER THIRTEEN

When Robin arrived at the Multnomah County Courthouse the next morning, Barry McGill was waiting for her with a heavyset woman in a threadbare coat. Robin judged the woman to be in her early fifties, but she looked much older and had obviously seen hard times.

"Robin Lockwood, Mary Goins," McGill said.

Robin hid her surprise. "Are you related to Willis Goins?"

"I'm that asshole's wife," she answered.

"I'll leave you two to get acquainted," McGill said, walking off before Robin could thank him.

"How do you know Barry?" Robin asked.

"Church," Goins answered tersely.

"And what can you tell me about your husband?"

"Plenty."

The spectator section of the courtroom was packed for the hearing on Robin's motion to bar Willis Goins from testifying. Judge Wright took the bench and told Rex Kellerman to call his witness.

"Please tell the Court your name," Kellerman said when a

heavyset, jowly man with bushy eyebrows and close-cropped salt-and-pepper hair took the stand.

"Rocky Stiller."

"Are you an investigator with the Multnomah County District Attorney's Office?"

"I am."

"Have you had any contact with a man named Willis Goins?"

"I have."

"Please tell Judge Wright about that."

Stiller turned to the judge. "I was in my office around five thirty on Wednesday evening when I received a call from the Justice Center jail. The caller was Mr. Goins. He said he had information that would help the prosecution of Everett Henderson, so I went to the jail and talked to him."

"What was the gist of what Mr. Goins told you?" Kellerman said.

"Mr. Goins said he'd had a conversation with the defendant during a recreation period, and Mr. Henderson told him that he was going to say he killed Greg Schaefer in self-defense, but he really hadn't. Goins said that the defendant told him that he was making up a story so he could win his case and had bribed his friends to back him up."

Everett Henderson leaned over and whispered in Robin's ear. "That's bullshit. We did talk, but it was about sports."

Robin laid a hand on Henderson's massive forearm. "Don't worry, Everett. I've got this covered."

"What did you do after you spoke to Mr. Goins?" Kellerman continued.

"I called you and told you what Mr. Goins said."

"What did I do after we spoke?"

"You came to the jail around nine o'clock and interviewed Mr. Goins."

"Were you in the room with me during the interview?"

"I was."

"What time did we finish speaking to Mr. Goins?"

"It was late, around ten, ten thirty."

"No further questions, Your Honor," the prosecutor said.

"Miss Lockwood?" the judge said.

"Thank you, Your Honor. Mr. Stiller, who is Terry Powell?"

Robin was watching Kellerman, and she was pleased to see the blood drain from his face.

"He's another investigator in our office."

"Nothing further," Robin said.

"Do you have any more witnesses, Mr. Kellerman?" the judge asked.

"No, Your Honor."

"Miss Lockwood?"

"I have two. I'd like Mary Goins to take the stand."

The bailiff went into the hall and returned with Mrs. Goins.

"What is your relationship to Willis Goins?" Robin asked after the witness was sworn.

"He's my husband."

"How long have you been married?"

Mrs. Goins sighed and shook her head. "It seems like forever, but I guess it's sixteen years."

"Do you have an opinion about Mr. Goins's ability to tell the truth?"

Mrs. Goins laughed. "He ain't got that ability. If Willis tells you it's high noon, you better get ten astronomers to back him up before you believe him."

"Now, we've had testimony that your husband called the DA's office and claimed that he and my client were in jail together and my client confessed to making up a story about acting in self-defense so he could win his case. Does this sound familiar?"

"It sure does," Mrs. Goins said. "He pulls this sh . . . stuff all the time when he gets arrested. He finds out about a case and gets friendly with the defendant. Then he rats him out."

"Isn't that a good thing to do?" Robin asked. "Shouldn't a good citizen contact the authorities if they know something that will help put a criminal behind bars?"

"Sure, if it's true, but Willis makes this stuff up. He lies about it so he can get a deal in his case."

"How do you know that?"

"He's bragged to me about lying to get out of jail."

"No further questions," Robin said.

"Mrs. Goins, if your husband is so dishonest, why are you still married to him?"

Mrs. Goins shook her head. "I've asked myself that question a lot, but a divorce costs money, and, besides, Willis ain't around that much. He's either in jail or gone most of the time, so it's like a divorce."

"Mrs. Goins, do you know anything about this case, the case involving Everett Henderson?"

"No, except what I found out when I talked to Miss Lockwood."

"So, you never talked to your husband about it?"

"No."

"Is it fair to say that you don't know if Mr. Goins is lying or telling the truth about his conversation with Mr. Henderson?"

Mrs. Goins started to say something. Then she stopped herself. "No. I got no idea."

"No further questions."

"Any more witnesses, Miss Lockwood?" the judge asked.

"One more, Your Honor. I call Jeff Hodges."

"Mr. Hodges, are you the investigator for the firm of Barrister, Berman, and Lockwood?" Robin asked as soon as Jeff was sworn.

"Yes."

"Did I tell you that Assistant District Attorney Rex Kellerman wanted to call a rebuttal witness named Willis Goins, who was not on his witness list?"

"Yes."

"Did I also tell you that Mr. Kellerman told Judge Wright that he learned about Mr. Goins for the first time on Wednesday night when Rocky Stiller, one of his investigators, told him that Mr. Goins had called him earlier on Wednesday evening from the jail with information about Everett Henderson?"

"Yes."

"What did you do after I gave you this information?"

"I went to the jail and looked at the visitors' log."

"What days did you look at?"

"Monday, Tuesday, and Wednesday."

"Did you confirm Mr. Kellerman's and Mr. Stiller's claims that they spoke to Mr. Goins on Wednesday night?"

"Yes."

"Did anyone else visit Mr. Goins on any of those days?"

"Yes. Terry Powell visited Mr. Goins on Tuesday afternoon at three thirty and left at four thirty. Then he returned an hour later and spoke to Mr. Goins again."

"Who is Terry Powell?" Robin asked.

"An investigator in Mr. Kellerman's office."

"Did you try to contact Mr. Powell about these visits?"

"I did."

"What was the result?"

"He refused to take my call. This morning, I went to the district attorney's office and asked for Mr. Powell, and I was told that he was out sick. I had his cell phone number from another case, and I called it."

"What happened?"

"The call went to voice mail."

"No further questions."

Judge Wright looked angry when he turned to Rex Kellerman. Kellerman's face was bright red.

"Did you learn about Mr. Goins on Tuesday?" the judge asked the prosecutor.

"I . . . Well, uh, not exactly, Your Honor. Mr. Powell told me that a prisoner at the jail had some information about the case, but I was too busy to follow up. So, I didn't know what the information was until Mr. Stiller called on Wednesday night."

Judge Wright looked like he could barely contain his anger. "I want to be certain I understand what happened, because there may be serious consequences. On Tuesday, did Mr. Powell, an investigator for the Multnomah County District Attorney's Office, tell you that he had spoken to Willis Goins?"

"Yes."

"Did he also tell you that Mr. Goins told him information relevant to Mr. Henderson's case?"

"Yes, but he didn't say what it was. I didn't learn the information until after I rested my case."

Judge Wright stared at Kellerman until the DA broke eye contact. Then he turned to Robin. "Do you have anything you'd like to say, Miss Lockwood?"

Robin had plenty she wanted to say, but she restrained herself. "I think it would be interesting to talk to Mr. Powell, but it appears that Mr. Powell has made himself scarce. In any event, I believe that it doesn't matter when Mr. Kellerman learned what Mr. Goins had to say. Terry Powell works for the Multnomah County District Attorney's office and is an agent of the office and Mr. Kellerman. Mr. Kellerman should be charged with knowing everything Mr. Powell knew on Tuesday. Mr. Kellerman can't put his hands over his ears and then spring a surprise witness on the defense. As soon as Mr. Kellerman learned about Mr. Goins from Mr. Powell, he had a duty to list Mr. Goins as a potential witness.

"In light of what Your Honor has learned from Mrs. Goins and Mr. Hodges, I think Your Honor should bar Willis Goins from testifying in this case."

CHAPTER FOURTEEN

Rex Kellerman stared straight ahead to avoid looking at Robin when Judge Wright read the *not guilty* verdict. Even though losing to a bitch like Robin Lockwood was unbearable, he congratulated her with a broad smile as soon as the jury was dismissed. A mob of reporters was waiting in the corridor outside the courtroom, and Kellerman gave them clichéd answers about the American system of justice before begging off and heading for his office.

Kellerman knew that news of his defeat had reached his fellow prosecutors because people averted their eyes and no one spoke to him as he passed their desks. Kellerman walked with his head up to preserve his dignity, but as soon as he shut the door to his office, the façade disappeared and he smashed his fist into the wall.

The murder of a policeman by a member of a racist prison gang had been headline news, and Rex had counted on a highly publicized win to make him a front runner when the district attorney announced that he was not going to run again. Now the voters Kellerman hoped would make him the county's district attorney would think of him as a loser.

Kellerman squeezed his eyes shut and dropped his head into

his hands. Vanessa Cole, the chief criminal deputy, was putting a campaign team together. He imagined the satisfied smile on Cole's face when she heard the news of his defeat.

When Kellerman opened his eyes, he saw the time on his wall clock and remembered that he would be fucking Douglas Armstrong's wife in half an hour. Kellerman had arranged to meet Marsha tonight so they could celebrate his victory in the *Henderson* case. There was nothing to celebrate now, but sex might help him forget his humiliation for a while.

Marsha was good in bed, but more than the sex, Kellerman enjoyed cuckolding her wimp of a husband. Whenever he and Armstrong met at the courthouse, it gave Kellerman great pleasure to remember the way Marsha's body felt.

Armstrong's first wife had died unexpectedly from cancer. A year later, he'd married his secretary. Kellerman had met Marsha for the first time at a bar function. She wasn't very bright, and she seemed a bit lost amidst all the legal brain power. Kellerman knew she wasn't a lawyer, but he had asked where she practiced and pretended surprise when she said she was a legal secretary. By the time they'd parted, Kellerman had convinced himself that she was attracted to him. He hadn't made a move during that first meeting, but he'd filed the memory away for further exploration at a date to be determined.

Nine months later, Kellerman had run into Marsha while she was waiting outside a courtroom where Doug was in trial. She seemed sad, and Kellerman sensed an opening. Not really thinking she'd accept, he asked Marsha to meet for a drink in a hotel over the river in Vancouver, Washington, where they were not likely to be seen. He'd been surprised when she accepted.

At the hotel, Marsha had been reluctant to do more than talk. Kellerman learned that her marriage was not working for reasons Marsha would not reveal. He pretended to be sympathetic, and Marsha agreed to meet him at the same hotel when Doug was in

Los Angeles, taking depositions. This time, they ended up in bed. Kellerman was pleasantly surprised by how aggressive Marsha had been, and he'd concluded that her husband left a lot to be desired in the sack.

They had not met again for a month, and their next tryst was less satisfying. Still, the combination of conquering a body like Marsha's and the secret thrill Kellerman experienced from cuckolding Doug Armstrong had made his experience enjoyable.

Imagining Marsha naked and waiting made Kellerman feel powerful. He looked at his watch. Marsha had probably arrived at the hotel by now. He would be at least fifteen minutes late. It would be good to make her wait.

When Kellerman walked into the hotel room, Marsha Armstrong was sitting in a chair on the other side of the room from the bed with her coat on. Kellerman stood in the doorway and frowned. Not only was Marsha dressed but she also wouldn't meet his eye.

"What gives?" Kellerman asked.

"I'm . . . I wanted to tell you in person," Marsha said in a voice that was barely above a whisper.

"Tell me what?" Kellerman asked, trying not to sound annoyed and not completely succeeding.

Marsha looked up. He could see she'd been crying.

"What's the matter, honey?" he asked with faked sympathy.

"I can't do this, Rex. I . . . Cheating on Doug . . . It's eating me up."

Kellerman knelt by her side and took Marsha's hand. "That's a natural feeling, Marsha. But we both know your marriage isn't working."

"It's not that. That's not why I agreed to . . . to do this." Marsha looked down at her lap. "When we first made love, I was very depressed. I'd . . ." Marsha took a deep breath and looked up. "I miscarried, Rex. It was our baby and . . . and the doctor said . . ." She started to cry again. "He told us I couldn't have another baby. And after that, when Doug wanted to make love . . . I couldn't do it. And I just wanted to see if I made love to someone else, maybe I could have a baby. But I wasn't thinking straight, and I know you've been kind to me, but I can't do this anymore."

"I can see why you're sad, baby," Kellerman said, not willing to give up, "but you know I care for you, and we're so good together."

Marsha shook her head. "I can't, Rex, I just can't."

She stood and Kellerman stood with her. "This is bullshit, Marsha," Kellerman blurted out. "We agreed to have sex tonight. I paid for the room. You can't just walk out."

Marsha's mouth dropped open, shocked by Kellerman's callousness. "I can't believe you just . . ." She shook her head and turned toward the door.

Kellerman grabbed her elbow. "I'm sorry. I didn't mean that. You know I care for you. Come on back."

Marsha wrenched her arm away. "This has been a mistake," she said. Then she left the room.

Kellerman clenched his fists and cursed. He knew he'd handled the encounter badly, but his sexual frustration piled on top of the humiliation he'd suffered in court had been too much.

Kellerman dropped onto the chair Marsha had vacated. He let his head fall back. First that bitch Lockwood, and now this. No one treated him like this and got away with it. Someone was going to pay.

CHAPTER FIFTEEN

Doug Armstrong worked late at his office, preparing a case he was hoping to settle in Seattle, Washington. He had plenty of time to prepare, but his work provided an excuse to stay away from home. Until Marsha had miscarried, the Armstrongs' home had been a joyful place to which he had always been happy to return. But miscarrying had hit Marsha hard, and the doctor's opinion that she would not be able to have children had driven Marsha into a deep depression.

Doug had waited for Marsha to rebound, but life at home had grown darker and darker. Several months ago, Marsha had told Doug that she wanted him to move into the guest room. Doug moved out of their marriage bed without complaint after telling Marsha that he loved her and would do anything that would help her get better. But the brave face he put on was a mask that hid the horrible way he felt, knowing that the woman he loved could no longer stand his touch.

Doug parked in his garage a little before eight. When he walked into the hallway, he could see Marsha sitting in the living room on the sofa with her hands clasped in her lap. The television—often her only companion—was not on, and the room was lit by a solitary lamp.

Marsha looked up when Doug walked into the living room. There were tears in her eyes.

Doug hesitated before walking toward her. "What's wrong, honey?"

"Me, I'm wrong. The way I've treated you . . ." Marsha began to sob. Her shoulders folded in, and she bent forward.

Doug moved closer, but he was afraid to hold his wife because he didn't know how she would react.

Marsha looked into Doug's eyes. "All you've ever done is love me, and I've been horrible to you. I've been so selfish."

Doug sat next to Marsha and placed a hand on her shoulder. "I can't understand what you've gone through, but I've seen how hard losing your child hit you."

Marsha didn't reject his touch. She turned toward him. "It was *our* child, not just mine. And I could see how badly you wanted a child. I had no right to throw you out of our bed. I've been a monster."

Doug took a chance and embraced Marsha. She melted into his arms. After a while, she stopped crying and nestled against Doug. They stayed that way for an eternity.

Then Marsha pulled back and looked at Doug. "Please take me to bed. I need you to make love to me, so I know you forgive me."

"There's nothing to forgive," Doug answered.

Marsha stood up, took Doug's hand, and led him toward their bedroom.

CHAPTER SIXTEEN

Carrie Anders found Patrol Officer Maggie Collins waiting in the hospital corridor.

"I understand you were the first responder," Anders said after the introductions had been made.

"Yes, ma'am."

"Bring me up to speed."

Collins took a notebook out of her back pocket and flipped to the relevant pages. "The victim's name is Jessica Braxton. She's Caucasian, twenty-two, single, and lives alone."

"Employed?"

"Not steadily. Mostly low-paying jobs. She clerked at a convenience store, cooked at a McDonald's. That sort of work."

"How is she doing?"

"The doctor says her only physical injuries are a black eye and split lip."

"And her mental state?"

"She was scared and nervous, but she's holding it together."

"Will she make a good witness?"

Collins frowned. "Yeah, I think so."

"Do you have reservations?"

"Not really. I don't know if this means anything, but she seemed more nervous than scared. I haven't been on the force long, but I have interviewed two rape victims, and they were terrified. Of course, I saw them right after the rape and not two hours later, when they'd had some time to calm down."

"So, she didn't call 911 right away?"

"No. She says she was disoriented by the beating and the alcohol and very frightened."

"Did she contaminate the crime scene?" Anders asked.

"No, and she did give us the panties. She says Ray threw them under the bed after wiping himself."

"Ray?"

"The perpetrator."

"Okay. So, what about these panties?"

"Miss Braxton told me that she didn't discover them until she'd called 911. She was going to throw them out when she remembered seeing a crime show on TV in which semen on a pair of panties was used to convict a rapist."

"Where are the panties?" Anders asked.

"They're at the crime lab. They also found semen when they did the vaginal swab for the rape kit."

"Okay," Anders said. "You did a great job. I'll talk to you again if it's necessary. Who's in with her now?"

"No one. The doctor and a nurse left a few minutes ago."

When Anders walked into the hospital room, Jessica Braxton's eyes went wide.

Anders flashed her shield. "Hi, I'm Carrie Anders. I'm a detective with the Portland Police Bureau."

Braxton stared at Anders's badge for a moment; then she relaxed. "I'm sorry. I'm just scared."

"You have every right to be," Anders said. Anders pointed at a metal chair that was sitting against the wall. "Mind if I sit down?" she asked. "I've been on my feet all day."

"No, please."

"Thanks," Anders said as she pulled the chair next to the bed. "So, how are they treating you?"

"Good. Everyone has been very nice to me."

"That's great. Do you mind if I ask you some questions about what happened so I can start hunting down the person who did this to you?"

Braxton looked down at her covers. "I don't like talking about it," she said quietly.

"I don't blame you. I've never met a woman yet who's been raped who enjoyed reliving the experience, but I can't find this bastard if I don't have your information. So, can we talk? I'll try to make it quick."

Braxton thought for a moment before nodding. "Go ahead."

"I think the easiest way to do this is for you to tell me what happened like you were telling a story. Start at the beginning."

"There's a club I like to go to, the Blue Unicorn, and I went there last night."

"Were you by yourself?"

"Yes."

"Okay, go on."

"I went out back in the alley to smoke, and this guy came out."

"Did this guy have a name?"

"Ray. At least that's what he said it was."

"Did he tell you his last name?"

"He might have, but I don't remember if he did." Braxton blushed. "I was drinking and . . . If I did something illegal, can I get in trouble?"

"Does this have to do with drugs?"

Braxton nodded.

"Not from me."

"Okay, well, I did snort some coke in the ladies' room. Between the two, I was a little high."

"Can you describe Ray?"

"He was handsome. He had blond hair, blue eyes, and an athlete's build. He was muscular and over six feet tall."

"Okay, so you're talking."

"Yeah, and after a while, he suggested we go to my apartment. I live alone on the second floor of a duplex not far from the club."

"Is that where it happened?" Anders asked.

Braxton swallowed and nodded. "As soon as we were inside, he hit me in the stomach and dragged me into the bedroom. Then he hit me again, threw me on the bed, and covered my mouth. He said he'd kill me if I screamed, and he asked me if I understood. I nodded and he ripped off my panties and . . ." Braxton licked her lips and took a breath.

"Did he penetrate you? That's important in a rape case. We can't convict if he didn't."

Braxton nodded. "He did."

"Did he use a condom?"

"No."

"Okay, what happened next?"

"When he was done, he wiped himself on my panties and threw them on the floor. Then he threatened to kill me if I told on him. Then he hit me again and left."

"You've done great, Jessica. I'm going to leave you now. Ray may have done something very stupid. I understand he left semen on your panties and they found more when they did the vaginal swab. That means we've got DNA, and that should give us a great chance of getting this bastard."

PART THREE

DNA

CHAPTER SEVENTEEN

Vanessa Cole, Multnomah County's Chief Criminal Deputy, was a slender, fifty-two-year-old black woman with sharp features and fierce brown eyes. She'd grown up in a wealthy area of Portland's West Hills and gone to Stanford for college and law school. Cole was known for her smarts and high ethical standards, and stood out from the moment she joined the Multnomah County District Attorney's Office, moving quickly from trying misdemeanors to trying felonies to handling murder cases and then death penalty murder cases.

Vanessa had always been anal. She almost never missed a school assignment from elementary school through law school, and a rare B had caused endless soul-searching. Her office reflected her obsession with order. The case files on her blotter were arranged in neatly squared stacks, and her computer monitor sat in the exact center of her desk.

Carrie Anders knew how much Vanessa detested chaos, and that was why she dreaded explaining the results of the lab tests in Jessica Braxton's case.

"Have you got a moment?" Anders asked from the doorway to the prosecutor's office.

Cole looked up from the memo she'd been reading and motioned the detective in. As she took a seat, Anders tried to think of
the best way to explain what had happened. She decided to be
blunt.

"We've got a problem in one of Rex's cases."

"Which one?"

"Hastings."

Cole's brow furrowed. "That case was open and shut. What's
the problem?"

"A bad one. A woman named Jessica Braxton was raped last
week by a guy who said his name was Ray. She met Ray at the Blue
Unicorn nightclub. Does that name ring a bell?"

It took Cole only a few seconds to make the connection. "Isn't
that where Hastings's victim, Randi Stark, says she was when she
saw the man who attacked her behind that gas station?"

Anders nodded. "It's a club she said she went to a lot. Now, get
this: Braxton described the rapist she met at the Blue Unicorn as a
handsome blond who was over six feet tall and very muscular."

Cole frowned. "That could be a description of Blaine Hastings.
But he's in jail. So, what's the problem?"

"That *is* the problem. Braxton says she and Ray went back to
her apartment and that's where he raped her. According to Braxton,
Ray penetrated her without a condom, ejaculated inside her, wiped
himself with her panties, and left after throwing the panties on the
floor. That meant that the lab had plenty of semen to test for DNA."

Anders looked directly at Cole. "Ray's DNA and Blaine Hastings's DNA match."

"What do you mean 'match'?"

"They're identical."

"That's impossible!"

"The lab retested Ray's DNA as soon as the computer made the
match between Ray's DNA and Hastings's DNA. When they got the

same result, they sent a sample of the semen in the Braxton case to a private lab, and that lab got the same result."

"Fuck!" exclaimed Cole, who never swore. "It's got to be a mistake."

"It's not.

"Can two people have the same DNA?" asked Cole, who already knew the answer but hoped that she was wrong.

Anders nodded. "If they're identical twins. But Hastings doesn't have an identical twin. He's an only child. And no, he and his evil twin were not separated at birth. I went to the hospital where he was born with a search warrant. Gloria Hastings gave birth to one child and only one."

"What explanation do the lab techs have?"

"The only thing they can think of is that someone screwed up Hastings's DNA test."

"What's the implication if that's true?"

"One possibility is that Randi met Ray at the Blue Unicorn and had sex with him. Then she went to the frat party and accused Blaine of rape."

Vanessa shook her head. "That still doesn't explain why the two DNA samples match."

"Correct."

"So, we're back to square one."

"More like one to the nth degree."

"Have you told Rex yet?"

"No."

"Then let's go break the news."

"He's not going to like it," Anders said.

Vanessa led the way down the hall to Rex's office. He looked up when the women walked in and started to smile. But the smile faded when he saw the looks on their faces.

"That's not possible," Kellerman said when Anders finished explaining the DNA match.

"Everyone I talked to agrees with you," Anders said, "but the samples match."

Kellerman shook his head. "It's a trick, a scam. Have you checked the visitor logs? Did this Braxton woman visit Hastings? Could they have fucked in the jail?"

"Hastings's only visitors were his new lawyer, Les Kreuger, and his parents."

"There's got to be an explanation."

"The crime lab is working on it. They've hired Paul Baylor at Oregon Forensics to run tests on the semen in the two cases."

"Does Kreuger know about this?"

"I've got to tell him, Rex."

Kellerman looked lost. "He'll try to get Hastings out of jail. He'll move for a new trial."

"I expect so," Vanessa said. "You better brush up on DNA because bad things will happen if we can't figure out how two people can have the same DNA."

CHAPTER EIGHTEEN

Tyler Harrison III watched Frank Nylander walk toward the elevator before closing the door to his office. Nylander had come to New York assuming that Leonard Voss's case would be settled by the end of their meeting. That hadn't happened, and both lawyers were upset by the intransigence of Nylander's client.

Harrison walked over to his window. Twenty stories below, the traffic crawled along Park Avenue. As he watched it, Harrison thought about how he was going to break the bad news to Marvin Turnbull. A few minutes later, he returned to his desk and dialed Turnbull's private number at Norcross Pharmaceutical.

The CEO picked up after one ring. "What happened?" Turnbull asked.

"Voss rejected the offer."

"You're kidding! It was more than generous."

"Voss sees this as a matter of principle. He's on a crusade."

"Is there any way we can keep the case from going to trial? The publicity could be disastrous."

"I'll take another shot at a settlement," Harrison said, "but Nylander told me both Voss and his wife are dead set on—and I quote—'exposing Norcross.' He didn't seem any happier about having to take the case to trial than I am."

"Fucking fanatics," Turnbull mumbled. There was silence for a moment. Then Turnbull said, "Okay, take another shot at settling. It looks like that's all we can do."

Marvin Turnbull hung up on Harrison. Then he took out a disposable cell phone and dialed a number in Portland, Oregon.

"Yes," Ivar Gorski answered.

"We've hit a snag, and I may need you to implement plan B, so be prepared."

CHAPTER NINETEEN

Robin was in her office when Vanessa Cole phoned.

"Are you representing Randi Stark in her civil suit against Blaine Hastings?" Cole asked.

"Yes."

"Les Kreuger is Blaine Hastings's new attorney. He filed a motion for a new trial and release on bail, and Judge Redding is hearing it this afternoon. You should be there."

"Why?"

"I'll let it be a surprise."

"Should I bring Randi?"

"No."

"Why the heads up?"

"You'll find out."

Judge Redding's courtroom was packed, and Robin guessed that someone in Blaine Hastings's camp had tipped off the press. Robin found a seat just as Les Kreuger called Paul Baylor, a slender, bookish African American, as his first witness. Kreuger was a bear of a man with a florid complexion and gray-streaked black hair. He had trained for the opera in his youth and used his deep voice for dramatic emphasis.

"Mr. Baylor, are you self-employed?" Kreuger asked.

"I am."

"What is your business?"

"I own Oregon Forensic Investigations."

"What do you do there?"

"I provide forensic expertise to individuals and institutions."

"With regard to criminal investigations, do you work for the prosecution and defense?"

"I do."

"What are your credentials?"

"I have a degree in forensic science and criminal justice from Michigan State University, and I worked at the Oregon State Crime Lab for ten years before leaving to open my own business."

"Can you tell the Court a little about DNA?"

Baylor turned to Judge Redding. "DNA is shorthand for deoxyribonucleic acid, a chemical entity that is found in all living things. With regard to human beings, DNA is an instruction manual that helps us carry out all the necessary life processes.

"DNA is also genetic material that we inherit half from our mother and half from our father. In addition to being life's instruction manual, DNA is capable of copying itself so that new cells in the body have identical content."

"Is DNA consistent throughout a person's body?" Kreuger asked.

"Yes."

"So, a sample taken from a person's hair, blood, skin, or semen will give the same result upon DNA testing?"

"Yes."

"Mr. Baylor, will two human beings ever have the same DNA?"

"No. The only exception we know of is identical twins. So, other than identical twins, no two human beings should have the same DNA."

"Let's move on to the subject of this hearing. A short time ago, were you contacted by the Oregon State Crime Lab and asked to conduct DNA testing on samples of semen obtained in two rape cases involving two different individuals?"

"Yes."

"Why did they contact you?" Kreuger asked.

"There is a database for DNA in which samples from an unknown individual can be compared to DNA from known individuals to see if they match. If semen from a rapist is found on his victim, a lab can determine the structure of the DNA in the semen and compare it to the DNA from people whose DNA is in the database."

"Did the State Crime Lab have semen from an unknown person known only as Ray who was accused of rape?"

"Yes."

"Were they puzzled by the results when they fed their information into the DNA database?"

"Yes."

"Why?"

"I was told that the DNA was a match for a man known as Blaine Hastings Jr."

"Why was that a problem?"

"Mr. Hastings was incarcerated at the time of the rape. The lab wanted me to conduct an independent test because they knew this result was impossible."

"What was the result of your test?"

"It was the same as the crime lab. Ray's DNA and Mr. Hastings's DNA are identical."

"How do you explain that?" Kreuger asked.

"There is a theoretical possibility that there are two humans who are not identical twins with identical DNA, but the odds are so astronomical that it is not a possibility in the real world. Therefore, the only explanation I can think of is that there were errors in the DNA tests conducted on one or both samples."

"Has any police lab ever made errors when testing DNA?"

"The Houston Police Department shut down the DNA and serology section of its crime laboratory in early 2003 after a television exposé revealed serious deficiencies in the lab's procedures, a Seattle newspaper documented DNA testing errors in the Washington State Patrol lab, and there have been similar problems detected in independent labs that test for DNA."

"Have these errors led to the conviction of innocent individuals?"

"Yes."

"Mr. Baylor, as an expert in the field of DNA testing, can you say with any certainty that the test of the semen in the case in which Blaine Hastings was convicted was an error-free test given the fact that identical DNA was found in semen ejaculated in a rape case in which it was physically impossible for Blaine Hastings to have been the perpetrator?"

"No. I cannot."

"Thank you. No further questions, Your Honor."

"Mr. Kellerman?"

"Mr. Baylor, if an error occurred, can you say whether it occurred in the tests in the Ray case or in the test in Mr. Hastings's case?"

"No."

"Then the DNA test in Mr. Hastings's case may be accurate?"

"Yes."

"No further questions," the prosecutor said.

After Paul Baylor was dismissed, forensic experts from the crime lab were examined. Robin heard the testimony, but she had a hard time believing it. It was obvious that Judge Redding was also having difficulty accepting the only conclusion that could be drawn from the evidence.

When all the witnesses had been questioned, Les Kreuger pitched his argument for his client's release on bail and a new trial.

"It is obvious, Your Honor, that my client has suffered a grave injustice. Defense Exhibit Three is a copy of the lawsuit filed by Randi Stark against my client after Mr. Hastings was convicted. She is suing for millions of dollars, which gave her a very strong motive to lie about what happened between her and my client.

"One explanation of what happened in this case is that Miss Stark had intercourse with the man identified by Miss Braxton as Ray. Miss Braxton met Ray at a club Miss Stark frequents and Miss Braxton's description of Ray could be a description of Mr. Hastings. After having sex with Ray, Stark went to the fraternity party and saw Mr. Hastings. She realized that he resembled Ray and this gave her a diabolical idea.

"During cross-examination at Mr. Hastings's trial, Your Honor heard Miss Stark admit that she bore a grudge against Mr. Hastings for beating up a former boyfriend. I suggest that she saw a way to avenge herself against Mr. Hastings and make a pot full of money in the process.

"Mr. Hastings was intoxicated. Miss Stark lured him into a bedroom with the promise of sex. There were no other witnesses in that bedroom and no one to contradict her when she accused my client of rape."

"How do you explain the fact that the DNA identified in the sample in Miss Stark's rape kit matches your client's DNA?" Judge Redding asked.

"I do not have the scientific training to answer that question, Judge, but none of the witnesses with that training have been able to answer it either. All I can say is that the evidence in the Braxton case raises a reasonable doubt about my client's guilt.

"Your Honor should grant Mr. Hastings bail and a new trial,"

Kreuger continued. "I don't think it's a stretch to say that any jury would have had a reasonable doubt about Mr. Hastings's guilt if it heard the evidence concerning the DNA in the Braxton case that you heard today."

"Mr. Kellerman?" Judge Redding said.

"I urge the Court to deny the request for bail. Mr. Hastings is a very dangerous man. If he's freed, Miss Stark may be in danger, as may other women Mr. Hastings may assault."

"Mr. Kellerman, you are arguing that Mr. Hastings is dangerous, but is he? The crucial evidence in your case against him was the DNA evidence that has been called into serious question by the testimony we heard today. Do you concede that there is an excellent chance Mr. Hastings would have been acquitted if the jury had heard this evidence?"

"I . . . There was Miss Stark's testimony."

"True, but the case boiled down to a 'he said, she said' situation with Miss Stark admitting that she had a grudge against Mr. Hastings and her lawsuit giving her a reason to present false testimony. It's clear to me that it was the DNA evidence that tipped the scales in favor of a conviction. Can you convince me otherwise?"

Kellerman started to say something. Then he stopped and shook his head. "I can't disagree in good conscience with your analysis, but the fact is that the DNA in Miss Stark's rape case matches Mr. Hastings's DNA."

"I can't accept that as a fact, given what I heard today," the judge said. "There's a real scientific mystery here, and I'm going to give you time to solve it by setting a hearing on Mr. Kreuger's motion for a new trial for a month from today. In the meantime, I am going to release Mr. Hastings on one million dollars' bail."

Blaine Hastings didn't move a muscle until the judge left the bench. Then he leaped to his feet and pumped Les Kreuger's hand. "You were amazing! I can't thank you enough for getting me out of that hellhole."

"We're not out of the woods yet, Blaine," Kreuger cautioned. "All the judge did was set bail. It will take a lot more to convince her to give you a new trial."

Before Blaine could say anything else, Blaine's father and mother swarmed Kreuger.

Vanessa Cole had been sitting in the back of the courtroom. Robin followed her up the marble steps to the DA's office.

"What's going on, Vanessa?"

"I have no idea. Rex and I spent a good part of yesterday afternoon talking to some of the top scientists who deal with DNA, and they're all stumped. All they could say was that we were describing something that was not possible and that one of the tests had to be in error."

"Do you have any idea which one?"

"Not at this time. But if it's the test from Blaine Hastings's case, your client could be in a lot of trouble. So, I suggest that you try to figure out why Blaine Hastings's DNA and Ray's DNA are identical."

CHAPTER TWENTY

As soon as Robin was back in her office, she called Randi Stark, who put the call on her speakerphone so her mother could hear.

"There's been a development in your case," Robin said.

"What happened?"

"Blaine Hastings is free on bail."

"How could that happen?" Maxine shouted. "He's supposed to be locked up."

"A woman was raped while Hastings was in jail. The rapist didn't use a condom, so they found his sperm and tested it for DNA. The DNA in the rapist's sperm is a match for Blaine Hastings's DNA."

"So, this other rapist has the same kind of DNA. What does that matter?" Maxine said.

"That's impossible, Mrs. Stark. Except for identical twins, no two people can have the same DNA."

"I don't understand," Randi said. "I know Blaine raped me, so it has to be his DNA."

"There's been a suggestion that you had intercourse with someone else before you went to the party," Robin said. "That it was this man named Ray, the man who raped this other woman."

"They're calling my Randi a liar?" Maxine spat out.

"No, but everyone, including the forensic experts, are very confused. This has never happened before."

"I did not lie," Randi said forcefully. "And I did not have sex with any man that night before Blaine."

"I believe you, but everything is up in the air until the scientists figure out what's going on."

"Are we going to get police protection while that animal is out?" Maxine demanded.

"The police don't protect citizens unless there's something concrete like a threat or an assault."

"So, my Randi has to be brutally murdered before the police will act?" Maxine asked belligerently.

"I don't think it will come to that," Robin said. "Hastings knows he'll be right back in jail if he calls Randi or comes near her. But you should be on your toes. Record any calls you get and call me if you see someone suspicious hanging around."

"Blaine is smart. He won't do anything himself," Randi said. "He'll get someone else to hurt me, someone like Marlon Guest."

Robin knew Randi was right. She'd seen Hastings's hair-trigger temper in court, and she'd saved Randi when Marlon Guest attacked her. Hastings was violent, and he'd want revenge on the person who put him in prison.

"I can talk to Vanessa Cole about protecting you, but I want to be honest. The police don't have the manpower to assign someone to Randi twenty-four hours a day."

"And meanwhile, that animal is free and we're in danger," Maxine said.

CHAPTER TWENTY-ONE

Doug Armstrong had just flown in from Seattle, where he'd nego-tiated a very favorable settlement in a difficult case, so he was in a great mood when he walked into the reception room of his law of-fice at five thirty on Tuesday evening. Doug would have been in a great mood even if the case hadn't brought the firm a terrific attor-ney fee. His law practice was prospering and, more important, his marriage was on the mend.

Doug remembered how depressed Marsha had been after her miscarriage and the dark days when he'd been banished to their guest room because she didn't want to make love anymore. But, miracle of miracles, Marsha had asked Doug to come back to her. The lovemaking had been tentative at first, but it hadn't been a one-time thing and he had high hopes that they would be able to rekindle the passion that had ignited the early years of their mar-riage.

Kate Monday, the firm's receptionist, was getting ready to leave when Doug walked in. "Welcome back," she said. "How did it go?"

"Fantastic. I can't wait to tell Frank. Is he back from the Big Apple yet?"

"Yes. He got in this afternoon. He's in his office. He wanted to see you if you got back before he left for the party."

"What party?"

"Did you forget? Chad is getting married this weekend, and there's a party."

"Damn, I did forget. Where is it?"

"The Monaco steak house."

Doug walked down the hall to his office. His good mood continued until he answered a voice message from Vanessa Cole.

"Blaine Hastings is free on bail," Cole said as soon as they were connected.

"How is that possible?"

Vanessa explained what had happened at the bail hearing. "Judge Redding is holding off on deciding if Hastings should get a new trial until we get a handle on how the two DNA samples could match. But I thought you'd want to know what happened."

"Thanks. I have to admit that I don't feel safe with Hastings on the street. He threatened me when the trial went south."

"Do you think you're in danger?"

Doug thought about Cole's question for a few seconds. "Probably not," he answered. "Hastings is a mean son of a bitch, but he was probably just blowing off steam."

"If he gives you any problems, call me immediately. I might be able to get the judge to revoke his bail."

"Will do. And thanks for the call."

Doug hung up and stared out the window of his corner office. Below, the lights of Portland were starting to wink on, and the high hills that loomed over the city were beginning to fade into shadow as the sun set.

Was he really in danger? Blaine Hastings Jr. was not someone to take lightly. Despite the question raised by the DNA tests, Doug was convinced his former client was a vicious sociopath. But Hastings wasn't stupid, and he had to know that attacking an attorney could only work to his disadvantage. No, Doug decided, he was probably safe.

Doug dialed Marsha. "Hi, hon."

"Did everything go okay?" Marsha answered.

Doug smiled because Marsha sounded happy. "Yeah, better than I thought it would."

"Will you be home soon?"

"I can't come now. Chad Spenser is getting married, and there's an office party at the Monaco. I forgot all about it, but I've got to go. You eat without me."

"Okay," Marsha said. She sounded disappointed.

"I know, babe. I miss you, too. I won't stay late. I promise."

They talked some more. Then Doug hung up and started to go through his mail. That's when he remembered that Frank wanted to talk to him.

Doug smiled. The luckiest thing that had ever happened to him occurred twenty years ago. He'd moved to Oregon from Arkansas looking for work, and Frank Nylander had taken a chance on him when no one else would hire him.

Doug's personal life had also profited because of Frank. His partner had introduced him to Lois, his first wife, and later, after Lois passed, he'd hired Marsha as his secretary.

Doug sobered when he remembered Lois's final days. There had been endless rounds of chemo and the beyond-sadness moment when she'd passed. Doug didn't know how he would have survived without Frank's support in the dark days of depression and grief that had followed Lois's death. Frank was his best friend, and Doug owed Frank everything.

Doug decided that the stuff on his desk could wait. He got his coat and headed down the hall to Frank's office. They could talk about Seattle and New York on the way to the restaurant.

CHAPTER TWENTY-TWO

A narrow hallway ran between two banks of elevators on the eleventh floor of the Pacific Northwest Bank building. The hallway connected an insurance company with offices that took up one side of the building with the law offices of Douglas Armstrong and Frank Nylander, which took up the other side. At the request of the police, the building had blocked all the elevators save one from going to the eleventh floor.

A deputy district attorney was always dispatched to the location of a homicide so he could see the scene before the body was removed. Rex Kellerman was squeamish and he hated going to crime scenes, but he was excited to discover the identity of the body that was waiting for him in the offices of Nylander & Armstrong. What if the victim was Douglas Armstrong? He smiled as he imagined Marsha Armstrong's tears.

Kellerman assumed a serious demeanor when he entered the firm's reception area. Roger Dillon, Carrie Anders's partner, a lanky African American with close-cropped salt-and-pepper hair, was talking to someone from the crime lab, but he cut the conversation short when he spotted the DA.

"Sorry it took me so long," Kellerman said. "Traffic was awful coming in."

"Not a problem."

"So, what do we have?"

"There was a party last night at a steak house for one of the firm's associates, who's getting married. Most of the employees left the office Tuesday evening between four thirty and five to go to the party. Kate Monday, the receptionist, says that Frank Nylander returned from New York around four fifteen and Douglas Armstrong came back from Seattle around five thirty. They were the only ones left in the office when she left for the party around five forty-five. Neither Nylander nor Armstrong showed up at the restaurant, which surprised everyone.

"Ken Norquist, one of the associates, came in around seven this morning because he had been doing some work on one of Armstrong's cases. Armstrong wasn't in his office, so he went to Nylander's office to see if he was there. He found Nylander's body and called 911."

"Cause of death?" Kellerman asked as he hid his disappointment.

"That one is easy. Unless the autopsy turns up an exotic poison, I'm going with massive head trauma inflicted by the bloodstained stone sculpture we found on the floor next to the body."

"Was the sculpture from Nylander's office?"

Dillon nodded. "It's some abstract thing with a lot of curves. Unfortunately, it also has a lot of heft. The receptionist told me that Nylander's wife got it for him as a birthday present and he kept it on his desk."

"Fingerprints?"

Dillon shook his head. "It was wiped clean."

"Do we have an estimate for the time of death?" the prosecutor asked.

"Sometime last night between five thirty and ten."

"Where is Armstrong?"

"He hasn't shown up yet."

"Does anyone know where he is?" Kellerman asked.

"No. The receptionist called Armstrong's house to tell him that Nylander was dead. Armstrong's wife said he wasn't home and didn't come home last night."

"Hmm."

"The receptionist said that Mrs. Armstrong was very upset."

"Let me take a look at the body," Kellerman said. "Then let's talk to the employees."

Kellerman tried to breathe through his mouth as he followed Dillon down the hall, but he still smelled the cloying scent of death before he arrived at Nylander's spacious corner office. Inside the office, Carrie Anders was talking to a lab technician who was snapping photographs of the room. Another forensic expert was taking measurements and placing an occasional object in a Ziploc bag.

"Morning, Rex," Anders said.

Kellerman didn't answer. He was stunned by the violence that greeted him. It was so extreme that it was hard for the DA to take in.

Frank Nylander was sprawled across a Persian rug. His arms were stretched out in front of his head with the palms of his hands touching the carpet as if he'd tried to break his fall. His legs were spread apart and his shoe tips were pointing toward the windows. It was his head that commanded Kellerman's attention. The back of Nylander's skull had been crushed to pulp, and his face was surrounded by a halo of blood. The lawyer's hair was drenched in blood, the scalp had been split in two places, and Kellerman thought he saw a piece of brain peeking through where the bone had been crushed.

"Jesus," Kellerman whispered. "Someone really had it in for this guy."

Dillon and Anders didn't respond. Kellerman looked around the room. Most of the objects on the desk had been swept to the floor, files and desk drawers had been wrenched open, and furniture had been overturned.

Anders noticed another member of the team from the crime lab standing in the door. "Do you need to see anything else in here? If not, we should leave so these guys can do their job."

"I want to see Armstrong's office," Kellerman said, eager to get away from the fetid odor and the gore.

Dillon led the way to the other end of the suite and the second corner office. A photographer was leaving when the detectives and the district attorney arrived. The contrast between the two offices was stark. Armstrong's desk was a bit messy. He'd thrown his attaché on top, and mail and files were spread across the blotter, but the rest of the room was orderly.

Kellerman looked at the walls. The one behind the desk was floor-to-ceiling glass. A colorful abstract oil hung on the wall opposite the windows and over a couch. The wall to the left of the desk held diplomas from West Virginia University, the Warren E. Burger School of Law at Sheffield University in Arkansas, and certificates attesting to Armstrong's membership in various state and federal bars. The fourth wall was covered with clippings from Armstrong's successful cases and plaques from civic organizations and the bar. Under the plaques and clippings was a bookcase. Most of the books were law-related, but Kellerman spotted several old-time mysteries including a number by Erle Stanley Gardner, Ellery Queen, Dorothy Sayers, and Agatha Christie. Next to *Murder on the Orient Express* was a biography of Dame Agatha.

"Let's interview the employees," Kellerman said when he was satisfied that nothing of importance to their case had occurred in Armstrong's office.

Dillon led the way to the conference room, where several people sat around a long table, talking quietly, sipping coffee, or staring at the tabletop. After he introduced the DA, he asked Ken Norquist to follow him to another room.

Norquist was a short, stocky man in his late twenties who was sitting at the far end of the table. The associate wore his blond hair short and sported a trim beard and mustache. He was dressed in a tan suit, white shirt, and tie. The top button of his shirt was undone, and the tie had been pulled down so that the skin at the base of his neck showed. He looked pale and shaky, and sweat beaded his brow.

Dillon led the way to an empty office and closed the door. "Have a seat," he said.

Norquist sat down and began tapping the toes of his right foot rapidly.

"Are you okay?" Anders asked.

"No. I keep seeing Frank's head." He shivered. "I've never seen so much blood."

"Do you want some water?"

Norquist shook his head.

"Mr. Kellerman would like to ask you some questions. Do you feel up to answering them?" Anders asked.

"Yeah, go ahead."

"Can you tell me the last time you saw Mr. Nylander alive?" the prosecutor asked.

"It was four something. I left early to pick up my date for the party. I passed him coming in when I headed out."

"How did he look?"

"Normal, I guess. Maybe a little distracted. I said hello, but he didn't answer me." Norquist shrugged. "I just saw him for a second, though. I thought he'd show up at the restaurant, but he and Doug never made it."

"Did that surprise you?"

"Yes, it did. We're not a big firm, and Frank and Doug always show for stuff like this."

"I notice that you call the partners by their first names."

Norquist smiled sadly. "Doug and Frank encouraged everyone to be informal. They wanted everyone to work hard but have fun."

"Did you see Mr. Armstrong last night?"

"No."

"Why did you come in so early this morning?"

"Doug called me before noon from Seattle and gave me a research project. He said it wasn't a rush, but I knew he wanted it done as soon as possible. I finished most of it yesterday, but I still wasn't through when I left. I wanted to get it done first thing."

"Was Mr. Armstrong in at all this morning?" Kellerman asked.

"Not that I know. I went to his office shortly after I finished my work. He wasn't there, so I went looking for him." Norquist took a deep breath. "That's when I found Frank."

"You seem to think highly of Mr. Armstrong and Mr. Nylander," Kellerman said. "Was there anyone in the firm who didn't like them?"

"Honestly, everyone thought they were great."

"Were there any former employees who might hold a grudge?"

"I've been here three years, and I never heard anyone say anything bad about them."

"What about the people they sued or represented?" Kellerman asked.

Norquist paused. "You know, recently there was a client who fired Doug."

"What case was that?" Kellerman asked.

"The rape. That athlete, Hastings. I did a little work on it, so Doug and I talked about Hastings. I think he said something to Doug that scared him."

"Was Mr. Nylander involved in the case?" Kellerman asked.

"Not that I know."

"Can you think of anyone else who might have a reason to do this?"

"No, I can't. I mean, no one likes to be on the losing side of a case, but I can't remember anyone talking about being afraid of a client or someone we sued."

"How did Mr. Armstrong and Mr. Nylander get along?" Kellerman asked.

Norquist's mouth gaped open, and he stared at the prosecutor. "If you're thinking that Doug . . . That's ridiculous. Frank and Doug were like brothers. They did everything together. It was a mutual admiration society."

"They never argued?" Kellerman asked.

"Well, yeah, about cases. But it wasn't angry arguing. It was strategy or whether to take on a client. Business stuff."

"Was the firm doing well?"

"I'm just an associate. But from what I picked up, this was their best year."

"Do you have any more questions, Rex?" Dillon asked.

"Not now."

"Have you given a statement already?" Dillon asked Norquist.

"Yes, to one of the officers."

"Then why don't you go home. You look pretty upset."

"Thanks. I really don't want to stay here any longer than I have to."

Kellerman, Anders, and Dillon talked to the other employees. They all said that the partners were the best of friends, and no one could think of anyone with a grudge against Nylander or Armstrong.

When they were through, Kellerman motioned the detectives into the hallway outside the law office. "Get names and addresses, then send everyone home," the prosecutor said.

Dillon nodded.

"What do you think?" Kellerman asked. "Could Norquist have killed Nylander this morning when they were alone in the office?"

"I thought of that," Dillon said, "but he's a really good actor if that's what happened."

"So, who did kill Nylander?" Kellerman asked.

"My gut says it's a robbery gone wrong," Dillon said. "Nylander's wallet, cell phone, watch, and keys are missing. I tried to have his secretary walk through the office to do an inventory, but she lasted two minutes before she ran to the ladies' room. I'll have her come back when the body is gone."

"What about Armstrong, Roger?" Kellerman asked. "He and Nylander were the only people in the office after the receptionist left."

"I don't know. Every person we talked to said they were best friends."

Anders chimed in. "If I killed Nylander, I would have made the office look like it had been robbed. Then I would have gone to the party and pretended Nylander was fine when I left."

"Carrie's right," Dillon said. "It doesn't make sense for Armstrong to run away when he could have deflected suspicion by going to the party."

"Maybe he panicked," Kellerman said.

"That doesn't fit the facts," Anders said. "If Armstrong killed his partner, he was cool enough to wipe his prints off the murder weapon and mess up the office."

"There is Blaine Hastings," Dillon said. "He's violent, he threatened Armstrong, and he's out on bail."

"Okay. Look, I've got a court appearance. Why don't you two go to Armstrong's house. Then talk to Hastings and Nylander's wife. Let me know what you find out," Kellerman said as he rang for the elevator.

Kellerman smiled as soon as the elevator doors closed. Wouldn't it be great if Doug Armstrong killed his partner and he was the one who sent the wimp away? Rex's smile widened as he pictured the suffering that would inflict on Marsha Armstrong. Just before the car arrived at the lobby, Kellerman remembered a phrase he thought was from the Bible. Something like, "The Lord works in mysterious ways."

CHAPTER TWENTY-THREE

The Armstrongs lived in an early-twentieth-century Tudor home in Portland's West Hills, one of the city's premier residential areas. The house was close to the top of the hill and looked out across the city and the river to the mountains. The lawn was manicured, and there was a wide variety of flowers in the garden. Anders spotted rhododendrons, roses, tulips, and some other varieties she couldn't name.

Anders figured the blond woman who answered the bell for her early thirties. Marsha Armstrong was wearing jeans and a man-tailored white shirt. She hadn't bothered to put on makeup or jewelry, but she was still very attractive and she looked very worried.

"Mrs. Armstrong?" Anders asked.

"Yes. Are you the police?"

Anders nodded as she and Dillon showed Marsha their shields.

"Do you know where Doug is?" Marsha asked.

"We were hoping you could tell us," Anders said.

"I can't, and I'm very worried. This isn't like him."

"Do you mind if we come in?" Dillon asked.

"Yes, please. I'm sorry. I'm just upset."

Armstrong's wife led the detectives into a living room and gestured toward a sofa. The detectives sat. Marsha was stiff-backed, her hands clasped in her lap and her body rigid.

"Kate Monday called. She told me that Frank was murdered."

"I'm afraid that's true, and no one seems to know where your husband is," Anders said. "When was the last time you saw him, or spoke to him?"

"I saw him on Sunday, when I drove him to the airport. He had a case in Seattle."

"How did he seem?"

"Fine."

"He wasn't worried about anything?"

"No, the opposite. He was excited about how he thought the case would go."

"When was the next time you spoke to him?"

"He called that evening from the hotel after he checked in."

"Was there any change in his mood?"

"Not that I noticed. He was upbeat because he was certain that the case was going to settle to his client's advantage. Then he called Monday night to tell me that everything was going the way he thought it would and he anticipated wrapping things up on Tuesday morning and flying back Tuesday afternoon, then taking a taxi to the office."

"Did you talk to him after that conversation?"

"Doug flew back from Seattle on Tuesday afternoon and called me when he got into his office. He said the case had ended better than he thought it would. He also told me that Chad Spenser, one of the associates, was getting married and there was a party for him at a restaurant. He said he had to go and I shouldn't wait for him to eat dinner." Marsha teared up. "He never came home."

"Mrs. Armstrong," Anders said, "we have no evidence that your husband has come to harm."

"Then, where is he?"

"We're looking for him."

"In hospitals and the morgue? You can be honest with me, Detective. Kate told me that Frank was beaten to death and his office was wrecked. If Doug was there when that happened . . ." Marsha choked up and pulled out a handkerchief.

"We don't want to jump to conclusions," Anders said. "Can you think of someplace he might be?"

"No. This is his home. He'd come here."

"Do you know someone who might want to harm your husband or Frank Nylander?"

Rex Kellerman came to mind immediately, but she couldn't imagine he would murder Doug or his partner to get back at her for breaking off their affair. And she didn't want anyone to know she'd cheated on Doug.

"I can't think of a soul who would want to harm either of them," Marsha said. "Unless . . ."

"Yes?" Dillon asked.

"There was a client who scared Doug."

"Who?"

"Blaine Hastings, the football player who raped that girl. Doug told me that he threatened him when the case started to go bad. I think he was relieved when Hastings was denied bail."

Norquist had also mentioned Hastings. Anders definitely wanted to know if Hastings had an alibi for the evening of Nylander's murder.

"How did Mr. Nylander and your husband get along?" Dillon asked.

"They were the best of friends. Doug believed he owed everything to Frank."

"Why did he feel that way?" Dillon asked.

"Doug grew up in West Virginia. He was an only child, and his family was not well off. His father worked in a coal mine and died when Doug was in high school. His mother worked in a department store and passed away before I met Doug.

"Doug went to the state university. He always wanted to be a lawyer, but he didn't do that well in college, so he ended up at the only place that accepted him, a third-tier law school in Arkansas.

"Doug took a trip to the West Coast in the summer before his senior year in college, and he fell in love with Oregon. After he graduated from law school, he drove to Portland. He passed the bar exam, but he didn't know a soul—and no one would hire him, because he didn't go to a great law school.

"Doug told me that he was terribly depressed and ready to go back home when he met Frank at a bar. Frank had just opened his own office after leaving a big firm where he'd worked for several years. Frank didn't have a lot of business, and he couldn't afford to hire an associate at the going rate. Doug said he'd work for a secretary's salary and a share of what he brought in. Frank took a risk when no one else would and hired him.

"Doug and Frank took court appointments and anything that came in the door. At the end of his third year, Doug won a big personal injury case, and the business started to grow. Doug always told me how grateful he was to Frank for taking a chance on him and how proud he was of being able to pay him back by helping the firm grow."

"Is there any reason you can think of that would lead your husband to attack Mr. Nylander?" Carrie asked.

"I can't imagine a situation where Doug would do anything to harm Frank. He owed him everything. He's told me that more than once."

Anders and Dillon talked to Marsha for twenty minutes more. Then Anders stood and handed Marsha her card. "If Mr. Armstrong contacts you or you think of somewhere he might be, call me anytime, day or night. Don't worry about waking me up.

"And if you remember anything—and I mean anything—you think may help us solve Mr. Nylander's murder, tell us, even if you think it's silly. Let us decide. Sometimes the smallest clue can break open a case."

"Finding your husband and bringing in Mr. Nylander's killer is a priority with both of us," Dillon assured her.

Marsha showed the detectives to the door.

"Let's drive to Hastings's house and have a talk with him," Dillon said as they walked to their car.

"Mrs. Armstrong wanted us to believe her husband had nothing to do with Nylander's murder. Do you think she laid it on too thick?" Dillon asked.

"I think she was being straight with us. Everyone we've talked to says the same thing. Have you met Armstrong or Nylander?"

"No," Dillon said.

"I've never met Nylander, but Armstrong tried the *Hastings* case and I did some work on it. I also worked two other cases he handled. He seemed like a nice guy, very ethical. He also seemed—I don't know—soft. I really can't picture him bashing his best friend's head in."

Dillon smiled. "We don't have time for me to go through a list of people I've arrested for the most heinous crimes who I had a hard time imagining committing them."

Anders sighed. "I know, Roger. If criminals looked like criminals, we wouldn't have to work so hard."

"Amen to that."

CHAPTER TWENTY-FOUR

The Hastingses lived in an estate across the Willamette River from the Westmont Country Club. The detectives called the house on an intercom attached to a stone pillar. Moments later, a wrought iron gate swung open and they drove up a paved driveway to a four-story Italianate McMansion.

Blaine Hastings Sr. was waiting at the front door. He greeted the detectives with a scowl. "What do you want?"

"We'd like to speak to your son," Anders said.

"About what?"

"A case that has nothing to do with his conviction."

"What case?"

"It's a homicide, Mr. Hastings. Douglas Armstrong's partner was murdered in his office last night, and we've heard that your son threatened Mr. Armstrong."

"Now you people are trying to frame Blaine for a murder? You've got some balls coming here. Do you have a warrant?"

"No, sir," Dillon said.

"Then get off my property."

"Your son is a convicted rapist who has been released on bail," Dillon said. "It would be to his advantage to cooperate with us."

Hastings laughed. "Do you think I'm stupid enough to fall for that? You're not talking to my boy, so get lost."

Hastings watched the detectives drive away. When they were out of sight, he went inside and slammed the door.

"What did they want, Dad?" Blaine Junior asked.

"Armstrong's partner was murdered, and they wanted to know where you were last night."

"Me?! Why do they want to know about me?"

"They know you threatened Armstrong. I guess that faggot whined to someone and they heard about it."

"What's that got to do with his partner getting killed?"

"I don't know. I didn't ask them. I told them to shove off as soon as I heard what they wanted."

"Well, I didn't murder anyone."

"But you were out last night," Senior said. "Did you go anywhere near Armstrong's office?"

"Of course not. Why would I want to go there? I was at a club. I've been locked up, and I wanted a night out."

"You've got to be smart, Blaine. You can't go clubbing. There's drugs, someone might pick a fight with you just because you're famous. You're out now, but the cops will use any excuse to put you back in."

"You're right, Dad. No more clubbing. I'll stay home at night until this blows over."

CHAPTER TWENTY-FIVE

Jessica Braxton spotted the buyer sitting at the end of the hotel bar where Harry said he would be. He was a big dude in a leather jacket and black turtleneck who looked like a character in *Shaft,* one of those blaxploitation movies out of the seventies. Jessica scanned the bar for anyone who looked like a cop before taking the stool next to him.

"A Cuba Libre," she told the bartender, using the code Harry had instructed her to use.

"That's a pretty powerful drink for a little woman," the man said, giving her the response she was expecting. They made small talk until Jessica finished the Cuba Libre. Ten minutes after she walked to her car, the buyer was sitting in her passenger seat.

"You got the stuff?" he asked.

"You have the money?"

The man handed Jessica a wad of cash. She counted it and gave him the heroin. That's when he showed Jessica his badge.

"Hi, Miss Braxton," the chubby young man in the mismatched jacket and slacks said. "My name is Ron Jenkins, and I've been appointed by the Court to represent you."

Jessica was sick and she had trouble paying attention. Withdrawal was a bitch, and she was in its throes. "Can you get me out?" she asked. "I gotta get out of here."

"That may be a problem. The amount of heroin the police say you delivered to the undercover agent was large enough to warrant sending this case to the feds."

Jessica put her head in her hands. "I gotta get out. I'm really sick. I'll do anything."

"I did talk to the district attorney, but they have such a strong case against your supplier, Harry Newcomb, that they aren't inclined to deal."

Jessica ran her tongue across her lips. "What if I had something bigger than Newcomb to trade? Could you get me help? I really need help."

"Big like what?"

Carrie Anders opened the door to the interview room. Jessica Braxton was sitting on one side of a wooden table, and her public defender was sitting beside her. Anders thought Braxton looked awful. She was a lot skinnier than she'd been when Anders had interviewed her at the hospital about her rape case, and she was twitching and scratching like someone who was really hurting.

"Hi, Jessica," the detective said. "I'm a little surprised we're meeting under these circumstances."

"Yeah, well, I fucked up big-time, but it's not my fault."

"Whose fault is it?"

"I'm an addict, Detective Anders. I wasn't thinking straight. You can see that, can't you? I'm not a criminal. I'm sick and I need help."

"Being an addict and being a criminal aren't mutually exclusive, Jessica. The way I see it, you're an addict who needs medical help *and* you're a criminal who sold a shitload of heroin to an undercover agent. You're facing a ton of jail time."

"But you'd help me get into rehab if I told you something important, right? Mr. Jenkins says that we could make a deal."

"That depends on what this important thing is."

"This is all off the record until we have a deal?" Jenkins interjected.

Anders nodded. "I'm here to listen. If Miss Braxton has something useful to trade, I'll work with her. So, Jessica, what do you want to tell me?"

"It's about Blaine Hastings."

"What about him?"

"It was a scam."

"What was?"

"I wasn't raped. His father paid me to say I was raped. He told me to say a guy named Ray did it, and he gave me a description of this Ray I was supposed to give to the cops."

"You had a black eye and a split lip. How did that happen?"

"Blaine's father did it. He said it would make the story more believable. He gave me a little extra. He called it combat pay."

"Let's back up here," Anders said. "When did Mr. Hastings ask you to say you were raped?"

"Right after his kid was convicted."

"How do you know the Hastingses?"

"I was working at his company and I got in a little trouble."

"What kind of trouble?"

"I took some money to buy drugs, and he found out—so I had to go to a motel and work it off."

"You had sex with Mr. Hastings so he wouldn't call the police?"

"Yeah."

"When was this?"

"About a year and a half ago."

"Did you keep working for the company?"

"No, he fired me."

"Did you see him after that?"

"Not until he called me after his kid went down. He said he would give me five thousand dollars if I told the cops I'd been raped. I was down on my luck and out of a job, so I said I would."

"This doesn't make sense. The DNA test showed a match to Blaine Junior's DNA. How did they figure out a way for you to have sex with him while he was in jail?"

Braxton laughed. "It was simpler than that. Junior jacked off into a ketchup packet and slipped it to his dad when Senior visited him in jail. Then I put some of it inside me and wiped the rest on my panties."

Anders stared at Braxton, dumbfounded. Then she started laughing, too. "A ketchup packet?"

Braxton nodded. "We sure fooled everybody."

"You sure did," Anders agreed.

CHAPTER TWENTY-SIX

Rex Kellerman was reviewing the police report of Carrie Anders's interview with Jessica Braxton when Les Kreuger walked into Judge Redding's courtroom.

"What's going on, Rex?" Kreuger asked when he walked through the gate that separated the bar of the court from the spectator section.

Rex suppressed an urge to gloat as he handed Kreuger a copy of Carrie Anders's report. "There's been a new development in Mr. Hastings's case. Read that. Then we can talk."

Kellerman watched Kreuger's face. When he got to the paragraph where Braxton described the scam, Kreuger's mouth opened and Kellerman grinned.

"Interesting, huh?" he said.

"A ketchup packet," Kreuger said.

"Yeah, that's everyone's reaction."

"You can do that?" Kreuger asked.

"We ran it by the people at the crime lab, and they agreed that it would work. One of the lab guys even remembered hearing about a perp in Milwaukee who ran the same scam about twenty years ago."

"What are you going to do?" Kreuger asked.

"I'm asking the judge to revoke Hastings's bail, of course."

Rex checked his watch. "And speaking of Mr. Hastings, where is your client? It's almost two."

"I called his house as soon as you notified me about the hearing. I assume his folks are driving him down."

"You didn't speak to him?"

"I told Mrs. Hastings." Kreuger looked at the clock on the courtroom wall. "He's still got a few minutes."

Rex was about to reply when the bailiff called the Court to order and Judge Redding took the bench.

The judge surveyed the courtroom and frowned. "Where is Mr. Hastings?" she asked Les Kreuger.

"On the way, Your Honor."

"He'd better be."

Kreuger took out his phone. "Let me check."

At that moment, Gloria and Blaine Senior walked in. They both looked upset.

"Where is your son?" Judge Redding asked.

Senior looked flustered. "We don't know, Your Honor."

"What do you mean, you don't know?"

"I told him about the hearing when your clerk called yesterday, but he wasn't in his room this morning," Gloria said.

"Are you telling me that he's run off?" the judge asked.

"We don't know that," Blaine said, straining to sound reasonable. "There may be some explanation."

Judge Redding looked grim. "If there is, he'll be telling me about it in prison clothes. I'm revoking bail and denying the motion for a new trial."

The judge turned to Kellerman. "You tell your people to bring him in."

"It will be the first thing I do as soon as I get to my office. But there's another matter I'd like to take care of right now."

"What is that, Mr. Kellerman?"

The DA nodded toward Carrie Anders and Roger Dillon, who had been sitting in the back of the courtroom. "I am placing Blaine Hastings Sr. under arrest for obstruction of justice."

CHAPTER TWENTY-SEVEN

Robin was talking about a case with Jeff Hodges when the receptionist told her that Carrie Anders was on the phone.

"Hey, Carrie, what's up?" Robin said.

"I have some news about Blaine Hastings."

"What about him?"

Anders told Robin about the Hastingses' scam.

"That is ingenious," Robin said. "But why are you telling me about it?"

"You know Doug Armstrong was Hastings's lawyer?"

Robin nodded.

"I assume you know that Armstrong's partner was murdered."

"Yeah, it was on the news."

"Frank Nylander was beaten to death, and Armstrong is missing. Hastings threatened Armstrong. He's a suspect in Nylander's murder and Armstrong's disappearance. You had a run-in with Hastings at the sentencing, and I wanted to give you a heads-up in case he decides to go after you."

Robin's features hardened. "I hope he does."

"I know all about your martial arts background," Anders said, "but Hastings is a beast, and he doesn't have any qualms about hurting women."

"We'll see who hurts who."

"Don't handle this by yourself, Robin. You call 911 if Hastings comes anywhere near you."

"I will, and thanks for warning me."

Robin told Jeff what Anders had told her.

"You have a gun, right?"

Robin nodded.

"Don't go anywhere without it until this shakes out."

"I won't."

Jeff hesitated. "Look, I know you can take care of yourself, but I'd like to babysit you until we have a clearer picture of what's going on."

"I appreciate the offer, but—"

Jeff smiled. "Face it, Robin. You're a damsel in distress, and you need a brawny knight to protect you. I'm also a terrific cook. From what I know about your eating habits, you need a decent meal even more than you need a bodyguard."

Robin couldn't help smiling. Even if she wasn't in danger, she found the thought of spending an evening with Jeff appealing.

"Are you going to be stubborn?" Jeff asked.

"I don't need a he-man to protect me, but I can use a good meal."

"Good. Let's finish up our work on this case. Then I'll see you home."

CHAPTER TWENTY-EIGHT

Randi Stark had been a mess ever since Robin's call. It was terrifying to think that Blaine Hastings was on the loose, and her mother's wails and hand-wringing didn't help. When she couldn't stand to be in her mother's presence another minute, Randi said she was going to bed. She was so anxious, she didn't see how she could sleep—but she had to get away from Maxine.

As soon as she was in her room, Randi texted Annie Roche and told her the news. Annie panicked. She wanted to know if she was in danger. Randi told her that Blaine wouldn't go after her, but Randi cautioned Annie to be careful. Randi would be the one he went after if he went after anyone,

After she turned off her phone, Randi tried to do some schoolwork, but she couldn't concentrate. She had a television in her room. She turned down the sound so her mother wouldn't hear it and come barging in. Then she tried to find a show that would distract her and eventually put her to sleep. Nothing worked.

Randi got into bed and turned out the lights. She closed her eyes and Blaine Hastings glared at her. Randi got out of bed and walked to her window. She pulled the edge of the shade aside and gazed into the night. Then she froze and her heart started tripping. Halfway down her block was a streetlight. Someone was leaning against it; someone with a build like Blaine Hastings's. Randi leaned forward. Was it Blaine?

Robin had given Randi her cell phone number, and she punched it in.

"Yes?" Robin answered after several rings.

"It's Randi Stark. I think Blaine is watching my house."

"Calm down and tell me why you think he's watching you."

"There's a man standing under the streetlight. He's staring at the house."

"And you're certain it's Blaine?"

"I . . . No, but who else would be watching my house at this hour?"

"Okay, here's what I want you to do," Robin said. "I'm coming over. Meanwhile, call 911 and tell them Blaine was outside your house. If he's still there, the cops will either arrest him or he'll run."

Randi called the police, but the person who had been watching her house had vanished by the time the squad car arrived. Robin and Jeff showed up soon after and explained the situation to the two officers. When they drove away, Robin sat at the kitchen table with Maxine and Randi.

"Do you have someplace safe where you can stay?" Robin asked.

"My aunt," Randi replied.

Maxine nodded. "Camille will put us up."

"Good. Call her now. Then pack and go while Hastings is not around."

CHAPTER TWENTY-NINE

Marvin Turnbull had just come back from a contentious meeting with his board when Tyler Harrison called.

"I have bad news, Marvin," Harrison said.

"What happened?"

"I called Frank Nylander in Portland on the *Voss* case. He's dead, murdered."

"You're kidding?"

"I wish I were."

"What happened?"

"He was killed in his office the evening he got back from our meeting."

"Do they know who killed him?"

"I just talked to the receptionist. She told me that no one has been arrested."

"Where does that leave the case?"

"It's too early to say. Nylander had a good relationship with Voss. If anyone could convince him to settle, it would have been Frank."

"Shit," Turnbull muttered.

"Yeah," Harrison agreed.

"So, what happens now?"

"Barring a miracle, we prepare for trial."

"And the newspapers get hold of the story, which means we're fucked."

"I'm afraid so. I could try to get a gag order, but I had an associate research the question, and our chances would be almost zero."

Turnbull's end of the line went silent and Harrison waited.

"Voss will need a lawyer," Turnbull said. "It will probably be someone in Nylander's firm, but he could hire someone else. Either way, it will take a while for the new attorney to get up to speed, and that gives us time. Hell, a new lawyer might even be able to convince Voss to settle."

"You're right. If two lawyers advise the same thing, he might see the light."

"This might work to our advantage, Tyler. Let me know what happens."

"Will do," Harrison said.

Turnbull disconnected and closed his eyes. The board had been informed about Leonard Voss's refusal to settle, and they were in panic mode. Turnbull had sounded confident during his conversation with the firm's attorney, but he was a realist. Voss was on a mission. He would never settle. If his lawsuit made headlines, the company would be ruined. More important, he would lose his job, and his stock would be worthless. Something had to be done, and he could see only one solution that would solve his and the company's difficulties.

Ivar Gorski's burner phone rang while he was in his motel room, performing katas, dancelike exercises that karate practitioners use to simulate combat. Gorski stopped in mid-kick and answered the call.

"We need to implement plan B," Turnbull said.

Gorski hung up without saying anything in case someone was listening. He knew this wasn't likely, but Gorski had stayed alive by being paranoid.

As soon as he ended the call, he continued his exercises. They calmed him and helped him think clearly. By the time he was showered and shaved, he had decided how he would carry out his mission.

CHAPTER THIRTY

Marsha Armstrong called Carrie Anders at seven in the morning on Tuesday.

"I just got a call from Saint Francis Medical Center. Doug's there on the third floor. I'm getting ready to drive over."

Carrie was headed to work, but she changed direction. Anders's phone rang again just as she was about to get out of her car, in the hospital parking lot.

"Carrie?" Robin said.

"What's up?" Anders replied.

"I wanted to give you a heads-up. Randi Stark called me last night. She was very upset. She thought she saw Blaine Hastings watching her house."

"Is she sure it was Hastings?"

"No. She told me she saw a man from her bedroom window. He was about a block away, it was dark, and his face wasn't illumi-nated. The best she can do is say that the person she saw had a build similar to Hastings's."

"Do you want me to have a car drive by tonight?"

"That won't be necessary. They're staying with a relative for a while."

"Okay. Give Randi my number, and tell her to call if she thinks she's in danger."

"Will do."

Marsha had not arrived when Anders walked into Reception, so she went to the nurses' station on the third floor and had the doctor who was treating Armstrong paged.

Moments later, a young man wearing a white coat walked down the hall.

"Dr. Sanchez?" the detective asked as she flashed her ID.

The doctor nodded. "You're here about Mr. Armstrong?"

Anders nodded in turn, and the doctor started walking toward a room that was halfway down the corridor. "Can you tell me what happened to him?" Anders asked.

"Mr. Armstrong was wandering around downtown at three in the morning. An officer spotted him and brought him here. He told me he didn't know who he was or what had happened to him, and he didn't have a wallet or phone we could use to identify him. This morning, he remembered his name and we called his wife."

Anders stopped in front of the room. "What injuries does he have?"

"There's some superficial damage to his face—a gash on his forehead, a split lip, black eyes, and cuts and abrasions on his nose, but nothing serious."

"Does he remember how he was injured?"

"No. He told me the last thing he remembered before the police found him was flying back from Seattle last Tuesday."

"Do you think his injuries caused his amnesia?"

"Neurological amnesia can result from a brain injury, but I found no sign of that."

"Last week, Mr. Armstrong's partner was beaten to death in an extremely violent manner. I've heard that amnesia can be caused by witnessing a traumatic event. If Mr. Armstrong witnessed his partner being bludgeoned to death, could that have brought on the problem?"

"There is a rare type of amnesia called dissociative amnesia, which is caused by emotional shock or trauma, such as being the victim of a violent crime."

"Can a person who develops dissociative amnesia recover lost memories?

"Loss of memory caused by emotional shock is usually brief."

"Can I talk to Armstrong?"

"Yeah, but I'll want to be in the room to observe. If I think he's getting too upset, I'm going to stop the interview."

Anders started to open the door to Armstrong's room. Then she thought of something. "Can I tell Mr. Armstrong that his partner is dead?"

Dr. Sanchez frowned. "I don't think that's a good idea right now. If he remembers, you can ask him what happened. But the news that his partner was murdered would probably upset him."

"Okay," Anders said as she opened the door.

When the detective walked into the room, Doug stared at her.

"Good morning, Mr. Armstrong," Anders said as she walked to the side of the bed and displayed her shield. "How are you feeling?"

"Not great."

"Do you know who I am?"

Armstrong's brow knitted and he looked closely at Carrie. "Did you work on one of my cases?"

"Yes. My name is Carrie Anders, and I'm a detective with the Portland Police Bureau. We've met on a few occasions in connection with some of your cases."

Doug shook his head. "I'm sorry, but my memory . . ."

"No need to apologize. Dr. Sanchez told me that you're experiencing some memory loss. In spite of that, I'd like to ask you a few questions. Do you feel up to answering them?"

"I'll try."

"Can you tell me how you were injured?"

"No."

"What is the last thing you remember?"

"I . . . There was a plane. I was at the airport. I think I flew from Seattle. After that, nothing."

Anders was about to continue when Marsha Armstrong rushed into the room. Dr. Sanchez blocked her.

"Please, I'm Doug's wife."

The doctor looked at Anders. The detective nodded. Sanchez stepped aside. Marsha walked to Doug's side. She took his hand and teared up.

"Hey, I'm okay," he said. "Don't cry."

Marsha wiped her eyes. "When I heard Frank was dead and you disappeared, I thought you were dead, too. I was so scared."

Doug stared at Marsha. "What do you mean, Frank is dead?"

"Oh God, you don't know?"

Doug looked bewildered. "How could he be dead? What happened?"

Dr. Sanchez stepped forward. "Mrs. Armstrong, you don't want to excite your husband. This is too much information right now."

Doug looked desperate. "You can't just leave it like that. Does Frank's death have something to do with what happened to me?"

Anders looked at the doctor.

"Go ahead," Dr. Sanchez said.

"Frank Nylander was killed in his office on Tuesday evening, the night you returned from Seattle," Carrie said. "We have no idea who killed him. We're hoping you can help us when your memory returns."

Doug closed his eyes and let his head sink into his pillow. "How could this happen?" Doug muttered. "It makes no sense."

"This is enough for now," Dr. Sanchez said. "I'd like everyone to leave me with Mr. Armstrong."

"Wait!" Doug said. "I do remember something. Is . . . Was Blaine Hastings . . . Is he still in jail?"

"No," Carrie answered. "There was a problem with some of the evidence in his case, and he was released the day you flew back to Portland from Seattle."

Doug closed his eyes for a moment. Then he looked at Carrie. "My memories are all jumbled. But I'm sure I told Frank that Hastings was out." Doug's brow furrowed and he looked upset. "That's all," he said after a moment. "I can't even be sure it happened."

"That's enough for today," Dr. Sanchez said.

"I'll come back tomorrow," Marsha said after casting an anxious look at her husband. When she and Carrie were in the hall, Marsha said, "I'm sorry. I thought Doug knew that Frank was dead."

"He does now."

"You don't think . . . I didn't hurt him, did I?"

"No. We had to tell him sometime."

"What did the doctor tell you? Is Doug going to be okay?"

"Dr. Sanchez says his memory loss is probably temporary. You can see that it's starting to come back already."

"But will he remember who killed Frank?"

"I hope so. That would make my job a hell of a lot easier."

CHAPTER THIRTY-ONE

Roger Dillon parked in a lot next to the Oregon State Medical Examiner's office. When Rex Kellerman got out of the car, he put on his game face. He hated attending autopsies, but he couldn't let Dillon and Anders see that he was afraid of making a fool of himself when the medical examiner started cutting into dead flesh.

Roger Dillon's phone rang as the detectives and the prosecutor approached the front door. Dillon paused to take the call. He frowned when he disconnected.

"What's up?" Anders asked.

"Frank Nylander left his car in the economy lot at the airport when he flew to New York. Nylander's secretary assumed that he drove from the airport to the office on Tuesday afternoon and parked in his reserved space in the building garage. On Friday, she remembered that Nylander's keys were missing, so she checked the space. The car wasn't in it. The secretary called Mrs. Nylander. The car wasn't at their house, and it just turned up in a parking lot, two miles from downtown."

"This is beginning to look more and more like a robbery gone bad," Anders said.

"I'm starting to lean that way," Dillon agreed.

The receptionist told Dr. Sally Grace, the assistant medical examiner, that she had visitors. Moments later, a slender woman with frizzy black hair and sharp blue eyes walked down the hall with a big smile on her face.

"You guys ready to slice and dice?" she asked.

"Always," Rex lied, hoping that he had successfully disguised the dread he felt at the thought of seeing a corpse disemboweled and its skull sawed open.

Dr. Grace led Kellerman and the detectives to the back of the building, where they put on blue, water-impermeable gowns, masks, goggles, and heavy black rubber aprons. When they entered the autopsy room, Frank Nylander's naked body lay on one of the two stainless steel autopsy tables that stood on either side of the room. He had been cleaned up, but there was no way to disguise the injuries he'd suffered.

"Mr. Nylander had some interesting things to tell me," Dr. Grace said.

"Oh?" Anders replied.

"When you were in his office, he was lying facedown, so you only saw the damage to the back of his skull. Those were the blows that caused his death. But he was struck on the front of his face first."

Dr. Grace pointed to a large gash over the dead lawyer's left eye, then at his nose, which had been crushed. "Now, look at his knuckles and the bruises on his forearms."

Kellerman studied Nylander's hands and forearms and saw the bruises and abrasions to which Dr. Grace was referring.

"I think Mr. Nylander fought with his killer but was stunned by blows to his face inflicted by the stone statue. Based on the blood spatter, I'd guess that the killer drove him to the floor with one or more of the blows to the front of his head, then finished him off while he was facedown on the carpet."

"Did you find any trace evidence the killer may have transferred to Nylander?" Kellerman asked.

Dr. Grace lifted Nylander's right hand. "I did scrape a minute sample of blood from one of his fingernails. It may not be enough to work with, but that's not my job. You'll have to ask the techs at the crime lab."

"Anything else—hair, saliva?" Dillon asked.

Dr. Grace shook her head. Then she flipped on her goggles, pulled up her mask, and picked up an electric saw. "Shall we?"

Kellerman felt his gut clench.

"Peter?" Kellerman asked when Peter Okonjo answered his call to the Oregon State Crime Lab.

"Hi, Rex. What can I do for you?"

"I'm calling about Frank Nylander's case. I just attended the autopsy, and Sally told me she sent over a small sample of blood that was scraped from one of Nylander's fingernails."

"She did."

"Has it told you anything?"

"It was a microscopic amount, Rex. Way too small to work with."

"And you didn't find anything else at the crime scene we can use to identify the killer?"

"There were a ton of fingerprints, but they all matched the people who work at the firm."

"So, no one who didn't belong?"

"No, but there were no prints on the statue, so the killer may have worn gloves."

"Okay," Kellerman said, unable to hide his disappointment. "Let me know if you come up with anything."

Kellerman was just about to hang up when Okonjo said, "There is something we might try with the blood."

"Oh?"

"There's a lab in town that uses low-template DNA analysis to determine genetic probabilities when analyzing minuscule amounts of genetic material that other methods can't interpret."

"Okay," said Kellerman, who had no idea what the forensic expert was talking about.

"I don't remember the name of the lab offhand, but I can look it up and see if they can do something with it. It's a long shot."

"Try it. We've got nothing to lose. And Peter, if they can analyze the sample, have the lab call me with the result. No sense making you act as a middle man."

CHAPTER THIRTY-TWO

After Blaine Hastings Jr. went on the run, life at Robin's condo fell into a routine. In the morning, Jeff would drive Robin to her gym or the office. In the evening, he would drive her home. After checking to make sure no one was inside Robin's apartment, Jeff would whip up a delicious meal. Then Jeff and Robin would read, work, or watch TV. When they got tired, Robin would go to sleep in her bedroom and Jeff would sack out on the couch.

"This has gotten very domestic," Robin joked one night when they were seated side by side on the couch, watching a movie.

Jeff smiled. "We have started acting like an old married couple."

Robin returned the smile. "That's not so bad, is it?"

They looked at each other, and Jeff stopped smiling. Then he looked away.

Robin put a hand on his arm. "I really appreciate what you're doing."

"Hastings is dangerous," Jeff said.

Robin took a deep breath. "Vanessa called this afternoon, right before we left the office. They think Hastings is probably out of the country."

"Why didn't you tell me?"

Robin looked directly at Jeff. "I was afraid you'd stop staying with me."

When Jeff didn't say anything, Robin said, "You don't have to sleep on the couch tonight. You can stay with me."

Jeff looked nervous. "We discussed this in Atlanta, Robin."

"I almost died in Atlanta. When I asked you to make love to me, you were right when you said it was my adrenaline talking. It's not now. I care about you, Jeff. And I think you care, too, or you wouldn't be here every night, protecting me."

"An office romance is a bad idea," Jeff said, sounding like a man torn between duty and desire.

"It can be, but it doesn't have to be. Making love isn't a trivial decision for me. I don't sleep around, and I don't think you do. If you care about me as much as I do for you, you shouldn't be sleeping on the couch tonight."

Jeff hesitated.

Robin gathered her courage. Then she leaned into Jeff and kissed him.

Jeff tensed for a second. Then he said, "God damn it, Robin," and he crushed her in his arms.

Robin woke up with a big smile. She'd wondered what Jeff would be like in bed, and now she knew.

"Wipe that stupid grin off your face," Jeff said.

"Who put the stupid look on my face, Mr. Hodges?" Robin said as she reached under the covers.

Jeff slapped her hand. "Stop that. You have to be in court at nine, and we don't have time for any more debauchery."

"Not even for a quickie?" Robin asked with an evil smile.

"Cut it out or I'll dial 911."

Robin faked a frown. "You're no fun."

Jeff kissed her and rolled out of bed.

Robin had been relieved to find out that the explosion that had scarred Jeff's face had not impaired his other functions, and she'd been right when she guessed that he would be a considerate lover. Actually, he'd been much more than considerate. He'd been downright accommodating.

PART FOUR

OCCAM'S RAZOR

CHAPTER THIRTY-THREE

A month after Frank Nylander's murder, Blaine Hastings Jr. was still a fugitive. Hastings or an unknown burglar were the popular choices for the person who had murdered Frank Nylander, but Rex Kellerman was not satisfied that Hastings had murdered Nylander. His focus had always been on Douglas Armstrong, who still claimed to have no memory of where he was or what had happened on the evening his law partner was killed. Then, just as Nylander's murder was about to become a cold case, Kellerman received a call with some very interesting news.

"Is this Rex Kellerman?"

"Yes."

"I'm Greg Nilson with Nilson Forensics. Peter Okonjo told me to call if I got a result on that blood sample he sent me."

"What blood sample is that?"

"Mr. Okonjo said it was in a murder case. The victim was a Frank Nylander."

Kellerman sat up. "What did you find?"

"Well, it's inconclusive, but the DNA might be a match for a man named Douglas Armstrong."

Now Kellerman was really interested. "Mr. Nilson, I have to be in court in fifteen minutes. Do you have some time later today to talk about this? It's very important."

"I'm free after two."

"That's perfect. Why don't I buy you coffee, and you can walk me through what you did?"

Kellerman had suggested meeting at Patty's Cafe, a locally owned coffeehouse on the outskirts of downtown. Ten minutes after he sat down in a booth in the back, a thin young man with sandy hair walked in. The man halted at the entrance and looked around.

Kellerman raised a hand, and the man walked to the booth. "Thanks for coming, Mr. Nilson."

"It's Doctor, actually."

"Sorry," Kellerman apologized. "What's your field?"

"Computer science, but I've studied biology and genetics."

"Impressive. When did you start your company?"

"Seven months ago. I spent a few years in the crime lab in Cleveland, Ohio, and decided to move to Portland to provide forensic services."

Kellerman sensed that he was hearing a sales pitch. "How's it going?"

Nilson smiled. "Slow, like most start-ups. That's why I was excited when Mr. Okonjo called. This gives us a chance to get our name out there."

Kellerman had done some research on Nilson Forensics and its owner in the time between taking Nilson's call and coming to this meeting. He knew that Nilson had sunk his life savings into the business and that he was shy on customers to the point where he might have to declare bankruptcy.

"Dr. Nilson, can you explain what your lab does that the Oregon State Crime Lab can't do? And please remember that I'm an idiot when it comes to science."

"How much do you know about DNA?"

"It's come up in other cases, but I'm no expert."

"Let's start with the basics: DNA is a molecule containing genetic material that codes for the unique physical characteristics of human beings. DNA is composed of four chemicals called nucleotides, or bases. The shorthand for them are A, C, G, and T. These bases pair together in the following way: A with T, and C with G. These pairs repeat in varying lengths and form rungs on the double helix that constitutes the DNA molecule.

"Now, the double helix is wound very tightly into a chromosome. A *gene* refers to a sequence of base pairs along a given portion of the DNA double helix which code for a certain trait, like blue eyes. Different genes are located in different places along a chromosome.

"An allele is one of several alternative forms of a gene that occurs in the same position on a specific chromosome. In other words, an allele is a variation in the number of times the base pairs of DNA repeat at a particular location on a particular chromosome. This number of repeats varies among humans. Modern forensic analysis focuses on the number of times the base pairs repeat at a variety of spots along a person's chromosomes. By measuring and comparing the number of repeats at given locations, an analyst can distinguish one individual from another."

"Okay, I get that. But what do you do that the crime lab can't?"

"The normal type of DNA analysis is performed in a laboratory, like the Oregon State Crime Lab," Nilson said. "DNA is extracted from the evidence, which can be a person's saliva or a sample of semen or blood. I won't go into the whole procedure, but you can get a graph of the DNA that can be used for comparison purposes.

"The problem for your crime lab in Mr. Nylander's case was that the amount of blood found under Nylander's fingernail was so small that the normal procedures for extracting and analyzing it didn't work. And that's where we come in.

"Nilson Forensics has developed a probabilistic genotyping software program. Probabilistic genotyping software uses computer science algorithms to perform complex mathematical and statistical calculations that are designed to calculate likelihood ratios or LRs. LRs reflect the relative probability of a particular finding under alternative theories about its origin. In forensic DNA analysis, the LR can be stated as, 'The profile is x amount of times more likely if the prosecutor's hypothesis is true than the defendant's hypothesis.' Your hypothesis is that the defendant contributed the sample, and the defendant's hypothesis is that someone else contributed the sample."

"So, you make guesses about the probability of the DNA in the blood under Nylander's fingernail matching the DNA of a particular person?" Kellerman said.

"Exactly." Nilson beamed like a teacher who has discovered a particularly apt pupil.

"You told me that the DNA in the sample matched Douglas Armstrong's DNA."

"Not exactly. There is some indication we have a match, but the probability isn't high enough for me to make a conclusive statement that the blood came from Mr. Armstrong."

"That's too bad," the prosecutor said. "If you were certain enough to testify that the blood is Armstrong's, it would give your company a real platform. This case is going to be front-page news. Media coverage is going to be huge."

Nilson frowned. "Of course, I'd love the publicity, but I can testify only about what the science shows."

"Certainly, but you said you deal in probabilities, not absolute facts. Is there a chance that a retest would show a different result?"

"I'm not certain what you're suggesting."

"I'm not suggesting anything. Like I said, I'm a real dummy when it comes to science. I was just wondering if it would be worth using your software again to see if you can get a more definitive result. My office would compensate you for the extra work, and I'll certainly spread the word about your business regardless of the outcome of a retest."

CHAPTER THIRTY-FOUR

Ivar Gorski parked a block away from the Vosses' house and got a tire iron and a can filled with accelerant out of the trunk. The lights in the Voss home had gone out shortly after eleven, but Gorski waited until two in the morning to go along the side of the house to the back door. There were no lights on in the houses on either side of Voss's house, but Gorski didn't believe in talking chances, so he was wearing dark clothing and a ski mask in case a nosy neighbor got up to go to the bathroom and happened to peek out a window.

Opening the lock on the back door was child's play. The door opened into a small kitchen. Gorski waited so his eyes could adapt to the dark interior. When he was ready, he walked down the hall to Leonard Voss's bedroom.

An officer moved the sawhorses that blocked the street to rubberneckers, and Carrie Anders parked her car behind an ambulance that had pulled up in front of a one-story bungalow. Roger Dillon got out of the passenger side, and the detectives walked over to

Miguel Montoya, the first officer on the scene. Montoya was waiting for them on the narrow front lawn.

"What happened?" Anders asked.

Montoya shook his head. "It's not pretty. The neighbor heard screams a little after two A.M. on Saturday. Then she saw the flames and called 911. The fire department reacted very quickly and saved the house. They found Mrs. Voss in the hall in front of her husband's bedroom. Someone bashed her head in."

"Do you have the murder weapon?"

"No."

"Go on."

"The husband is in his bedroom. He's a stroke victim, and he and Mrs. Voss sleep in different rooms. His face was beaten to pulp."

"How did the killer get in?" Dillon asked.

"The back door opens into the kitchen. It was jimmied."

"Let's go inside," Anders said.

They found Rita Voss sprawled on her stomach. The detectives studied the body before edging around it and going into Leonard Voss's bedroom.

"Jesus," Dillon said when he saw the damage to Voss's face.

After a few moments, Anders and Dillon went into the hall to let the lab techs do their work.

"I'm guessing the killer went after Mr. Voss first," Dillon said. "Mrs. Voss hears screams and comes out of her bedroom. The killer chases her down the hall, and *bang*—" Dillon imitated someone raising a club overhead and smashing it down.

"Seems right," Anders said.

"Then the killer starts the fire to destroy evidence."

Anders nodded. "Any sign of a burglary?"

"Mrs. Voss's purse was open. There was no cash in her wallet,"

Montoya said. "There's a jewelry box on her dresser, and it's open and empty."

"Okay," Dillon said. "Let's talk to the neighbors and see whether anyone saw anything."

CHAPTER THIRTY-FIVE

Rex Kellerman loved to tell anyone who would listen about the brilliant flash of insight that led to the solution of Frank Nylander's murder. He thought it was a great story, especially given the fact that Agatha Christie, the Queen of the Mystery Novel, had given him a clue that helped solve the case.

A week after meeting with Greg Nilson, Kellerman received a report from Nilson Forensics that concluded that there was a high probability that the DNA in the blood sample found under Frank Nylander's fingernail matched the DNA of Douglas Armstrong. And that was when Kellerman remembered the mystery novels in the bookcase in Douglas Armstrong's law office. There had been a lot of Agatha Christies in the bookcase, and there had also been a biography of Dame Agatha.

Kellerman had never been much of a reader. When he did read a book, it was usually a military history. But he remembered something he'd heard or read about Agatha Christie. He did a web search for her on his computer, and his smile grew even wider when he read Christie's biography. As soon as he finished, Kellerman ran

down the hall to the office of his boss, Multnomah County District
Attorney Paul Getty.

Getty was balding and had a sallow complexion. A heart condition brought on by the stress of his job made him look ten years
older than his sixty-two years and had led to his decision to retire
before the next election.

"He's faking!" Kellerman said as soon as he was admitted to
Getty's office.

"Who's faking?" Getty asked as Kellerman dropped into a seat
across from him.

"Armstrong," Kellerman said, leaning forward in his chair and
fixing Getty with a diabolical grin. "The son of a bitch killed his
partner."

"Slow down, Rex. If I recall correctly, you're the only one who's
pushing that theory."

Kellerman flashed a satisfied smile. "I've got proof." Kellerman
told his boss about the result of the low-template DNA analysis of
the blood found under Nylander's fingernail.

"What kind of method is that?" Getty asked. "I've never heard
of it."

"It's cutting-edge stuff, Paul."

"Can you even get the results into evidence?"

"Sure, no problem," Kellerman said with more confidence than
he actually felt. "And there's something else," Kellerman said in
an effort to divert Getty's attention from the scientific evidence.
"Armstrong is still claiming he can't remember anything about
what happened on the day of the murder and the week following.
Well, I think he's full of shit."

"And why is that?"

"He's a big fan of Agatha Christie. He's even got some of her
mystery novels in his office. And," Kellerman said, pausing for
dramatic effect, "he also has a biography of Christie on his office
bookshelf."

"So?" asked Getty, who looked genuinely puzzled.

"Christie's maiden name was Miller. She married Archibald Christie in 1914. In late 1926, Archie asked Agatha for a divorce because he was in love with another woman. On December 3, 1926, the Christies quarreled and Archie left the house. That same evening, Christie disappeared from her home. Her car was later found on the edge of a chalk quarry along with an expired driver's license and clothes."

"I'm still not following you, Rex."

"Christie's disappearance was big news, Paul. Rewards were offered for information, over a thousand police officers, fifteen thousand volunteers, and several airplanes searched for her. Arthur Conan Doyle even consulted a medium.

"Then, ten days later, Christie was found at the Swan Hydropathic Hotel registered as Mrs. Teresa Neele, the surname of Nancy Neele, her husband's lover. Christie never gave an explanation for the missing days, and two doctors diagnosed her as suffering from amnesia."

"You've lost me," the DA said.

"I think Armstrong killed his partner. Then he remembered Christie's disappearance and decided to fake his own disappearance and claim amnesia like Christie did."

"Well, Rex, that's, uhm, interesting, and a very creative theory, but I don't see where that gives you probable cause."

"What about the DNA? It's Armstrong's blood under Nylander's fingernail. They fought, Paul. Armstrong killed Nylander during the struggle. That's why he ran away. He panicked and ran. Then he faked amnesia to cover up his crime."

"The DNA is interesting."

"You learned about Occam's razor in college, right?"

"Sure. In a complex situation, the simplest explanation is probably the right solution."

"Exactly. Armstrong and Nylander were alone in the office

during the time span the ME set out as the parameters for the murder. There's no evidence anyone else was in the office after the receptionist left. All the employees were at a party, and they can alibi each other. But Armstrong has no alibi for the time of the murder."

"What about a motive? As I recall, everyone says that Nylander and Armstrong were the best of friends, and Armstrong repeatedly told people that he owed everything to Nylander. Hell, Rex, I know Doug, and I've seen him and Frank together at parties and bar functions. I've never heard a word about any animosity between the two of them."

"Even good friends fall out."

"If they have a reason. According to the receptionist, Armstrong was in a great mood when he came back from Seattle. What made him turn into a homicidal maniac moments later?"

"I don't know. But something happened. Think, Paul. Armstrong's blood is under Nylander's fingernail, and Armstrong had injuries to his face when he was brought to the hospital. That's proof they fought."

"Or that Doug was attacked by the same person who killed Frank. Doug Armstrong is an influential member of the bar and most probably a victim of the same person who murdered his partner. I've got to see more before I let you go after him."

"Don't get hung up on motive, Paul. We don't have to prove motive to get a conviction. There's not a scintilla of evidence that anyone but Armstrong and Nylander were in that office when Nylander was murdered. It's Armstrong, Paul, I know it. Once he's under arrest, I'll get his motive out of him. Let me go to a grand jury with this. Let's see what they say once they hear all the evidence."

The stress of being the Multnomah County district attorney had exhausted Getty and destroyed his health. He was tired and he didn't have the energy to fight with Kellerman.

"Okay," Getty said. "Run it by the grand jury. But get someone working on a motive. If you do get an indictment, keep it quiet and don't make a move before you tell me everything you've got."

Kellerman stood up, anxious to leave before Getty changed his mind. "Thank you, Paul. You'll see. You won't regret this."

CHAPTER THIRTY-SIX

Robin worked out before going to the courthouse, where she had a short appearance. Robin had the law on her side and had given the judge a brief supporting her position before arguing. The district attorney didn't support her argument with a single case, so Robin didn't have to concentrate too hard while the DA droned on. Instead, she passed the time thinking about last night's lovemaking with Jeff.

Robin didn't sleep around, and she'd had very few lovers, none of whom were as adventurous as her investigator. Actually, when she thought about it, Jeff was as good an investigator in bed as he was in the field. That thought brought a smile to Robin's face and a scowl to the DA's, who was insulted by the idea that her argument was amusing her adversary.

The judge ruled in Robin's favor. To celebrate her victory, she treated herself to a latte on the way back to her office. When she walked into the reception area at nine thirty, an attractive blond woman stood up.

"Miss Lockwood?" the woman asked.

Robin was certain that she'd seen the woman before, but she couldn't place her.

"I'm Marsha Armstrong."

Robin didn't think she'd ever talked to Marsha, but she remembered seeing her at a few bar functions. "Of course, Doug Armstrong's wife. Are you here to see me?"

"Yes." It was obvious that Marsha was upset.

"Come on back," Robin said.

While Marsha took a seat, Robin shut the door to her office. Doug's wife sat up straight, her back rigid and her hands tight on her purse like a drowning woman clutching a lifeline.

"How can I help you?" Robin asked as soon as she was seated.

"Doug's been arrested."

"What! Why?"

"They're saying he killed Frank."

"His partner?"

Marsha nodded. "Doug told me to ask you to come to the jail." She opened her purse and took out her checkbook. "I don't know what you charge, but Doug said to pay your retainer."

"Why don't we hold off on that until I've talked to your husband? When did Doug call you?"

"Around nine. He said that two detectives were waiting for him at his office when he got in."

"Did he know the detectives?"

"I don't know."

"Did he give you any names?"

"No. He just said they were taking him to jail to book him in and to have you come as soon as possible."

"Okay. I'm going over right now. You give my receptionist your contact information. I'll call and let you know what's up when I get back from talking to Doug."

• • •

Robin thought about Doug Armstrong as she walked to the jail. Her general impression was that Doug was a nice guy and a decent lawyer. She had never co-counseled a case with him. She remembered talking to him at a few continuing legal education seminars, but she couldn't remember the conversations. Robin had watched Doug try Blaine Hastings's case because she was representing Randi Stark, but she hadn't talked to him, because the interests of their clients were adverse. It wasn't fair to judge Doug on the result in the *Hastings* case, because the facts were so bad and Doug's client was so awful on the stand.

Robin concluded that she really didn't know Doug very well, and she knew even less about Frank Nylander, who didn't handle criminal cases. Robin also realized that she knew very little about Frank Nylander's murder. She rarely read about other lawyers' murder cases because she tried murder cases for a living. She did recall scanning an article after Nylander was killed, but all she remembered was that the murder had been committed in Nylander's law office.

After checking in at the jail reception area, Robin took the elevator to the floor where Doug was being held. A guard let her into the area where attorneys met their clients. While the guard was opening the door to the contact visiting room, Robin studied Armstrong through a wide pane of shatterproof glass that let her see into the room. Doug was wearing an orange, jail-issue jumpsuit that was a size too big for his pudgy body, and he slumped in his chair. When the guard ushered Robin inside, he looked at her with red-rimmed eyes.

"How are you doing?" Robin asked as soon as the guard was gone.

Doug just shook his head. "How could they do this?" he asked, choking up as tears filled his eyes. "Frank was my best friend. How could anyone think I would hurt him, let alone kill him?"

"That's what I'm going to find out, Doug. But it's going to

be a lot harder to do if you don't pull yourself together and help me."

Doug wiped his eyes with his sleeve. "I'm sorry."

"No need to apologize. I can't imagine the stress you're under. But you've got to take a deep breath and morph into lawyer mode. You're a bright guy, and I'm going to need your help if I'm going to get you out of this mess."

Doug gave Robin a weak smile. "I'll be okay."

"Good. Now, who were the detectives who arrested you? Do you know them?"

Doug nodded. "It was Carrie Anders and Roger Dillon."

"How did they treat you?"

"I was a little surprised. They were very considerate. I don't think they had their heart in it."

"What makes you say that?"

"They told me they were sorry they had to arrest me, and they waited until we were in the elevator to cuff me so no one in the office would know I was under arrest. Carrie even asked if the cuffs were too tight."

Robin frowned. Something was going on, and she made a mental note to talk to the detectives to find out what it was. "Did they tell you the basis for the arrest?" Robin asked.

"Roger said he couldn't tell me what the evidence was, but he did say that Rex Kellerman had gotten the indictment."

Doug looked down. "I don't know what Rex has against me, but for some reason, he doesn't like me."

"Rex treats everyone like crap," Robin said.

"This is something different. He goes out of his way to humiliate me. He alerted the press, and they were waiting outside my building, so everyone who watches the evening news would see me perp-walked to the police car.

"Carrie told me she didn't know that Rex had done that, and she pulled my coat over my face as soon as she saw the TV cameras."

"Did Carrie or Roger say anything else?" Robin asked.

Doug nodded. "Yes, they did. They said that I should tell my lawyer to get the reports from the crime lab. Especially the one about the DNA evidence."

"Interesting." Robin made a note. "They seemed to be bending over backward to be nice to you."

"That was my impression."

"Look, I know you know this, but I'm going to tell you that anything you say to me is confidential and warn you not to talk to anyone, including the other prisoners, Marsha, or anyone in law enforcement. You're a lawyer and you've given this advice to your clients, but now you're a defendant, and the pressure to unburden yourself—to try to convince others that you're innocent—is going to be overwhelming."

Doug smiled. "Don't worry, Robin. I'm upset, but I do have my wits about me."

Robin smiled back. "Good. Can you tell me about your relationship with Frank? I've known you two for a while, but I don't know you very well."

Doug told Robin about his dismal academic record at West Virginia University, his attendance at the law school at Sheffield College in Arkansas, his infatuation with Oregon, and the depression he suffered when his attempts to get a job in Portland failed.

"I'd hit rock bottom, and I was ready to pack it in and go back home. That's why I was quietly getting drunk on a barstool in the Cascade Tavern when Frank sat down on the stool next to mine. There was a basketball game on the tube and we started talking about it."

Doug smiled as he remembered that first meeting. "Have you ever met someone and immediately hit it off? After a few minutes, I felt like I'd known Frank my whole life. When he found out I was a lawyer, he told me about opening his own firm and how tough it was to break through financially. But he said things were looking up and he was starting to get some decent clients.

"I told him my tale of woe, and he told me that he had an extra office in his space and could use some help. I told him I wouldn't be able to pay the rent. Frank said he'd hire me, pay me a small salary, and let me keep a percentage of what I brought in. I had nothing to lose, so I said I'd give it a go. Other than marrying my wives, it was the smartest move I've ever made."

Robin grinned. "Your story sounds like a love affair."

Doug laughed. "In a way, it has been. We've been there for each other at every step of the way for twenty-odd years."

"So why are you suspected of killing Frank?"

Doug looked completely lost. "The only thing I can think of is that I don't have an alibi."

"That can't be all there is."

"How much do you know about my case?"

"Other than that Frank was killed in his law office, not much."

"Then you don't know that I have amnesia for the week of the murder."

"What do you mean?"

"I remember going to Seattle to negotiate a settlement in a case, and I remember landing in Portland. I also have a vague memory of talking to Frank in his office about Blaine Hastings being free on bail. But that's it until I was found by the police wandering around downtown about a week after Frank was killed."

"You can't remember anything?"

Doug shook his head. "Believe me, I've tried, but there's nothing there."

Robin asked Doug to tell her everything he remembered after he was brought to the hospital. Doug told her that he'd remembered his name and recognized Marsha. His house seemed a little strange at first, but he felt comfortable there now. When he returned to his office, he'd studied his cases and recalled details. But he had not re-covered any memories of the events surrounding Frank's murder, with one exception: he thought he might have told Frank that Blaine Hastings had been released on bail.

Robin made a note to talk to an expert on amnesia.

"I think this is enough for now. You'll be arraigned tomorrow. I'll set a bail hearing then. I want you out of jail if that's possible. Get me a list of character witnesses and anything else you think will help convince the judge to set bail. I'll also get you a copy of the discovery. When you've studied it, call me and we'll brain-storm."

"I told Marsha to write you a check for your retainer. How much will it be?"

Robin told him, and he said he would be able to pay her.

When they were finished discussing business, Robin reached across the table and laid her hand on top of Doug's. "You have a very good reputation in the bar. Use your lawyer smarts. I want you thinking like an attorney, not a defendant. Got that?"

"I do. And I appreciate the way you're treating me."

Robin smiled. "I'm treating you the way I treat everyone who has been accused of a crime they didn't commit."

CHAPTER THIRTY-SEVEN

There was a big smile on Rex Kellerman's face when he walked down the corridor toward the courtroom of the Honorable Sylvester Greenwood. What better revenge could he have on Marsha Armstrong than to send her husband to death row, where she could watch him languish for years?

Kellerman made the smile disappear as soon as he spotted the reporters waiting outside the courtroom. Death cases should be serious business, and it would be unseemly to appear to be enjoying himself. Kellerman maneuvered his way through the crush while spouting innocuous answers to the shouted questions from the press. Then he walked down the aisle and through the low gate that separated the spectators from the trial participants.

Robin Lockwood was conferring with her client at the defense counsel's table, and Marsha was sitting behind them. Lockwood had called Rex to let him know she was representing Armstrong, but Kellerman had told the receptionist to say he was unavailable. He was still furious with Lockwood for humiliating him in the *Henderson* case, and he didn't want to talk to her. But knowing she was Armstrong's lawyer had thrilled him because it would give him an opportunity for revenge.

The arraignment went quickly, as they usually did. Armstrong waived a reading of the charges and entered a *not guilty* plea. Lockwood filed constitutional objections to the death penalty, requests for discovery, and other motions. The judge set a date for a bail hearing and a tentative trial date. It was all over in twenty minutes. Then the guards took Armstrong away, and Kellerman heard Marsha choke up when she told Doug she loved him.

Kellerman left the courtroom quickly and headed for the elevator. As the doors started to close, a slender hand blocked them and Marsha Armstrong stepped into the car. There were tear tracks on her cheeks and she was flushed.

"Why are you doing this?" she demanded.

"Doing what, Marsha?" Kellerman asked innocently.

"Do you hate me so much that you'd kill my husband to get back at me?"

"I don't hate you and *I* didn't do anything. A grand jury heard the evidence against your husband and decided that there was enough of it to indict him for murder. He has a good lawyer. If he's innocent, he'll be acquitted."

"You know he didn't kill Frank. You're going after Doug to get back at me for walking out on you."

"Marsha, we're two adults. We had a brief fling and you decided to go back to Douglas. That was your choice, and I don't hold it against you."

Kellerman stepped out of the car, and the doors closed on Marsha. The prosecutor broke into a wide grin. What a lovely way to end his morning, Rex thought as he walked to the Multnomah County District Attorney's Office.

Dr. Margo Schatz was waiting for Kellerman in the reception area. Schatz had been a prosecution witness in several of Kellerman's trials. The psychologist was in her early sixties. Her silver-gray hair fell to her shoulders and framed a pleasant oval face. Soft blue eyes, lips that were quick to smile, and an appealingly plump body gave her a grandmotherly appearance that played well with jurors.

"I hope you haven't been waiting long," Kellerman said as they walked to his office.

"I just got here."

Kellerman closed his office door and motioned Schatz into a seat across the desk from him. "Did you read my memo?" the prosecutor asked.

"I did."

"Do you think Armstrong is faking amnesia?"

"There's no way I can answer that question without interviewing him and administering a series of tests."

"So, you can figure out if a defendant is faking amnesia?"

"It's possible. Crime-related amnesia is common in cases involving extreme violence. It's not unusual for perpetrators to fake amnesia to obstruct a police investigation or reduce their responsibility. I've seen studies that posit that twenty percent of criminals who claim no recollection of their crimes are feigning their memory loss and other studies that argue that the percentage is higher. One study found that twenty-nine percent of all criminals sentenced to life imprisonment who claimed amnesia at their trials admitted they were faking."

"How could you figure out if Armstrong is faking?" Kellerman asked.

"Faking amnesia has been linked to increased brain activity in the prefrontal cortex of the brain, and increased pupil dilation."

"Armstrong's not going to submit to an MRI or CAT scan or whatever you'd use to see that stuff."

"Symptom validity testing, or SVT, can also be used as a tool to assess whether people are faking when they claim to have no recollection of crimes they've committed."

"How does that work?"

"SVT asks defendants to answer a number of questions about the details of the crime with which they're charged. In answering each question, they must choose between two equally plausible answers, one of which is correct and one which is incorrect. If the defendant really has amnesia, the results should be random. In other words, correct and incorrect answers should be selected approximately equally. If the performance is significantly below chance—the incorrect answer is chosen significantly more than the correct answer—this indicates deliberate avoidance of the correct answer. That means the defendant most likely has an intact memory of the crime and is faking his amnesia."

"So, we can trip up Armstrong if we can get him to take the test!" Kellerman said.

"Not necessarily. Armstrong is a lawyer, so he probably has above-average intelligence and good research skills. If he researched how to fake amnesia, he probably researched the methods you could use to prove he was faking. If he's read the studies, he would understand the rationale behind SVT and how to game the test by giving random answers."

"So, you're saying that there's no way we can figure out if he really has amnesia."

"Not if he's faking and has done his homework."

CHAPTER THIRTY-EIGHT

Robin went back to her office after Doug Armstrong's arraignment and called Carrie Anders. Anders was reluctant to discuss the Armstrong case, but she finally agreed to talk to Robin that evening at the Log Cabin, a tavern located on a country road, a half mile from the entrance to a state park, where they were not likely to run into anyone who would know them.

At five, Robin picked up some sushi and ate at her desk while working on a case she'd been neglecting. At eight, she turned out the lights. Thirty minutes after she left her office, Robin was sitting in a booth in the dimly lit interior of the Log Cabin.

The meeting was supposed to take place at eight thirty. Robin checked her watch. It was nine. By nine fifteen, Robin decided that Anders was going to be a no-show. She was getting ready to leave when the detective walked in. It was hard for a woman as big as Anders to be incognito, but she was trying her best by wearing jeans, a quilted ski jacket, and a baseball cap that was pulled low on her forehead. Anders stopped in the entrance to adjust her eyes to the dim light. The tavern was only a quarter full, and most of the patrons were regulars who lined the stools at the bar. Anders scanned the rest of the room. Moments later, she was sitting across from Robin.

"Thanks for coming," Robin said.

"I bet you thought I wouldn't show."

"You didn't seem crazy about talking to me."

"I'm not."

"Can I get you a beer as a thank-you?"

"I'm not going to be here long enough to drink it. And before I talk to you, I need you to agree that this meeting never happened?"

Robin nodded.

"Why did you think I'd agree to meet?" Anders asked.

"Doug told me how you and Roger treated him when you made the arrest. He also said you told him you wanted me to check into the DNA test the crime lab conducted. That struck me as a strange way to act if you were convinced Doug was a murderer."

"I'm not."

"Why?"

"Can we agree that Rex Kellerman is an unscrupulous asshole?"

"Definitely," Robin said, using all her willpower to keep her facial muscles from forming a smile.

Anders leaned forward and lowered her voice. "No one but Kellerman thinks your client murdered his partner, and no one can figure out why he's so intent on convicting Armstrong. The firm's receptionist left Nylander and Armstrong alone in the office on the evening of the murder—so he could have done it—but no one we talked to can come up with a single reason why your client would kill the person everyone says was his best friend in the whole world. So, there's opportunity but no motive. And then there's the DNA."

"What about it?"

"They scraped a minuscule amount of blood from under Nylander's fingernails. The lab couldn't analyze it, because the sample

was too small, so Kellerman used a lab I've never heard of to analyze it. The report he read to the grand jury concluded it was Armstrong's blood. But the lab didn't use a conventional test. They used
a test I've never heard of that depends on algorithms."

"So, the DNA test might be flawed?"

"I don't know anything about the science. Suppressing the results is your job. I just thought you should know that the state's case
is flaky."

"Who do you have pegged for the killing?" Robin asked.

"There's a good chance this was a burglary gone bad. If it
wasn't, Blaine Hastings is the obvious choice, but we have no evidence that puts him at the scene of Nylander's murder."

"So, there are no solid suspects?"

"No. And it's time for me to go."

"I can't thank you enough for this, Carrie."

"Yeah, well, I've always thought of Armstrong as a pretty solid
guy. If he's guilty, I misjudged him. But this just doesn't sit right
with me."

Anders left and Robin waited fifteen minutes before going to
her car. While she waited, she decided that if she was going to save
Doug Armstrong, she had to find out everything she could about
the test that had been used to conclude that his blood was under
Frank Nylander's nail.

Jeff was sitting on the couch, watching a football game, when Robin
walked in. He smiled and used the remote to pause the game.

"Hi, kid," he said. "What kept you so late?"

"Doug Armstrong's case, and I need your help with something
odd that's popped up."

Jeff patted the sofa. "What do you want me to do?" he asked
when Robin was seated next to him.

"There's plenty of evidence that Doug and Frank Nylander

were alone in their law office around the time that the murder occurred, but Doug claims that he has amnesia for the evening of the
murder and several days after, so he can't tell me what happened
that night."

"Do you believe him?"

"I'm sure Rex Kellerman will claim he's faking. Kellerman
called me shortly after the arraignment and wanted Doug to take
some tests he claimed would show if he really has amnesia."

"What did you tell him?"

"What do you think?"

Jeff laughed. "I hope you were diplomatic."

"My answer was completely in Latin."

"Good for you. So. Do you think Armstrong is faking?"

"I don't have the training to give an opinion, but he seems genuinely confused."

"So what's this thing you need help with?"

"Doug has injuries that could have come from a fight. One piece
of evidence that suggests that the fight was with Nylander is a minute amount of blood that was found under Nylander's fingernail.
The blood sample is too small to be used in a conventional DNA
test, so Kellerman submitted the sample to an independent lab that
uses some kind of cutting-edge technology, and they concluded
that the blood is Doug's. I need you to find out what that lab did
and brief me on how valid the test is. I want to know if I can knock
out the DNA evidence pretrial by arguing that it's not been deemed
reliable in the relevant scientific community."

"Sounds interesting. Give me what you've got tomorrow, and
I'll look into it."

"Will do." Robin looked at the TV. "Who's playing?"

"Broncos and Colts, but the game's a snooze."

Robin smiled. "Does that mean you don't want to watch anymore?"

Jeff smiled back. "Why? Can you think of something we could do that would be less boring?"

Robin put her hand on Jeff's thigh and gave it a gentle squeeze.

"I might," she said, as she took the remote and switched off the set.

CHAPTER THIRTY-NINE

In the morning, Robin thought about Doug Armstrong's case as she walked from the gym to her office through a cold, damp drizzle. As soon as she got in, she gave the discovery she'd received from Rex Kellerman to her secretary with instructions to make copies for Jeff.

Moments after her secretary left with the reports, the receptionist told Robin that she had a call.

"My name is Herschel Jacobs," the caller said in a heavy New York accent. "I'm a homicide detective in Manhattan. Carrie Anders gave me your name. She says you represent Douglas Armstrong."

"That's right. What's your interest in Mr. Armstrong?"

"None, actually. I'm calling because he's Frank Nylander's law partner."

"Was," Robin corrected. "Mr. Nylander was murdered, and Mr. Armstrong is charged with his murder."

"Yeah, Detective Anders filled me in on the case."

"I still don't get why you're calling."

"I'm investigating the murder of Tyler Harrison III, an attorney in a firm with offices on Park Avenue. Mr. Harrison was found in a vacant lot Saturday morning, about five days after he met with Mr. Nylander to negotiate a case."

"I'm still confused. Mr. Nylander was killed on Tuesday evening, the day he returned from New York. That's several days before Mr. Harrison was murdered. So why do you want to talk to my client?"

"We're stuck, Miss Lockwood. The vacant lot is in a part of Manhattan where someone like Mr. Harrison wouldn't go. It's high crime rate, drugs, prostitutes. No one in his law firm or his acquaintances or his family can give us any reason why he would be there. And to answer your question before you ask it, no, he didn't have a drug habit and he was happily married."

"How about clients? Did anyone he represented live in the neighborhood?"

Jacobs laughed. "Mr. Harrison represented financial institutions and Fortune 500 companies. Aside from one bank with a branch that's fifteen blocks from the lot, there's nothing that connects his practice with the area. Our theory is that he was killed someplace else and the killer dumped his body in the lot."

"I still don't understand why you're interested in Mr. Armstrong."

"I'm talking to everyone who had contact with Harrison the week he was murdered, so I called to talk to Mr. Nylander and I found out he was murdered the same week. I don't like coincidences."

"Sometimes a coincidence is just a coincidence."

"True, but I'd still like to talk to your client to find out about the case Harrison and Nylander were working on and any guesses he can make that might help with Harrison's murder."

"I can't let you talk to Mr. Armstrong, for obvious reasons, but let me make a suggestion. Why don't you send me a list of questions you'd like him to answer? If he has no objection, I'll send you his answers."

"That sounds fair."

"And I'd like a copy of the Harrison case file so I can advise Mr. Armstrong on how he should proceed."

"The whole file?"

"You seem like a straight shooter, Detective Jacobs, but I don't know a thing about you. This could be a trap to get Mr. Armstrong to incriminate himself."

"He's not a suspect. We're just out of ideas, and I'm fishing around, hoping I'll latch on to something helpful."

"I believe you, but I find it's better to be cautious anytime there's a murder and a homicide detective wants to talk to one of my clients."

Robin didn't have any meetings or court appearances, so she decided to go to the jail and tell Doug about the call from New York. She didn't expect to learn anything interesting, but she thought that Doug would appreciate the break in his deadly dull jail routine.

"I had a call about an hour ago from Herschel Jacobs, a homicide detective from New York." Robin told her client. "He wants to talk to you."

Doug tensed. "About what?"

"Don't worry. It's about Tyler Harrison, the lawyer Frank met with in Manhattan. He was murdered."

"What's that have to do with me?"

"Nothing. The police in New York are stumped. They don't know who killed Harrison or why he was murdered. They're just talking to anyone he met with the week he was killed. Jacobs called your office to talk to Frank and found out he was dead. He wants to talk to you about Frank's case to see if it sheds any light on what happened to Harrison. So, what can you tell me about it?"

"Not much. Frank and I met for dinner once every week to talk about our cases. During dinner, we would discuss problems we were having and talk out solutions. It also helped for us to know about each other's cases in case one of us got sick or went on vacation."

"We do something like that in my firm. Did you talk about the case he was negotiating in New York?"

Doug nodded. "Right before he left, but all I remember him saying is that there was a good chance it was going to settle."

"What do you know about the New York case?"

"It wasn't really a New York case. We were suing a pharmaceutical company in Connecticut that was represented by a firm in Manhattan. It had something to do with a side effect. I think someone in Oregon had a stroke after using the drug, but that's all I know. You might want to talk to Ken Norquist, one of our associates. He did some work on the case for Frank."

"Okay. The detective is sending me the file on Harrison's murder and questions he'd like you to answer. I'll review the file and the questions before we talk about it."

CHAPTER FORTY

The file in the Tyler Harrison murder along with Herschel Jacobs's questions arrived two days later. Robin went through it while she ate a sandwich at her desk. The body had been found in a vacant lot, and Harrison had been shot in the back of the head. The crime scene and autopsy photos were gruesome, but Robin was used to gore and she had no trouble eating her lunch while she viewed them.

Interviews with members of Harrison's law firm, his friends, and his family had yielded no clues. Harrison was well liked in the firm and at his clubs. The fifty-eight-year-old attorney had been married for more than twenty years. He appeared to have loved his wife, and everyone said that he doted on his two children.

Harrison's wife had consented to a search of the victim's home office, and the firm had permitted a search of his law office—but the searches had yielded no clues. Robin studied the photographs of both offices and found them neat and well ordered, decorated with the college and law school diplomas and family pictures she would expect to find. She concluded that Harrison was a man who abhorred a mess and who liked to dot every *i* and cross every *t*— excellent traits for someone who dealt with contracts and corporate business.

One of Jacobs's interviews was with Marvin Turnbull, an executive at Norcross Pharmaceuticals. He told the detective that Harrison was defending a lawsuit filed by Leonard Voss, Frank Nylander's client. Harrison had called Nylander and asked him to come to New York to discuss settling the lawsuit.

After finishing with the file and going over Jacobs's questions, Robin walked across town to the offices of Nylander & Armstrong. The receptionist had been subdued when she used the intercom to tell Ken Norquist that Robin had arrived. Robin glanced in the offices she passed on the way to the conference room. The lawyers who glanced at her when she walked by looked grim.

Norquist was seated at a long conference table. Several folders and three-ring binders were stacked on it. The associate got up when Robin walked in. His handshake was limp and he looked depressed.

"Thanks for meeting with me," Robin said. "This has got to be awful for you."

Norquist flashed a humorless smile. "That's the understatement of the century."

"How is everyone in the firm holding up?"

"Not well. One associate left already and a few are looking around."

"What about you?" Robin asked.

"I can't believe Doug would kill Frank. You know better than I what his chances are, but I have to believe he'll be acquitted."

"So, you're staying?"

"Yeah. We've lost several clients, but enough are sticking with us so we can keep the firm afloat until Doug is back. Of course, if he goes to prison . . ."

"Let's hope he doesn't. So, Doug said that you worked with Mr. Nylander on the case he went to New York to negotiate?"

"I did."

"Can you fill me in?"

"The suit was against Norcross Pharmaceuticals."

"Why did you use the past tense?"

"Leonard Voss, our plaintiff, died recently. He and his wife were murdered during a burglary and they don't have any living relatives, so the suit is as dead as they are. That's a big hit for our firm."

"How so?"

"Norcross Pharmaceuticals manufactures an anticholesterol drug Voss was taking when he had a stroke. It hasn't been on the market long. Voss had a preexisting heart condition, but the claim is that the drug caused the stroke. There have been a few other cardiac problems and even one death by users of the drug, but Norcross's position is that the medical problems have been a coincidence and not the result of using their product."

"I understand that Mr. Nylander went to New York to try to settle the case."

Norquist nodded. "Mr. Harrison told him that a settlement might be possible. Frank thought that Norcross didn't want to litigate because of the bad publicity."

"Did they resolve the case?"

"I don't know. Mr. Nylander was killed shortly after he returned from New York. The only person who could have talked to him after he got back is Doug, and he said that he doesn't remember anything that happened on the evening Frank was murdered."

"Was the drug responsible for your client's stroke?" Robin asked.

"It's not clear. Our expert says yes, but there are other experts we talked to who told us they couldn't say for sure. In court, it would be a battle of the experts, and no one knows how that would come out. That's why Frank thought the case would settle, and the settlement would have been big. We're talking several million dollars. Our expert's opinion was in the minority, so Frank was playing poker with Harrison and Norcross, counting on them to want to avoid publicity enough to settle, even when the product might be okay."

"Can you think of any reason connected to this case that could account for Mr. Harrison or Mr. Nylander being murdered?"

"Norcross is relatively new, and this is their first big product. The company would take a big hit if a jury found that they were manufacturing a killer drug."

"Are you saying that you think Norcross may have been involved in a murder?" Robin asked.

"No, no. You just asked if I could think of a theory. Look, do you need me here? I've got a lot to do in our other cases, especially now that Frank and Doug . . ."

"I understand. I'll call you if I need you. And hang in there. I've just started representing Doug, but my gut tells me he's innocent. Hopefully, I can get him back to work soon."

Robin spent an hour going through the files Norquist had provided, but she didn't see anything that would help Doug. Still, on the way back to her office, Robin couldn't help thinking about her conversation with Detective Jacobs. He'd said that Harrison and Nylander being murdered so close together had raised a red flag, and Robin remembered responding that sometimes a coincidence was just a coincidence.

Voss, Nylander, and Harrison had all died violently within a short time, and Leonard Voss's death had ended his suit and may have saved Norcross Pharmaceuticals millions. She could see why the company would want Voss and Nylander dead, but Tyler Harrison was Norcross's attorney. Why would the company want to kill

him? Robin couldn't come up with a single theory that would connect all three murders. By the time she arrived at her office, she decided that it didn't matter who killed Voss and Harrison, since she
couldn't think of any theory that would help Douglas Armstrong.

CHAPTER FORTY-ONE

Robin had just returned from her meeting with Ken Norquist when Jeff walked into her office. She smiled.

"You interested in Thai, tonight? I'm treating," Jeff asked, as he dropped into a seat across from Robin.

"Sounds good"

"I've got interesting news on that DNA thing," Jeff continued.

"What did you find out?"

"You know that expert witnesses in an area of science are permitted to give opinion evidence only when their testimony is based on a scientific principle or discovery that has passed the experimental stage."

"Sure. The side that wants the jury to hear the evidence has to convince the judge that the science behind the evidence has been generally accepted as valid in the relevant scientific community."

Jeff nodded. "That's so junk science, like astrology, can't be used in court. Now, Oregon courts have long held that it's okay to admit DNA evidence in a trial when it's obtained in a lab, but no Oregon court has ruled on the admissibility of DNA evidence that uses mathematical probability to match a sample to a defendant."

"Do you think we've got a chance to knock out Rex's DNA match?"

"Probably not. Unfortunately for Armstrong, other courts have let a jury hear it."

"Are we dead?"

"There is an argument you can make. I just don't know if it will win."

"Explain it to me."

"There are courts in several states that have accepted conclusions based on analysis by probabilistic genotyping software. These courts have held that forensic biologists accept the method's validity. You can argue that this is not the scientific community in which the decision should be made. The method uses software, so the relevant community should be the computer science community, because it is inappropriate for forensic biologists with no or little training in software development or engineering to decide if the software works."

"Have you found an expert who can make our case for us in a hearing?"

"Yeah. There's a guy I know at Reed College. He needs to look at the source code for the software to see if it's been rigorously tested, validated, or verified using current software engineering practices. If it hasn't been, we can move to exclude the evidence. But I think it's a long shot given the number of courts that have accepted the use of the method."

"You said you had interesting information. What you've said would be interesting if I were prosecuting Doug."

"Sorry. There is something else. Nilson Forensics is the lab that did the analysis. The report Kellerman gave you in discovery was one page and didn't include any of the raw data about the tests Nilson conducted. I called the lab and spoke to Dr. Nilson. He sounded very nervous, and he told me he couldn't talk about the test without Kellerman's permission. I told him he didn't need the DA's permission, but he still refused to talk to me. So, I drove over to the lab to see if my incredible charm would melt his resistance."

"Did it?"

"His secretary told him I was in the waiting room, and he came out. I told him I wanted to see the raw data and the source code for the software. He refused. He said the source code is a trade secret." Jeff paused for emphasis. "Robin, he sounded scared."

"Can you think of any reason why he should be?"

"Maybe there's something about the test he doesn't want us to know."

"I'm going to move for discovery of the source code and the raw data that was used to determine that the blood under Nylander's fingernails was Doug's. Once we get it, we can try to see if there's a reason Dr. Nilson is scared."

CHAPTER FORTY-TWO

Robin was shocked by Marsha Armstrong's appearance when Doug's wife walked into her office. Marsha's eyes were red from crying, she'd lost weight, and it looked like she'd thrown on her clothes without any thought as to how they would look.

"Why are you here, Marsha?" Robin asked, not trying to hide her concern.

"I was just at the jail. Doug told me that they're going to say that the blood under Frank's fingernails is his. How bad is that for Doug's case?"

"It doesn't kill us. I may have a witness who will testify that there are flaws in the method that was used to make the match. I can argue to the jury that the results are unreliable."

"But the district attorney will argue they're not, and the jury might believe Doug was in a fight with Frank?"

"That's possible."

"And Doug won't be able to say anything, because he has amnesia."

"Yes."

Marsha looked at her lap. When she spoke, Robin had a hard

time hearing what she said, and she asked her to repeat it. Marsha looked up. There were tears in her eyes. "I did something terrible," she said. "It's why Rex Kellerman is trying to send Doug to prison."

Robin was confused. "I don't understand."

"I cheated on Doug with Rex."

"You what!?"

"I miscarried and I was depressed and Rex acted like he cared, but he didn't."

"Slow down and tell me what happened," Robin said.

Marsha told Robin about her miscarriage, her depression, and her brief affair with Doug's prosecutor.

"When I came to my senses, I realized that I'd made a big mistake and I broke it off. Rex didn't take it well. He was really angry, and I think he's going after Doug to get even with me."

"Jesus. Why did you wait to tell this to me?"

"I couldn't before. I thought this was all a mistake and you'd get Doug out and he wouldn't have to know. Even after he was denied bail, I kept fooling myself because I couldn't bear to hurt Doug. And I know this could kill him. But now he might really die and . . . Will this help? Can you use it against Rex?"

"I'm going to have to think about what you've told me. One thing is certain: Rex Kellerman has a big fat conflict of interest. The question is how to exploit it."

"You're kidding!" Jeff said.

They were in his office with the door closed, and Robin had just finished telling him about Marsha's affair.

"Interesting, huh?"

"Did you take a class in understatement at Yale?"

"What do you think I should do?"

"If Marsha isn't making this up to help Doug . . ."

"I don't think she is. You should have seen her. She was in tears and she looked awful."

Jeff grinned. "Rex is definitely fucked whether Doug is guilty or innocent."

Robin nodded. "This screams prosecutorial misconduct. No one but Rex was pushing the theory that Doug killed Nylander."

"Get me photos of Marsha and Rex," Jeff said. "I'll go to the hotel in Vancouver."

"If you can find evidence to back up Marsha's claim, I'll move to have the case dismissed."

Jeff shook his head. "Don't go to the judge. Set up a meeting with Paul Getty. If you work this out privately, Getty can say they've reevaluated the DNA evidence or give some other excuse for dismissing. That way Marsha can decide whether she wants to tell Armstrong about her affair and Paul can save face by dismissing without embarrassing his office."

"And if they don't dismiss?"

"Then you have no choice. You'll have to go before a judge and move for dismissal on grounds of prosecutorial misconduct. But if I know Getty, he'll want this settled quietly."

"I think you're right. But before I go to Getty, there's one other thing we need to do."

Robin and Jeff were waiting in the parking lot at Nilson Forensics when Greg Nilson walked to his car.

"Dr. Nilson?" Robin asked.

Nilson stopped and looked at Robin, then Jeff. "I'm Dr. Nilson."

Robin held out her business card. "My name is Robin Lockwood, and I represent Douglas Armstrong. I believe you've met my investigator, Jeff Hodges. We'd like to talk to you about a DNA test your lab conducted."

Nilson looked nervous. "I told Mr. Hodges that I wouldn't discuss the test without the district attorney's permission."

"When you say the DA, do you mean Rex Kellerman?"

"Yes."

"Well, Mr. Kellerman is going to be in a world of hurt very soon, and anyone who did anything even mildly dicey in Mr. Armstrong's case is going to be in big trouble, too. Do you fit into that category?"

"What . . . what do you mean?"

"I can't go into details, but Mr. Kellerman violated a number of ethical rules, and the odds are that Mr. Armstrong's case will be dismissed. When Jeff tried to talk to you, you refused and he got the distinct impression that you were scared. Why would that be if you had nothing to hide?"

"Look, I don't want any trouble."

"Then you better come clean about what you did," Robin said.

"What would happen if I told you about the test and you thought I'd done something I shouldn't have done?"

"You're not under oath right now, Dr. Nilson. But you will be if I start filing motions. If you lie under oath, that's perjury and you could go to jail. If you're honest with me, I will try to protect you if I can without hurting my client. Now, what did you do?"

CHAPTER FORTY-THREE

Rex Kellerman was in a great mood when he walked down the hall to Paul Getty's office. The day before, he had won a motion to suppress in a high-profile case. He guessed that Paul wanted to congratulate him in person for his coup.

Kellerman's mood changed from elation to confusion when he saw Robin Lockwood sitting across from his boss. Then he smiled. Maybe Lockwood was here to work out a plea in *Armstrong*.

"Close the door and have a seat, Rex," Getty said. He didn't sound happy.

"What's up?" Rex asked.

"Miss Lockwood has just given me some deeply troubling information," Getty answered.

Rex glanced at Lockwood. She looked grim. Rex frowned. "What did she say?"

Getty nodded at Robin.

She turned so she could look Kellerman in the eye. "Doug Armstrong's wife came to my office two days ago. She told me that you met her at a hotel in Vancouver, Washington, on four occasions. According to Mrs. Armstrong, the second and third time, you had sexual relations, and the fourth time you met, she broke off the relationship."

Kellerman looked stunned, but he recovered his composure quickly. "That's ridiculous."

Getty handed Kellerman several documents. "This is a sworn affidavit from a desk clerk at the hotel who identified you and Mrs. Armstrong from photographs Robin's investigator showed him. The other documents are copies of the hotel register signed by Mrs. Armstrong."

Rex kept his eyes on the paperwork so he wouldn't have to look at Robin or his boss.

"Well?" Getty asked when enough time had passed without a response.

"I . . ." Kellerman ran his tongue over his lips. "This is a setup, Paul. I mean, maybe Armstrong's wife was having an affair with someone at the hotel, but it wasn't me."

Getty handed more paperwork to Kellerman. "I sent a detective to the hotel," the DA said. "The clerk made another positive identification of you. He also gave us credit card receipts signed by you. Lying is just going to make this worse."

Kellerman was dizzy, and he felt like he might throw up. "Okay, yeah, we had a brief affair, but it was before Armstrong murdered his partner."

"Rex, you're a smart guy," Getty said. "Don't tell me you didn't understand that you had one hell of a conflict. Mrs. Armstrong thinks you're prosecuting her husband to get even with her for breaking off the affair."

"No, no. He did it. That's why I'm after Armstrong."

"We had a talk in this office before you went to the grand jury. I told you that I was dubious about Armstrong's involvement and so is everyone else who's had any part of this case. I think what Robin told me explains why you were so enthusiastic about indicting Doug."

"I know how this looks," Kellerman pleaded, "but Armstrong is guilty. I knew I might have a conflict, but no one else was willing to go after him. I couldn't let him get away with murder. He was alone with Nylander. Armstrong's blood is under Nylander's fingernails."

"The DNA evidence presents another problem," Getty said. "Robin spoke to Dr. Nilson, who runs the lab that conducted the DNA test you say supports your theory. He told her that you were informed that his initial test of the blood sample was inconclusive and that you offered him several incentives for him to retest it. Did you share the results of the first test with the defense?"

"No. I didn't think it was necessary. The retest showed it was Armstrong's blood."

Getty was starting to look angry. "You do know that the United States Supreme Court has ruled that prosecutors have to give any exculpatory evidence to the defense?"

"Yes, but the first test wasn't exculpatory. It was inconclusive."

"I'm not even going to respond to that ridiculous argument," Getty said. "But I am going to ask you if you offered a bribe in the form of extra payments and a chance for Nilson to get publicity for his company in exchange for a positive test?"

"No, never. I don't know what Nilson told you. I just asked him to retest the sample. I couldn't expect him to do it for free. And his company is new. I just let him know that the press would be covering the case and *if* he got a positive result and testified in court about it, people would learn about Nilson Forensics. But I never told him to fake a result."

Getty was shaking his head, and Kellerman stopped when he realized his boss's mind was set.

"I'm taking this case away from you," Getty said, "and I'm going to dismiss it with prejudice. That's the deal I've made with Robin in exchange for a promise by her to keep the reason for the dismissal between us.

"I'll go to Judge Greenwood in chambers and say we've reevaluated the evidence. That way the real reasons for the dismissal won't come out. I'm doing it this way to protect Mrs. Armstrong's reputation. Is that acceptable to you, Robin?"

"Yes. If Mrs. Armstrong wants to tell Doug what she's done, it will be her decision. My impression is that she greatly regrets the affair." Robin turned to Kellerman. "I don't trust you, Rex, so I'm warning you. If your affair with Mrs. Armstrong becomes public, I will have you disbarred."

"Okay, Robin," Getty said. "I think Rex gets the point. Now I'd like you to leave us. I have a few more things I want to discuss with Rex. I'll let you know when Mr. Armstrong can go home. I'll try to dismiss soon."

When they were alone, Getty looked at Kellerman. "I'm also keeping the reason for dismissal quiet so you can resign from your position without anyone knowing why you left."

"You're firing me?" Kellerman asked in disbelief.

"I don't see how I can keep you on after this. You're a good lawyer, Rex. You'll probably be able to get a job with a firm if no one learns why you quit. I wish you the best, but I can't have you on my staff anymore."

"Come on, Paul. It was one slipup."

"That's not true. Judge Wright met with me after the conclusion of the *Henderson* case and told me how you lied about your rebuttal witness. He wanted to file a bar complaint, but I talked him out of it. That was a mistake on my part. If you'd been forced to answer that complaint, maybe you would have understood that there are consequences if you violate your oath as an officer of the Court."

"Armstrong is a killer, Paul. Our job is to protect the public by putting killers where they can't hurt the citizens of Oregon."

Getty looked sad. "You don't get it, do you, so let me put this in plain English: *You fucked Doug Armstrong's wife.* By keeping that fact secret, you've forced me to dismiss his case with prejudice.

That means he can never be prosecuted for Nylander's murder. So, if he is guilty, you also fucked the people of Oregon.

"You should have taken yourself off the case immediately *and* you should have told me about the affair immediately. I'm not even going to get into the DNA evidence. You've left me no choice. There's no way I can justify keeping you on my staff after what you've done."

CHAPTER FORTY-FOUR

Robin and Marsha were waiting for Doug in the jail reception area. As soon as he walked out of the elevator, Marsha ran to him and threw herself into his arms. Robin waited while the couple had their moment.

When they broke their embrace, Doug saw Robin. He put his arm around Marsha's shoulders and the couple walked over. They were both smiling.

"I don't even know how to begin to thank you. You've been extraordinary."

"I just did my job, Doug."

"How did you get Paul Getty to dismiss my case with prejudice?"

"I had a lot of help from Rex Kellerman. The DNA test of the blood sample under Frank's fingernail was the only concrete evidence Rex had. The test results he gave to me said there was a match between your DNA and the DNA extracted from the blood. But there was a test that was conducted before the test results Rex gave us in discovery. That first test came out inconclusive.

"As you know, a prosecutor is required to give the defense any

evidence that supports an argument that the defendant is innocent, but Rex didn't do that. When he didn't like the result, Rex
bribed Dr. Nilson, the head of the lab, to do a retest. Dr. Nilson
shaded the results to come out with a positive match.

"When I confronted Dr. Nilson, he confessed to screwing
around with his calculations so the test came out positive. When
Paul heard what Rex had done, he was very upset."

Doug's face flushed with anger. "That little prick. I'm going to
see that Kellerman is disbarred."

Robin put a hand on Doug's forearm. "I think we should talk
about what you should do when you've had some time to think.
Getty has given Rex his walking papers. He also made Rex promise that he wouldn't run for Multnomah County DA."

"What about my reputation? Everyone is going to think I killed
Frank and got off on a technicality."

"I thought of that. Paul has agreed to hold a press conference.
He's going to apologize to you publicly, and he's going to tell everyone that there is no evidence that you killed Frank."

"Getting fired isn't enough punishment for what Kellerman did
to me."

"Agreed, but getting your life back on track and putting this
behind you might be better for your peace of mind than seeking
revenge." Robin squeezed Doug's forearm. "You hired me so I could
give you objective, unemotional advice, and that's what I'm doing.
Go home, take a shower, eat a good meal, and get a decent night's
sleep. Then call me. We'll talk about what to do with Kellerman
when you're calmer."

Doug sighed and the tension left him. "You're a really good
lawyer, Robin. I'm going to follow your advice. Especially the part
about the shower and the decent meal. The food in this place is
awful."

Robin laughed. Marsha hugged her. Then Marsha and Doug
walked out of the jail, into the sunlight. Robin headed back to her

office, praying that she could head off Doug before he did something that would force Rex to reveal his affair with Marsha.

Freeing an innocent man from prison was the greatest reward a criminal defense attorney could receive, but freeing Doug *and* saving his marriage were something she was going to work hard to achieve.

PART FIVE

SOMETHING ODD

CHAPTER FORTY-FIVE

Vanessa Cole waited until she had shut the door to her new office before breaking into a huge grin. She still could not believe the surprising turn of events that had made her the district attorney for Multnomah County. It all started with Rex Kellerman's startling resignation and his declaration that he had no plans to run for Paul Getty's seat. Two weeks later, Paul suffered a stroke and announced that he was retiring. Then, yesterday, the governor summoned Vanessa to tell her that she was going to follow Paul's recommendation and appoint her to the post.

Vanessa wondered if she would miss trying cases and how she would feel about being an administrator. She knew she would enjoy instructing her fellow prosecutors on the ethical standards she would demand that they follow—lessons Rex Kellerman could have used.

Vanessa detested Kellerman and was ecstatic when she learned he was leaving. Rex was smug, egotistical, condescending, and rude. Several women had complained that he'd made sexual advances or harassed them. What was far worse—though she could never prove it—was Vanessa's belief that Rex had manufactured evidence to gain convictions. Everyone knew about the *Henderson* case, and Vanessa was certain that *Henderson* wasn't the only time Kellerman had ignored the discovery rules; it was just the only case where he had been caught.

Vanessa didn't know the story behind Kellerman's rapid exit, but there were rumors galore. Paul had personally dismissed all the charges against Doug Armstrong the day after Rex quit, so Vanessa was pretty certain that something had happened in Armstrong's case.

Vanessa had inherited Paul's secretary. She told Vanessa that Robin Lockwood and Rex had met with Paul on Kellerman's last day, but she had no idea what was said in her boss's inner sanctum. She did say that Rex had looked like a death row inmate who was walking the last mile when he left the meeting.

Vanessa had a ton of things to do, but thoughts of Rex Kellerman kept distracting her. She worked through lunch. When the page she was reading began to blur, she told her secretary to hold her calls. Then she put her head back and closed her eyes, but visions of Rex Kellerman danced in her head like demented sugar plum fairies.

Paul Getty was convalescing at his home in Portland Heights. After work, Vanessa drove there for a one-on-one seminar on how to be *the* Multnomah County district attorney. Paul's wife, Sheila, greeted Vanessa with a warm hug and congratulated her on her new job. Then she led Vanessa to the sunroom, where Paul was reading in an overstuffed armchair.

"I see you survived your first day on the job," Getty said.

"Just barely. How are you feeling?"

"Much better. I went for a mile walk this afternoon, and I'm still here."

"Good. You had us all worried."

"The doctor says that stress was partly to blame for the stroke.

Let that be a warning to you. If the job starts getting to you, back off. I wish I had."

"Well, now you can be a bum and forget about protecting an entire county."

"Yeah. I'm resigned to spending the rest of my days eating bon-bons and watching daytime TV."

Vanessa smiled. "Somehow I don't think I see that in your future."

Paul grinned back. "Shall we get down to business? Sheila's preparing a gastronomic feast for you. I'm going to get the healthy, tasteless crap my doctor has prescribed."

Vanessa waited to talk about Rex Kellerman until Sheila told them that dinner would be ready in twenty minutes.

"Thanks for the crash course," she said.

"My pleasure."

"Can I ask you about something that happened in the office recently?"

"Sure."

"Why did Rex quit?"

Getty stopped smiling. "That's not something I want to discuss."

"Did he do something unethical in Doug Armstrong's case?"

Getty looked conflicted. Then he nodded.

"I'm DA now, Paul. If he did something that reflects badly on *my* office, I should know about it."

Getty sighed. "You guessed right. It was *Armstrong*."

"What did he do?"

"Before I tell you, you've got to promise me you'll let the matter stand the way it is now."

"I don't know if I can do that without knowing what happened."

Getty's lips formed a grim line. "Rex had an affair with Doug Armstrong's wife, and she broke it off."

Vanessa's jaw dropped. "He prosecuted an innocent man for revenge?"

"I think he's convinced that Armstrong is guilty."

"Based on what evidence?"

Getty told Vanessa about the blood under Frank Nylander's fingernail and what happened with the DNA tests.

"That's horrible, Paul. What if Armstrong had been executed? What if Robin hadn't figured out what Rex was doing?"

"Well, she did, and Doug is a free man."

"I have to think about this, Paul."

"Doug doesn't know that Marsha cheated on him. Think of the damage you'll do to their relationship if he learns what happened between her and Rex."

"Think of the damage Rex could have done. He's a criminal, Paul, and I don't know if I can sweep what he's done under the rug."

The next morning, Vanessa was the first person to arrive at the Multnomah County District Attorney's Office. There were two reasons for her early appearance. First, she wanted to know if there was a history of prosecuting district attorneys who intentionally withheld exculpatory evidence or offered evidence they knew to be false or questionable to a grand jury or trial jury. Second, she just couldn't sleep, knowing that Rex Kellerman had tried to put Doug Armstrong on death row to avenge being jilted by Doug's wife.

Vanessa found only a few cases where a prosecutor had been disbarred or jailed for withholding exculpatory evidence. In one case, a Texas prosecutor had intentionally withheld evidence in a murder case that could have cleared the defendant. The defendant was convicted and spent twenty-four years in prison before being exonerated. The ex-DA, who was a judge when his crime was discovered, was prosecuted and pled no contest. He left the bench and was disbarred, but he spent only ten days in jail.

Vanessa was furious when she finished reading about that case.

In *Brady v. Maryland,* the United States Supreme Court had made it crystal clear that prosecutors had an absolute duty to turn over exculpatory evidence to the defense. Every district attorney knew that. The Texas DA's dereliction of duty had robbed a man of twenty-four years of his life and forced him to spend those years in the company of hardened criminals. Ten days in jail was a woefully inadequate punishment for such a hideous crime. To Vanessa's mind, the DA was guilty of kidnapping, and Rex Kellerman was guilty of attempted murder.

CHAPTER FORTY-SIX

Blaine Hastings was still on the run, but Robin figured that he'd be behind bars soon. Fugitives were usually caught. Someone would recognize him and phone the police or he'd get desperate and use a credit card or he'd just get tired of being hunted and turn himself in. So, she began preparing Randi Stark's lawsuit. During a brainstorming session, Robin and Jeff drafted a witness list. Many of the witnesses in the civil suit would be the same witnesses who testified at Hastings's criminal trial, but there were some loose ends that Robin wanted tied up.

Jeff found the names of Hastings's high school teammates in Hastings's high school yearbook. Then he cross-checked the names with the Portland State roster. There were three boys at PSU who had played football in high school with Blaine.

Two days after his meeting with Robin, Jeff parked in front of Alpha Phi Sigma's fraternity house, a converted Victorian near the Portland State University campus. When Jeff started up the steps to the frat house, he spotted a young man with a blond crew cut, a thick neck, massive thighs, and ripped biceps sitting on a dilapidated sofa on the front porch. The young man stood up when he saw Jeff and walked toward him.

"Dino Portis?" Jeff asked.

"That's me," Portis said with a smile. "And you must be the PI."

"I am." The investigator handed Portis his card.

Portis pretended to look Jeff over. "Where's your trench coat?"

"I left it at home with my magnifying glass."

"That's cool," Portis answered with a laugh.

"Thanks for taking the time to talk to me."

"Yeah, well, Randi and I lived in the projects and went to school together. So why do you want to talk to me?"

"I was hoping to get some background on Blaine and Randi from someone who knew them. Can you tell me a little about Blaine? Have you had much contact with him since high school?"

"No. I didn't have much contact with him in high school either, except during football practice, and even then, not so much."

"Why is that?"

"We were on opposite sides of the ball. I was a running back and he was a linebacker, so there wasn't much interaction during practice. And I told you I lived in the projects. Blaine was partial to rich kids who were members of the Westmont Country Club."

"How did Randi and Blaine Hastings get along in high school?"

"Blaine never paid much attention to her, but he wasn't nice to her the few times I saw them together."

"What do you mean?"

"If we were in a group, he'd insult her or talk down to her, if he paid any attention to her at all. Then there was that thing with Ryan."

"Ryan Tucker, her boyfriend?"

"Yeah. That was fucking awful."

"Tell me about that."

"They had a fight after school. I came out of the locker room after it started. But, from what I heard, Ryan accused Blaine of forcing himself on Randi."

"Forcing himself how?"

"I'm not sure. Like I said, I wasn't there at the start."

"Okay, go on."

"Someone told me that Blaine called Randi a slut and Ryan took a swing at him. Blaine is a bully, but he can back it up. I'd never want to tangle with him. Ryan could fight but he wasn't in Blaine's league, and Blaine beat the shit out of him. It would have gotten really bad if me and a few of the guys on the team hadn't jumped in to stop it.

"What was worse than the beating was what Blaine did afterward. He had Ryan arrested. I mean, you don't do that. A fight is between you and the other guy. When it's over, that's that. But Blaine got the cops involved. Then he got his buddies to lie about what happened, and Ryan went to juvie."

"That's pretty low."

Portis nodded. "And it got worse, because Ryan committed suicide after he got out."

"I heard that."

"I doubt Blaine gave a shit. I had an abnormal psych class last semester. Blaine would have fit right in to our discussion of sociopaths."

"Tell me about Randi when she was in high school."

"She was always a little wild, always rebelling against something. She hung with the Goth crowd, smoked weed. I don't think she was into any other drugs. If she was, it didn't show. One thing you should know. She isn't dumb. She never did well in school, but that's because she never tried. But she was in a few of my classes, and I could tell she has it between the ears, even if she didn't use what she had up there."

"She's in community college studying to be a nurse, so maybe she's a late bloomer."

"Yeah, she told me about that at the game."

"The PSU–Oregon game?"

Dino nodded.

"Tell me about that."

"There's not much to tell. We got our butts kicked. But guys on our team knew a lot of the Ducks, so we were milling around on the field after the whistle blew. Randi and Annie Roche came up and we were talking, and Jerry Reyes told Randi about the party."

"Did he mention that Blaine was going to be there?"

"Yeah, he did."

"So, Randi and Annie knew that?"

"Yeah, probably. Annie was there, but she was talking to Nick Dominico. She had a thing for him in high school, and it looked like she was trying to rekindle the relationship." Portis laughed. "Nick told me later that he was afraid she was going to attack him."

"She might not have known?"

"It's possible, but we were all just inches from each other."

"Did you see Randi or Blaine or Annie at the party?"

"I saw them when they came in."

"Randi says that Blaine came over to her and started talking. Then they danced. Then he asked her to go to a bedroom to make out. Does that sound right?"

Portis thought for a bit. Then he frowned. "Okay. I remember Blaine talking to someone. There was a group of people from our class. Randi and Annie came over." Portis paused, and his brow wrinkled as he tried to remember what happened at the party. "You know, I do remember Randi and Annie looking at Blaine before they came over to our group."

"Looking how?"

"Just looking. And they were whispering. Then they'd look over again."

"And this was before they came over to your group?"

"Yeah."

"Do you know how Blaine and Randi got together?"

"Yeah. Blaine was talking to someone. I don't remember who. And Randi started talking to him, which I thought was odd given the way I knew she felt about him. Then they started dancing."

"Did you see the two of them go to the bedroom?"

"I wasn't paying that much attention, because I was talking about the game with some friends of mine. They go to Oregon and they were razzing me." Portis smiled. "That game will not be on my highlight reel."

"Okay. Is there anything else you can think of that might help?"

"No, I . . ." Portis paused again. "There was one other thing. While Randi and Blaine were talking and dancing, Annie was watching them. This is just an impression, and it was dark and I wasn't paying her that much attention, but I thought she looked nervous, but she also had this little grin on her face."

"What did Annie do after that?"

"I don't know. Like I said, I wasn't paying that much attention. I did see Blaine leave right before the girls did."

"How did Blaine look?"

"I can't say."

"And Randi and Annie?"

"You know, now that I think about it, Randi was bent over and Annie looked like she was supporting her."

"Is there anything else you can think of that bears on the rape?"

Portis thought for a moment before shaking his head.

"Okay, well, thanks," Jeff said as he stood up. "You've got my card. If you think of anything, give me a call."

CHAPTER FORTY-SEVEN

Rex Kellerman's second wife let him keep the house when she divorced him. Her dentist boyfriend had a much bigger house. Besides, the house wasn't anything to brag about. It was just a serviceable ranch in a decent middle-class neighborhood. The nicest feature was a back patio that had a view of the mountains. The rain had let up for a few days, and the weather had been unseasonably mild. When the detectives came to arrest him, Rex was on his patio nursing a glass of Scotch.

Even those who detested Kellerman agreed that he always looked as if he had just stepped out of a men's fashion magazine. Not today. The man Carrie Anders and Roger Dillon found on the patio sported a ragged three-day growth, unwashed hair, and was dressed in a sweatshirt, a worn T-shirt, and soiled jeans.

Kellerman had stopped shaving and showering when the fifth firm he'd interviewed with told him that they thought he was a hell of an attorney, but they just weren't hiring. That's when the light went on. He was persona non grata. Someone had talked. How else could you explain the lack of interest in a lawyer who, Kellerman firmly believed, was one of the best litigators in the state?

The disgraced assistant district attorney was so deep in his sea of misery that he didn't hear the detectives approach.

"Afternoon, Rex," Dillon said.

Kellerman wrenched sideways, startled, almost spilling his drink. When the identity of his visitors registered in his soggy consciousness, he smiled. "Hey, Rog, Carrie. Pull up a chair. Wanna drink?"

"Not right now, Rex," Carrie answered.

"Come on." Kellerman extended his arm and pointed toward the perpetually snowy summit of Mt. Hood. "What's the sense of having this view if you don't take advantage of it? Pull up a chair, let me get you a drink, and let's enjoy the day."

"I'd love to, Rex," Dillon said, "but we're here on serious business."

"Oh? What's up?"

Dillon held out an official document and Rex read it. Then he laughed.

"Is this a joke, Rog? Did you and Carrie cook this up?"

"It's no joke. We're here to arrest you for the attempted murder of Doug Armstrong."

Kellerman stared at the detective. Then he broke out laughing again. "Okay, who put you up to this?"

Carrie stepped in front of Kellerman and showed him her handcuffs. "It's time for you to get serious, Rex."

It suddenly registered that the detectives weren't the only law enforcement personnel on his patio. Two burly cops had moved behind him.

Kellerman stood on shaky legs. "You are serious?"

"Please turn around and put your hands behind your back so I can cuff them. Roger, read Mr. Kellerman his rights."

"It's that bitch Cole, right."

"I don't want to use force. Please don't resist," Carrie said.

"All right, all right, but I am going to sue her ass. I was promised. Paul promised."

Roger Dillon had read Rex his Miranda rights, but the detectives had
not tried to question him, because they knew he wasn't sober
enough to waive them. Rex had sobered up a little as soon as it
dawned on him that he was in handcuffs, in the back of a police
car, charged with a crime serious enough to land him in prison.

Kellerman's first instinct was to try to make the detectives
understand how ridiculous the charges were, but he had been on
the other side in enough interrogation rooms to know that talking to
the police was the quickest way to kill any chance of being cleared.
There was, however, one word he knew he had to say, and he said
"Lawyer!" loud and clear. The detectives allowed him his call as
soon as he was booked in.

Carrie made sure that Rex was put in isolation. She was afraid of
what would happen to him if the inmates discovered a DA in their
midst. Rex lay on his bunk, staring at the ceiling, too scared to sleep,
even though he was certain that he would be released on bail when
he was arraigned in the morning. Hell, the charges might even be
dismissed. Who had ever heard of such a thing? Charging a district attorney with attempted murder for trying to bring a killer to
justice? Vanessa was insane. She should be behind bars for even
thinking of throwing him in jail for pursuing Armstrong. He would
definitely sue her when this was over. He would get her disbarred.
Thinking about bringing down the haughty bitch made Rex feel a
little better, but his good mood soon faded when an inmate began
screaming, prompting other inmates to howl like banshees.

When the guards restored order, Rex made a serious attempt
at sleeping, but imagining everything that could go wrong kept him
awake. What if he ended up in prison? No, that couldn't happen.

He'd hired Les Kreuger, and Les Kreuger was brilliant. The charge was as flimsy as a spider's web, and Les would rip right through it. Rex took a deep breath. Everything was going to be okay. He was going to be okay. But what if . . . ?

CHAPTER FORTY-EIGHT

Blaine Hastings had been hiding in the bushes at the edge of the bar's parking lot for an hour before the back door opened and a man staggered out. Several men and women had gone to their cars while he waited, but they had been in groups. He needed a lone drunk, and he got one just after one in the morning.

The man leaned over the driver's door and made two unsuccessful attempts to insert his key into the door of an old Ford pickup. He was making his third attempt when Hastings hit him with a metal bar. As soon as the man collapsed on the asphalt, Hastings grabbed his wallet and ran. When he was far enough away from the bar to feel comfortable, he went through the wallet. There were thirty-four dollars and some credit cards. He took the cash and tossed the wallet with the cards into a Dumpster.

Hastings was very hungry. He'd been reduced to rolling drunks for cash because he didn't dare use a credit card. He'd been sleeping on the street in Seattle and Tacoma. He couldn't risk going to a shelter or a soup kitchen for fear of being identified.

This was his first evening back in Portland. He had gone to Mexico briefly and sent a letter to his parents, hoping it would be intercepted so the police would think he'd left the country, but he had planned to make his way back to Portland to kill Randi Stark, the lying bitch who was responsible for destroying his life.

After getting a burger, fries, and shake at a McDonald's, Hastings made his way to the Starks' house. He had spent a long time deciding what he would do when he got there. He was wearing a hairnet under a hoodie, and he'd shaved off his body hair in a gas station bathroom. He also had gloves and long sleeves to cut down on the possibility of leaving trace evidence for the cops to find.

When he got to the Stark residence, he would break in and beat the bitch and her mother to death. His only regret was that he'd have to kill them quickly. He would have loved to torture them for hours to avenge what they'd done to him. But the important thing was killing Randi.

Hastings had been to the house before, but the cops had been called and he'd had to run. This time he would be more careful. It took him three quarters of an hour to walk from the restaurant to the house. He noticed that there were no lights on. He tried the doors and found them locked. He didn't think the Starks could afford an alarm system, so he broke a pane in the back-door window and waited a minute. When no alarm screeched, Hastings reached through the window and opened the door from the inside.

When he was inside, he crept up the stairs to Randi's bedroom. He knew where it was because he'd seen Randi looking down at him the first time he'd been outside the house. He turned the doorknob slowly. Then he slid into the room. His hand closed on the iron bar he'd used to fell the drunk, and he walked to the bed. He wanted to stun Randi with the first blow so she could see who was going to beat her to death. Only he didn't get the chance, because the bed was empty and neatly made.

Hastings made his way through the rest of the house. No one was home, and there were few items of clothing in the closets. Hastings stifled an urge to scream. Then he closed his eyes and took several slow breaths until he'd regained control of his emotions. The Starks were hiding. But where were they and who would know?

One name came to mind immediately. Robin Lockwood, Randi's lawyer, would have to keep in touch because of the lawsuit. Hastings remembered the contempt she'd shown him in court. He hoped Lockwood would refuse to tell him where the Starks were hiding so he could beat the information out of her.

CHAPTER FORTY-NINE

"It's Vanessa Cole," Kellerman said as soon as he and Les Kreuger were alone in the contact visiting room at the jail. "The bitch has always been jealous of me."

"I talked to Vanessa," Les said. "She wouldn't tell me much, but she did tell me you were forced to resign because of the way you handled Doug Armstrong's case."

"Doug Armstrong killed Frank Nylander, but everyone is trying to protect him." Kellerman shook his head. "Paul and I had a deal. I can't believe he'd stab me in the back like this. I was supposed to resign, and that was supposed to be that."

"Vanessa knows about the deal. She told me that Paul tried to talk her out of bringing any charges against you, but she decided to charge you anyway. Once I know more about the case, I might be able to use Paul's promise to your advantage. Right now, I need to know what's behind these charges. If Armstrong is guilty, why were you fired for prosecuting him?"

"I may have cut some corners," Kellerman answered with a nervous laugh.

"Tell me about that, because the indictment alleges that you bribed a witness to falsify evidence so you could frame Doug for a crime that could have led to his being executed."

"Yeah, well, he wasn't framed. The DNA evidence proved he's guilty."

"I'm confused. If you had evidence, what was the problem?"

Kellerman told his lawyer about the inconclusive first test and his request for a retest. "It was all legal, but Paul misinterpreted what I did."

"Vanessa told me you had an affair with Doug's wife and didn't tell anyone about it. Did she 'misinterpret' that?"

"I didn't tell anyone, to protect Marsha. I didn't want to mess up her marriage."

"Wouldn't sending Doug to death row have messed up their relationship?" Kreuger asked.

Kellerman started to respond. Then he realized there wasn't much he could say. "Can the attempted murder charge stand?" he asked instead. "Have you ever heard of anything like this?"

"I had an associate work on the problem after you called from jail. He found a few cases where a district attorney was prosecuted for withholding evidence that led to the conviction of an innocent man. But there is a United States Supreme Court case that might hurt us. It held that the Civil Rights Act of 1871 did not authorize a convicted person to assert a claim for damages against a police officer for giving perjured testimony that helped the state get a conviction. The bad news is a statement by the Court that you don't need the possibility of damages to dissuade witnesses from lying, because they know they can be prosecuted criminally for perjury.

"Vanessa can argue that you convinced the DNA expert to commit perjury and should be criminally prosecuted for attempted murder since you knew that the jury might sentence Doug to death if it accepted the perjured testimony."

"That's a stretch," Kellerman said.

"I agree. I was just trying to play devil's advocate."

"What's the plan, Les? What are we going to do next?"

"Your arraignment is at ten. I'm sure Vanessa will alert the press, so be prepared for a circus."

"Can you get me out of here?"

"Teresa Reitman is presiding. That's good. She's smart and she doesn't choose sides. I'm fairly confident she'll grant bail that you can afford. After that, we hunker down and figure out how to get your case dismissed."

CHAPTER FIFTY

Marsha Armstrong turned on the television in the kitchen while she fixed breakfast for Doug. He had started going to his office again because he thought it would help to get back into a routine, but he still couldn't remember anything about the days surrounding Frank's murder.

The lead story on the news killed Marsha's appetite. Vanessa Cole had charged Rex Kellerman with attempted murder because he had bribed a witness to falsify evidence that could have led to Doug's execution. From the debate between the legal experts, Marsha gathered that no one had ever charged a prosecutor in this manner, but it wasn't the novelty of the legal action that made Marsha want to throw up. Now that he was under arrest, Rex would have no reason to keep their affair a secret, and Marsha was smart enough to realize that Vanessa would expose the affair to prove Rex's motive for framing Doug.

Marsha turned off the set and collapsed on a chair. By the time Doug walked into the kitchen, she had decided what she had to do.

Doug was smiling, but his smile faded when he saw Marsha's face. "What happened?" he asked.

"Sit down. I have something I have to tell you."

Doug was confused. Marsha looked like she was about to cry. "What's wrong, honey?"

"The police arrested Rex Kellerman for attempting to murder you by bribing that witness to lie at your trial about the DNA."

Doug brightened. "That's great! I hope they send the bastard to prison."

"It won't be so great for us."

Doug's brow furrowed. "I don't understand."

"There's a reason Rex went after you, why he tried so hard to frame you."

"What reason?"

Marsha looked down at the tabletop. "I . . . We . . . Rex and me, we had an affair."

"What?!"

"It was the miscarriage. I was so depressed about losing the baby. I wasn't thinking straight. I . . . I was sick, crazy with grief."

Marsha looked up. "I stopped when I came to my senses. When I realized how wrong it was." Her eyes begged Doug to understand. "I'm so sorry." Marsha started to cry.

Doug stared at her for a moment, stunned by what she'd told him. Then he walked around the table and took Marsha in his arms. "I love you, Marsha. I'll always love you. I know what losing our baby did to you. The affair means nothing. It's your happiness that means everything to me."

"I was so wrong."

"No, if that's what you needed to heal, it's what you had to do."

Marsha started to wail. She squeezed her eyes shut and threw back her head. She was crying so hard, she couldn't talk. Doug hugged her as hard as he could.

"You're so good," Marsha managed when she had enough air to speak.

"No, baby, you're the one who's good. You're the one who saved me. You brought me back to life after Lois died. I'd do anything for you. I love you so much."

Marsha rested her head on Doug's shoulders, and they stayed in an embrace for a while. When Marsha calmed down, she leaned away from Doug. "Paul Getty made a deal with Rex. He said he wouldn't make public the reason Rex was resigning if Rex promised to keep our affair secret. Now everyone will know I betrayed you."

"I don't care," Doug said. "All that matters is that we're back together."

"How can I face our friends? What will they think?"

"If they're really our friends, they'll forgive you like I have." Doug gripped Marsha's shoulders and stared into her eyes. "Be strong. Together, we'll get through this."

"Oh God, Doug," Marsha said as she threw herself back into his arms. "I will never deserve you. Never."

CHAPTER FIFTY-ONE

The arraignment went the way Les had said it would. Vanessa had pressed for a high bail, but Les argued that the case presented novel legal issues that might not survive pretrial motions, and the judge had agreed. Les posted bail, and Rex had been set free two hours after court adjourned.

One of Les's associates had been waiting for Rex in the jail reception area and drove him home, where he had showered and dropped into a deep sleep. The annoying tones of his doorbell woke him at seven thirty the next morning. He staggered downstairs and opened the door. A reporter from a local television station was standing outside, his cameraman aiming a lens at Rex. Rex slammed the door before the reporter could get his question out. Moments later, Rex's cell phone began to ring. It was another reporter. Rex disconnected and turned off his ringer.

Rex tried to get back to sleep, but the doorbell kept ringing. At eight o'clock, he gave up. After pulling down all the window shades so the reporters couldn't look into his house, Rex fixed a breakfast of bacon, eggs, toast, and black coffee. Eating this breakfast, after gagging on the slop he'd been fed in jail, proved to be one of the greatest dining experiences of his life.

While he ate, Rex booted up his laptop. The story of his arrest was featured on the local paper's webpage. Vanessa had told the press that Rex had faked evidence to frame an attorney against whom he had a grudge, which was bullshit. Rex knew Vanessa had planted this slanted and inaccurate story to poison the jury pool.

It was a cool but sunny day. Rex thought about going out on the patio, but the reporters could get to him there, so he went into his den, collapsing on the sofa, where his emotions yoyoed between anxiety and rage.

Before he left Rex at the courthouse, Les had told him that he wanted him to go through the files in Frank Nylander's case so he could tell him the strongest argument he could make that Doug had killed his partner. Shortly after three, a messenger from Kreuger's office arrived with copies of the discovery that Vanessa had turned over.

Rex spread the files across his kitchen table and fixed a cup of black coffee. While the afternoon slipped away, he read the files in the Nylander murder case, the New York City case file that contained the investigation into Tyler Harrison's murder, Nylander's file with the information about Leonard Voss's lawsuit against the pharmaceutical company that had brought him to New York City, and the file about the murder of Leonard Voss.

Kellerman made notes on his laptop during his initial read-through. He got hungry a little after eight and made a sandwich. It was already dark when he started to reread the files. By eleven, he'd finished the interviews with Ken Norquist and the other employees of Nylander & Armstrong, the Harrison murder file, and the forensic and autopsy reports. Rex's eyes were getting heavy and he was ready to pack it in when something occurred to him. He frowned. Then he went back to two of the files. His heart began to thud when he found what he was looking for. It was strange, but was it relevant?

Kellerman did a web search and found what he was looking for. He peeked through a window. The reporters had cleared out. He walked outside and stared into space. It was cold on the patio, but Rex was too distracted to notice. It was too late to follow up on his idea. He decided that he shouldn't be the one to investigate anyway. That was his lawyer's job. Les had crack investigators who could find out if there was anything that could help him.

Rex went back inside and found his cell phone on the kitchen counter. That's when he realized that he didn't have the number for Les's cell phone. He looked up the number for Kreuger's law office. A computer voice told him to leave a message.

"Les, this is Rex. I came across something odd in the files you sent me. I don't know if it means anything. Give me a call in the morning when you get this message."

Rex disconnected. He was tired, but it was too early to go to bed. He decided to watch some television and was headed for the den when he heard a noise. He paused. Someone had come in the door that opened onto the patio. It was probably a reporter. Rex was furious. He walked toward the rear door.

CHAPTER FIFTY-TWO

"It was definitely arson," Carrie Anders told Vanessa Cole.

They were standing in front of the charred remains of Rex Kellerman's house. The blaze had awakened the neighbors, but the house was badly damaged by the time the fire trucks arrived.

"Any leads on who did this?" Vanessa asked.

"It's too early."

"Any thoughts?"

"There are all the defendants he prosecuted," Anders said, "and no one I know liked Rex. Doug Armstrong comes to mind. He must hate Kellerman for framing him. If he found out that Rex was having an affair with his wife, that would give him another motive."

"If I were Doug, I'd want to see Rex go through the hell of a trial," Vanessa said. "Then I'd wait to see if he went to prison. That would give me more satisfaction than killing him."

"I'll check on his alibi anyway," Anders said just as Les Kreuger drove up.

"What's Les doing here?" the detective asked.

"I don't know. He was representing Rex," Vanessa said.

Anders and Cole walked to Kreuger's car.

Kreuger got out and stared at the ruins of Kellerman's home. "What happened?" he asked

"Rex was murdered last night, and his house was set on fire," Carrie answered.

Kreuger looked stunned.

"Why are you here?" Vanessa asked.

"Rex left a voice mail message last night. He said he'd found something odd in the files I gave him. I called when I got the message. He didn't answer. Then one of my associates told me he'd heard on the radio that Rex's house had burned down, so I drove over."

"Did Rex say what he'd found in the files?" Carrie asked.

"No. Only that he found something strange. I saved the message. I'll give you a copy."

"When was the last time you saw or talked to Rex?"

"When he was arraigned. One of my associates drove him home and dropped off the files yesterday afternoon. I can make him available if you want to talk to him."

"What files did you give him?"

"It was your discovery, Vanessa. The files in the Nylander case, the stuff the New York detective sent about the Harrison murder, some information about the case Nylander went to New York to negotiate."

"The arson investigator thinks the fire might have been started by setting the files aflame," Vanessa said. "Did you see anything in the files you gave Rex that can help us figure out why someone would want to destroy them or what Rex was talking about?"

"I've been through the files a few times, but I didn't see anything that struck me as 'odd.'" Kreuger looked at the house. "Did he die in the fire?"

"No," Carrie said. "His body was burned, but the ME says he was probably dead when the fire started."

"Thank God he didn't burn to death. That's a horrible way to die."

"Dr. Grace found an entry wound in his forehead, and forensics found a bullet lodged in a wall under a painting. His body was found near the back door. Dr. Grace thinks Rex was shot by someone who came in that way and that he died immediately."

"Do you have any more questions for Les?" Vanessa asked Carrie.

"No."

"Why don't you take off," Vanessa said. "If you think of something that might help, give Carrie a call."

Kreuger nodded. He took another look at the house and gave a sad shake of his head before walking to his car.

CHAPTER FIFTY-THREE

The doorbell woke Marsha Armstrong from a deep sleep. She looked at the clock on her end table. When she saw the time, she bolted up in her bed. Ten o'clock! How had she slept until ten o'clock? She was an early riser, out of bed by seven at the latest. She couldn't remember the last time she'd slept until ten. She looked at Doug's side of the bed. It was empty, the sheets rumpled and his blankets thrown back. Doug was also an early riser, so she guessed that he was at the office.

The doorbell rang again. Marsha grabbed her robe and rushed down the steps. When she looked through the peephole, she saw Roger Dillon and Carrie Anders. She had no idea why they would be here. She opened the door.

"Hi, Mrs. Armstrong," Roger said. "Is your husband home?"

"No. He's probably at work."

"I guess that means he's feeling much better."

"He is, but he still can't remember what happened on the night Frank was murdered, if that's what you're here to find out."

Carrie smiled. "It's not."

Marsha frowned. "Then what do you want with Doug?"

"Actually, we wanted to talk to the two of you."

"Oh?"

"Can you tell me what you and Doug did last night?"

Marsha's brow furrowed. "Why do you want to know?"

"I'll tell you in a minute."

Marsha hesitated.

"It's important," Roger said.

Marsha shrugged. "We stayed home. I fixed dinner and we watched some episodes of *Game of Thrones* Doug missed when he was in jail. Then we went to bed."

"About what time was that?"

"I don't know. Nine, nine thirty."

It suddenly dawned on Marsha that she couldn't remember what time she'd gone to bed or even going up to bed. She did remember seeing the episode where the dragons burned up the army, but even that memory was hazy.

"You were together all night?"

"Yes," she said, although she was guessing.

"Could Doug have left during the night?"

"Okay. That's enough. I don't think I should say anything else until you tell me why you're here."

"Rex Kellerman was murdered last night," Carrie said as she watched Marsha closely for her reaction.

Marsha's jaw dropped and she looked stunned. Then she realized why the detectives were at her door. "You think . . . ? That's ridiculous."

"We have to talk to everyone who had a grudge against Mr. Kellerman, and Doug had a powerful motive to kill Rex."

"Doug was home all night, and I don't think we have anything more to talk about."

"I'm sorry we upset you," Carrie said.

"You have some nerve, coming here after what you did to Doug. So just go."

Marsha slammed the door. The adrenaline generated by her anger had cleared Marsha's head a little, but not completely. Why did she feel so dopey?

Marsha had told the detectives that Doug was with her all night, but had he been in her bed all night? She could never swear to that, because she had been dead to the world until the doorbell roused her at ten in the morning.

Marsha thought about the previous evening. She had been tired, but not abnormally tired. So, what was the explanation for her foggy memory and deep sleep? Marsha did take sleeping pills on occasion. She'd taken them almost every night after her miscarriage and while Doug was under arrest. But she had not taken any since Doug forgave her for having an affair with Rex Kellerman.

Marsha strained to remember what had happened during their viewing of *Game of Thrones*. Doug had been very sweet, she recalled. He'd bought several flavors of ice cream for her, and she'd eaten a big bowl while the dragons were flying around.

It dawned on Marsha that this was her last clear memory. She frowned. Did Doug put something in the ice cream? Why would he do that? The answer that came to her was one she quickly rejected. Doug was no killer. He was a gentle soul. It was ridiculous to think that he would drug her, sneak out of their house in the dead of night, and kill Rex—wasn't it?

CHAPTER FIFTY-FOUR

Robin had a court appearance in another county, so she had to take her car. The case finished at three. When she got back to her office a little after four, she found Everett Henderson waiting for her in Reception. Robin broke into a big grin. She hadn't seen Everett since she'd won his case and humiliated Rex Kellerman, two very pleasant accomplishments.

"Hey, Rockin' Robin," Henderson sang when he stood up.

"What brings you here? Hopefully, not another run-in with the law."

"Nah. I'm keeping my nose clean." Henderson pointed to a man who was sitting next to him. "This is my good friend, Bill Carmody. He's got legal problems, which I'll let him explain. And he has money, so don't let him off cheap."

Carmody gave new meaning to the word *disreputable*. He was rail thin, dressed in stained jeans, a soiled black T-shirt, and a leather vest that displayed the colors of the Viper motorcycle gang. His beard was unkempt, as was his hair, and he couldn't sit still. As Robin drew near, she caught a whiff of a horrible stink resembling the odor of cat piss, which she knew from experience attached itself to people who cooked speed.

"Thank you, Everett," Robin responded, trying not to breathe.

Henderson stood. "I'll be waiting downstairs, Bill. You're in good hands."

"Mr. Carmody," Robin said, "why don't we go to my office, and you can explain why you think you need my help."

It was after six by the time Robin finished interviewing her new client. She was too tired to work, so she called Jeff to tell him she was on her way. He said he'd treat her to dinner at their favorite restaurant. Robin straightened her desk and headed down the street to her garage.

The lot had been packed when Robin arrived, and the first spot she'd found was far from the elevator, at the back of the eighth floor. By six thirty, most of the cars were gone and her car was the only one parked against the back wall. Robin was reaching for the driver's door handle when she heard footsteps. As she turned, a hand shot out and jammed her against her car.

"Where is Randi Stark living?"

"She moved after she saw you outside her house, Blaine. I don't know her new address."

"I don't believe you. Give me the address or I'll hurt you."

"You're in enough trouble already. Don't make it worse by piling an assault on top of a rape."

"I never raped that lying cunt."

"The evidence and the witnesses say otherwise," Robin said to stall for time.

"The witnesses lied and the evidence was planted."

"DNA doesn't lie."

"You moron, that scheming bitch rigged the DNA."

"What are you talking about?"

Hastings's features hardened. "I'm through talking. Give me the address or I'll beat it out of you."

Robin let her voice crack so Hastings would hear fear. She hoped he would relax enough to give her an opening.

"Okay, okay. But I don't have it memorized. It's on my phone. Give me some room. It's in my pocket."

Hastings stepped back, and Robin aimed a kick at his knee. Blaine had exceptional reflexes, and Robin's foot missed the mark. Robin smashed her fist into Hastings's stomach, but it was like hitting a wall. Hastings grunted. Then he swung. Robin blocked the punch, but there was enough force behind it to drive her back against her car. She raised her forearm to block the next punch, but Hastings was so strong that the blow drove her forearm into her face. The back of her head smacked into the side of her car, stunning her.

Hastings grabbed Robin by the throat with one hand and slapped her hard with the other. "The address, bitch, or . . ." Hastings's eyes went funny and he released Robin.

He started to turn, and a massive fist adorned with brass knuckles crashed into the side of his face. Hastings staggered and tried to raise his arms, but he was too dazed to get them up. The next punch flattened his nose and sent him to his knees. Everett Henderson's final punch put Blaine out.

"How you doing?" Henderson asked.

"I've been better. How did you know I needed help?"

"I was downstairs waiting for Bill when I saw this asshole watching the building. I didn't think about it until his hood fell back for a moment, and I recognized him. Then you came out and he started following you. I decided to tail him."

"I'm glad you did. He was way too big for me."

"Hey, you tried."

"I'm going to call 911. Those brass knuckles are illegal, so I think you should disappear."

Henderson smiled. "Good advice, Counselor."

"And thank you."

"No need after what you did for me. Hey, I just got an idea. We should go WWE. We'd make a good tag team."

Robin laughed. "Get lost."

Hastings started to come to before the police arrived. Robin hesitated. Then she remembered what Blaine had done to Randi, and she stomped his head hard enough to put him out again. Two police officers arrived moments before the ambulance.

Robin had told Dispatch who had attacked her and asked them to notify Carrie Anders and Roger Dillon. The detectives showed up fifteen minutes after the first responders. The EMTs had Hastings strapped down in the back of the ambulance. The detectives checked on the prisoner, then walked over to Robin, who was sitting in her car with the door open.

"You're going to have a tough time getting dates if you keep beating them up," said Anders.

"Blaine Hastings isn't my type, Carrie. I don't date rapists."

"I took a good look at Mr. Hastings's injuries. I didn't know you could hit that hard."

"I can't. A Good Samaritan came to my rescue."

"Did you get a name?"

"No. And I was too dazed to give you a description, so don't ask."

Anders studied Robin for a moment. Robin met her gaze and Anders smiled.

"Maybe Prince Charming can give us a description. But he's going to have his jaw wired shut for a while, so I'll have to wait. Why did he attack you?"

"He wanted Randi Stark's address."

"Lucky for her, he's in no condition to pay a visit." Anders frowned.

"What are you thinking about?" Robin asked.

"I was just wondering if Hastings murdered Rex Kellerman."

"Kellerman's dead?"

"You haven't heard. It's been all over the news."

"I was in court and out of town all day. What happened?"

"Les Kreuger gave Rex all the files in the case against Doug Armstrong, those New York cases, all that stuff. Someone shot him early this morning, then set fire to the files. His house burned down."

"And you think Hastings might have killed him because he prosecuted him?"

"It's possible. Especially now that you tell me he was going after Randi Stark."

"Why would Blaine or anyone burn case files? Plenty of people have duplicates."

"That's a question we've been asking. Les Kreuger told us that Rex left a message in his office voice mail last night. He claimed he'd found something odd in the files, but he didn't say what it was. I have someone going through our copies to see if he can figure out what Rex noticed."

Robin was about to say something when she grew dizzy and reached out to brace herself.

"Are you okay?" Carrie asked.

"I think my adrenaline tank just went dry."

"Do you think you have a concussion?"

"I hope not."

"Did you make a statement already?"

"Yeah, to the first officer who responded to my 911 call."

"Can you drive safely?"

Robin thought about calling Jeff but decided against it. She'd see him at the apartment. "I'll be okay. I'll just sit for a minute."

"Okay. Then go home. If I need anything more, I'll get in touch."

CHAPTER FIFTY-FIVE

When Robin walked in the door of her apartment, Jeff saw her black eye and swollen jaw.

"What happened!?"

"I had a run-in with Blaine Hastings."

Jeff looked shocked. "Are you okay? How badly are you hurt?"

"I'm good. Just a little shaken up."

"Did you go to the hospital?"

Robin smiled. "Relax, Jeff. I used to fight professionally. I've been hurt worse in the octagon, believe me."

"Not by someone who tried to kill you."

"Blaine didn't try to kill me. He just wanted information. And he's in jail, so I don't have to worry about him. He also got much more of a beating than I did."

Robin told Jeff about the attack and the rescue. By the time she finished, he'd calmed down.

Jeff wrapped his arms around Robin and pulled her tight. "I should have been there for you."

"It's not your fault Blaine got to me."

"We dropped our guard. I should have known better."

Robin pushed Jeff far enough away to look into his eyes. "I'm okay. Please don't beat yourself up."

"I love you, Robin. If anything happened to you . . ."

"Neither of us can live in a bubble. If I could go back in time, I'd keep you from going into that meth lab, but I can't, and you can't go back in time and walk me to my car."

Jeff started to say something, but Robin silenced him with a kiss.

"Who rescued you?" Jeff asked when they came up for air.

"I'm not saying, because I don't want to get him in trouble."

"I won't tell anyone."

"You won't be able to if I don't tell you the identity of my knight in shining armor."

Jeff decided it would be futile to pursue this line of questioning.

"Did you hear about Rex Kellerman?" Robin asked to divert Jeff.

"Yeah. Do you think Hastings killed him?"

"I don't know. And right now, I don't want to think about Kellerman, Blaine Hastings, or anyone but the sandman."

Robin had a splitting headache when she woke up the next morning. Jeff was concerned, but she told him that he shouldn't worry. Then she took two Advil and fixed a bagel and tea for breakfast. Jeff read the newspaper while they ate. Every once in a while, he would comment on an article, but Robin seemed miles away.

They were almost finished with breakfast when Carrie Anders called to see how Robin was feeling and to ask her to come in to give a formal statement. Robin called her secretary to tell her she'd be in late.

"Do you want me to drive you downtown?" Jeff asked.

"I'll be able to drive myself."

"Are you really okay? You seem a little spacey."

"More than usual?" Robin said, flashing a smile that made it look like she felt a lot better than she actually felt.

Jeff didn't return the smile.

"I'm okay, Jeff. Please don't worry."

"Will you promise me you'll see a doctor? You could have a concussion."

"I'll go right after I give my statement to Carrie."

Robin went back to her breakfast, and Jeff turned to the sports page. He was about to comment on an upcoming football game when he saw Robin staring into space.

"What is it?" Jeff asked.

Robin frowned.

"Out with it," Jeff said. "I know when a weird idea is whirling around in your little brain."

"It's something Carrie told me. Les Kreuger gave Rex copies of the files in Doug Armstrong's case. Rex left Les a message on his voice mail. He said he'd found something odd in the files, but he didn't say what it was. The person who killed Rex burned the files. Could Rex have been killed because he found something in them that put someone in danger?"

"There's another possibility," Jeff said. "Paper burns. Maybe the killer just used the files to start his fire."

Robin sighed. "That's the most likely possibility. But Frank Nylander went to New York to settle a case against a pharmaceutical company represented by a lawyer named Tyler Harrison. The files in that case were among the files that Les gave to Rex. Leonard Voss was the plaintiff in the case. Both Harrison and Nylander were murdered. Then Leonard Voss and his wife were murdered, and their house was set on fire, just like Rex."

"And you don't think that's a coincidence?"

"I'm starting to think that there are too many coincidences connected to the New York case."

"Did Rex have anything to do with the New York case?"

"Not that I know, but he might have stumbled onto something when he read the files. Norcross Pharmaceutical is a relatively new company, and the drug that Voss claimed caused his stroke is their first big product. If Voss's suit had been successful, it could have been devastating for Norcross."

"You think the company hired someone to kill Voss?"

"I don't know, but Voss and the lawyers who were representing Voss and Norcross were all murdered within a short time."

"Assuming Rex found a smoking gun in the files last night, how would Norcross even know about it?"

Robin grimaced. "You've got a point."

"This isn't our case anymore, Robin. Doug was our client, and you cleared his name. Why waste your time?"

"It just bothers me."

"If you're right, poking around in Rex's case could be dangerous."

Robin smiled. "You're sweet, but you don't have to worry. If I do find something, I'll tell Carrie and Roger."

Robin drove to police headquarters and gave a statement about Blaine Hastings's assault to Carrie Anders. She pretended not to know the identity of her rescuer, and Anders didn't push.

"Can I ask you a question?" Robin asked just before she left.

"Shoot," Carrie answered.

"Something has been bugging me. Does the way Rex died and the way Leonard and Rita Voss died strike you as being similar?"

"I did think about Voss when I drove up to Rex's house, but I haven't found anything that ties the two together."

"Have you had a breakthrough in the Voss murders?"

"Maybe. Mrs. Voss called the station before she died and said she thought someone was following her. She said she got suspicious when she saw the same car on two occasions. Then she spotted a car down the street from her house."

"Did she give a description of the car?"

"She said it was a red Honda Accord."

"Did she get a license number?"

"No, the car was too far away, and it sped off when she started to walk toward him. But we may have caught a break. A red Honda Accord ran a red light two blocks from the Voss home on the night they were killed. There was a traffic camera at the light, and we have a photo of the driver and the license. The car was a rental. The renter used fake ID, but we ran the photo of the driver through facial recognition software and we think his name is Ivar Gorski."

"Does he have any connection to Norcross Pharmaceuticals?"

"All we know now is that Gorski has a private detective agency in New York."

"You should call Detective Jacobs in New York and let him know. He can get on it from his end."

"Gee, Robin, I never thought of that."

Robin blushed. "Sorry."

"Why don't you let us do the detecting? That's what we're paid for. You concentrate on putting criminals back on the street so I can stay employed."

Robin laughed. "Don't worry. I'm not after your job."

"That's good to know," Carrie said as she flashed an answering smile.

"Have a nice day, Counselor."

CHAPTER FIFTY-SIX

Randi Stark and her mother moved back to their house as soon as Robin told Randi that Blaine Hastings was back in jail. Two days later, Robin filed Randi's lawsuit against Hastings in the Multnomah County Circuit Court, and the next day, Jeff ushered Annie Roche into Robin's office before taking a seat against the wall.

When Roche testified in Blaine Hastings's rape trial, she'd worn a long-sleeve blouse and an ankle-length dress, and her only jewelry had been conservative earrings and a tasteful turquoise ring. Today, her bare arms were covered from shoulder to wrist with tattoos, and she wore a nose ring and metal piercings in her ears and eyebrows.

"Have a seat, Annie. Can I get you coffee, tea, some water?" Robin asked.

"I'm good."

Robin thought Roche looked nervous. "Thanks for coming in."

"Yeah, about that. How come you need to talk to me? I saw you sitting in at Blaine's trial. You already know what I'm going to say."

"I do have a transcript of your testimony and the police report with your statement. But you're going to have to tell your story to the civil jury that will hear Randi's lawsuit. There may be different issues we have to cover in that trial, since we're asking for money to compensate Randi for her physical and emotional injuries."

"Okay. Go ahead."

"Why don't you tell me a little about yourself. How old are you, did you grow up in Oregon, are you in school or working? That kind of thing."

"Uh, I'm twenty-one. I grew up in Salem. Then my folks moved to Portland when I was thirteen. I'm going to community college and working part-time in a nail salon and also at a grocery store to pay tuition."

"That sounds hard."

Roche shrugged.

"How long have you known Randi?"

"Like forever. We went to middle school and high school together."

"So, you're good friends?"

"Yeah."

"One of the big issues in a civil suit is the pain and suffering the plaintiff has endured. This can be physical pain or mental and emotional pain. Have you had a lot of contact with Randi since she was raped?"

"Yeah, I have."

"And have you noticed any physical or emotional changes?"

Roche nodded.

"Why don't you tell me what you've seen."

"Uh, well, she's depressed, you know. She told me she has nightmares and has trouble sleeping. And, uh, she's scared all the time. Like she thinks it could happen again."

"Okay. That's helpful. What about physical pain?"

"Uh, after Blaine did it, she was sore. That's what she told me."

"Anything lasting?"

"You have to ask her."

"Okay. Let's talk about something else. Did you know Blaine Hastings in high school?"

"Yeah."

"Were you friends?"

"No. Blaine Hastings is a pig. He belongs in jail." Roche answered with more emotion than she'd shown since she walked into Robin's office.

"You really hate him, don't you?"

Roche looked away and shrugged.

"Did he ever do anything to you to make you feel this way?"

"Not to me, but to people I know."

"Tell me about that."

"There's a guy I knew. He framed him, and he went to jail."

"Was this Ryan Tucker?"

"Yeah."

"Randi told me he killed himself."

When Roche nodded, she looked grim.

"What about other times Hastings molested a woman? Have you heard anything like that?"

"Just rumors. I don't know anything specific."

"Okay. Let's move on to the PSU frat party. How did you know about it?"

"Portland State played Oregon. Some guys we knew from our high school play for PSU. They told me about the party when we saw them after the game."

"Did Randi know about the party when you were at the game?"

"Not until I told her."

"My investigator talked to several of the guys you talked to after the game. They say that Randi did know about the party."

"Then I guess Randi may have heard about it."

"Blaine Hastings said he found out about the party from some of the PSU players. It must be the same guys."

"Maybe."

"Did the guys tell you Blaine was going to be at the party?"

Roche's shoulders folded in. "Uh, no. Not that I remember."

"Dino Portis told my investigator that Randi knew and you were standing next to her when she found out."

"Maybe I did know. I'm not sure."

"If you and Randi hated Blaine, why did you go to a party he was going to attend?"

"There's a lot of people at those parties. We weren't going to hang out with him."

"But Randi did. She danced with him, made out with him, and went into a bedroom with him."

"So?"

"It just seems odd if she hated him so much."

Roche shrugged again.

Robin noticed that Roche was worrying the skin on one of her fingers. Robin was wondering what was bothering Roche when she remembered Blaine Hastings's cryptic statement about the DNA evidence that had been crucial to his conviction.

Robin studied Roche. A reason for Roche's nervousness occurred to Robin—a reason that made her feel a little sick.

"Let's go over some basic stuff about testifying, Annie. Did Rex Kellerman, the DA who prosecuted Blaine Hastings, talk to you about perjury and the consequences of lying under oath?"

Roche's cheeks reddened, and she squirmed in her seat. "He told me that it was important for me to back up Randi's story about Blaine raping her."

That would be typical of Kellerman, who was always more interested in a conviction than the truth, Robin thought. Out loud, she asked, "You know that the DNA evidence in Blaine's case was crucial?"

"Yeah." Roche looked uneasy, and that encouraged Robin to press her.

"Rex got in trouble because he bribed an expert to lie about the

DNA evidence in another case. He was facing serious jail time before he was killed."

"Why are you telling me about this?" Roche asked. "You're
Randi's lawyer."

"I am, but I'm also an officer of the Court, so I have a duty to
keep from putting on testimony if I know it's not the truth." Robin
paused and look Roche in the eye. "You've been very nervous since
you entered my office. Is there a reason for that?"

"No," Roche answered, but her answer didn't sound convincing.

"Did you hear about Blaine's scam, the way he got out of jail
after he was convicted?"

"Yeah, Randi told me."

"So, you know that Blaine's father paid a woman to put Blaine's
ejaculate in her vagina and claim she was raped."

Roche didn't move.

"Did you know that Blaine attacked me in my parking garage?"
Roche nodded.

"Here's the thing," Robin said. "While we were in the garage,
Blaine insisted that he never raped Randi. I said that DNA doesn't
lie. He said that the DNA evidence in his case had been rigged."

Roche twisted in her seat.

"Did Blaine get the idea for his scam from Randi? Did Randi
lure Blaine into a dark bedroom and jerk him off so she could get
his sperm? Did Randi shout 'Get off me' as a signal for you to come
into the bedroom so she could put his cum in her when you walked
in and distracted him?"

"Why are you cross-examining me like I'm some kind of criminal?"

"I'm just asking you questions Blaine's lawyer is going to ask
when you testify for Randi in her civil case, and I wanted to see how
you'd hold up. With millions at stake, Blaine's family is going to hire
the most vicious lawyer they can find. He'll try to rip you apart.

Doug Armstrong is a pussycat compared to the attorney who will be defending this case. He's going to try to make the jury believe that you lied on the stand to convict Blaine so you could get revenge and a share of the money Randi gets."

"Well, that's . . . that's not true."

"Good, because witnesses who lie in court get in a lot of trouble."

"Well, I'm not lying."

"So, Blaine didn't get the idea for his scam from Randi?"

"I have no idea how Blaine dreamed that up."

"Well, that's good to know. Now, let's go over the questions I'm going to ask you."

"Why did you lace into Roche like that?" Jeff asked as soon as they were alone.

"You weren't in the garage when Blaine attacked me, so you didn't hear the way he protested about being framed. He really sounded sincere."

"Blaine Hastings is a sociopath. You can't believe a thing he says. You sat through the trial. You heard the testimony. Hastings raped Randi Stark."

"Yeah, but Hastings has insisted that Randi gave him a hand job and that he never penetrated her. If he ejaculated in her hand and she put Hastings's cum in her vagina, the same way Braxton did, it would explain how his DNA got inside her and how he got the idea for his scam."

"You think Randi's smart enough to come up with a plan that complicated?"

"You told me that Portis kid said she's bright, and she's studying nursing. She told me that she has a 3.65 GPA. That's up there. I'm pretty sure that Randi would have the medical know-how to pull off something like this."

"You think she made up the rape?" Jeff asked.

"What do you think?"

"I think that Roche was nervous because you scared the hell out of her, and I think Blaine Hastings raped Randi Stark."

Robin thought for a minute. Then she shook her head. "You're right. I'm probably still concussed and not thinking straight."

CHAPTER FIFTY-SEVEN

"I found something you need to know," Peter Okonjo told Carrie Anders as soon as she answered her phone.

"Tell me."

"We dug a bullet out of the wall in Rex's place, and I ran it through the National Integrated Ballistic Information Network. NIBIN came up with a match to a bullet used to murder a lawyer in New York City named Tyler Harrison III."

"Now that's interesting. Can you match the bullet to a particular gun?"

"If we had the gun. Without it, all I can say is it's the kind of bullet that could be fired from a certain type of gun. This one could have been fired from an automatic like a Smith and Wesson, a Beretta, or a Glock nine-millimeter. Why, do you have a specific gun in mind?"

Anders had a thought. "Let me get back to you."

As soon as she disconnected, Anders phoned Roger Dillon and told him to meet her at the Nylanders' house.

•　•　•

Frank Nylander's widow lived a few blocks from the Armstrongs in a yellow and white Dutch Colonial. Janet Nylander had put on makeup, but it didn't completely disguise the dark circles under her eyes, evidence of the many sleepless nights she had endured since her husband was murdered.

"We're sorry to intrude, Mrs. Nylander, but we want to ask you about something that may help us figure out what happened to your husband," Anders said.

"Go ahead."

"Did Frank own a gun?"

"Yes, a handgun."

"Do you know where it is?"

"No."

"Where did he keep it?"

"I don't know. He bought it when there were a rash of home burglaries in our neighborhood. But that was a while ago."

"Could it have been in his office or his car?" Roger Dillon asked.

"I'm not sure where it is."

"Can you look for it now?" Dillon asked.

"Yes. Of course. Why don't you wait in the living room?"

Janet returned twenty minutes later. "I can't find it," she said. "I looked in our closets, the den. I'll keep looking after you leave. I could have missed it."

"Thanks," Carrie said.

"You know, I think Frank did tell me that he was going to take it downtown."

"Do you remember what kind of gun Frank owned?" Dillon asked.

Janet's brow furrowed. "It had a funny name."

"Beretta?" Dillon asked.

"No. Something that sounded German."

"Was it a Glock?" Carrie asked.

"Yes, that's it!"

"Thanks, Mrs. Nylander. You've been a big help."

"Are you any closer to finding out who . . . did that to Frank?"

"Maybe. And what you've told us may help."

CHAPTER FIFTY-EIGHT

Robin was in court, asking the presiding judge for a setover in one of her cases. The assistant district attorney had no objection, and the request was granted. When Robin walked into the corridor outside the courtroom, she spotted Les Kreuger talking to another lawyer. She waited for them to finish before walking over to Les.

"Carrie Anders told me you were representing Rex Kellerman. I thought Vanessa went way out on a limb, charging Rex with attempted murder. How do you think the legal issue would have shaken out?"

"I'm not sure. There are good arguments for and against." Kreuger shrugged. "We'll never know now."

"Have you ever had a client murdered before?"

"I've been practicing for twenty-seven years, and this is a first."

"I didn't like Rex, but I wouldn't have wished this on him."

Kreuger flashed a sad smile. "No one liked Rex."

"Carrie said that Rex left you a cryptic message about finding something odd in the files."

"He did, but I and my associates are stumped. If there's

something odd in those files, we haven't been able to discover what it is."

Robin got an idea. "Would you mind if I took a shot?"

Kreuger looked surprised. "Why would you want to do that?"

"I guess I'm just curious. I've been directly or peripherally involved in several of Rex's cases. I'm suing Blaine Hastings, whom Rex prosecuted. I also represented Doug Armstrong when Rex charged him with murder." Robin grinned at Kreuger. "Also, it's slow at the office so I need something to keep me occupied."

Kreuger laughed. "Knock yourself out. Come over to my office tomorrow. I'll have copies of the files waiting for you."

Les Kreuger's law firm was housed in an historic Victorian home in Portland's West Hills. One of Kreuger's associates showed Robin into a spacious conference room that was illuminated by high windows and dominated by a carved oak conference table. The conference table was piled high with copies of the files Rex had been reviewing.

Robin bought a latte before walking over. She took off the lid, took a sip, and started on the files. Two hours later, she was no closer to figuring out if the killer had set the files on fire because paper burns or because there was something incriminating in them. But reviewing the files had made her think about Tyler Harrison's murder, so Robin decided to call Herschel Jacobs in New York when she returned to her office.

"You told me to call if I got any ideas about the Harrison case, and I had a few thoughts."

"Let me hear them."

"Carrie Anders told me about that New York PI who was seen near the Voss house."

"Yeah."

"Do you know if he had any connection to Norcross Pharmaceuticals?"

"We're working on that."

"What if Voss wouldn't settle and the negotiations fell through? That would mean that any problems with Norcross's product would be aired in public. From what I've learned, that could have cost Norcross a fortune. With Nylander, Harrison, and Mr. and Mrs. Voss dead, the suit is dead, and there won't be any negative information about Norcross's anticholesterol drug coming out. That gives Norcross a powerful motive for murder."

"Detective Anders and I discussed that possibility."

"There's something else that happened in Portland that might be important. A DA named Rex Kellerman was murdered, and his house was set on fire. The modi operandi of his murder and the Voss murders are very similar, and he was going through files that included the files on Tyler Harrison's murder and the civil suit against Norcross. The only problem is that I haven't found any connection between Rex Kellerman and the case against Norcross Pharmaceuticals."

"Actually, there is one," Jacobs said.

"Oh?"

"Detective Anders called me with some interesting news. It seems that the bullet that killed Mr. Kellerman and Mr. Harrison came from the same gun."

"You're kidding!"

"The gun could have been a Glock nine-millimeter. Frank Nylander owned a Glock, and no one can find it."

CHAPTER FIFTY-NINE

When Herschel Jacobs picked up Carrie Anders at JFK Airport, she learned the dangers of stereotyping. When she'd spoken to Jacobs on the phone, his name and heavy New York accent had made her picture the actor who played a chubby, Jewish delicatessen owner on a TV sitcom. The man who greeted her when she got off the plane was a burly six-two with curly blond hair and bright blue eyes.

"Welcome to the Big Apple," Jacobs said.

"Thanks for picking me up."

"First time here?"

Carrie nodded.

"I'll point out some of the tourist attractions on our way to the Meatpacking District."

"What's there?"

"Ivar Gorski. I've had someone on him ever since you told me about the photo. My man just called. Gorski's in his office."

Ivar Gorski's office was on the second floor of an old brick building near the High Line and the new Whitney Museum and a few blocks from the Hudson River. Jacobs had determined that Gorski didn't advertise his services online or any other place. He surmised that the PI had a small list of clients who were willing to pay a lot for services that might cross the line between legal and illegal.

The lettering on the office door read GORSKI INVESTIGATIONS, and that door opened into an unmanned waiting room. Gorski was seated at a small desk in a room off the waiting area. He looked up when he heard the door open.

"Yes?" he said with obvious surprise. Anders guessed that Gorski was rarely visited by people he did not expect.

"We're here on police business, Mr. Gorski," Jacobs said as he flashed his shield.

Gorski didn't look alarmed.

"I'm Manhattan homicide detective Herschel Jacobs, and this is Carrie Anders, a homicide detective from Portland, Oregon."

"How can I help you?" Gorski asked in a heavy Eastern European accent.

The detectives took seats across from him.

"We have a few questions relating to a recent trip you took to Portland," Carrie said.

"Yes?"

"Why were you in Oregon?" Carrie asked.

"I'm afraid that's confidential."

Carrie smiled. "Come on, Ivar. We know you were employed by Norcross Pharmaceuticals to follow Leonard Voss, who was suing the company."

Gorski didn't respond.

"Would you care to explain why you rented the car you used in Oregon under a phony name?" Anders asked.

"These questions are very aggressive. I think I should consult an attorney."

"That's your decision, but let me show you something first." Carrie placed her laptop on Gorski's desk and ran her fingers over the keyboard. Then she turned it so he could see the screen. "That's you driving a block from the home of Rita and Leonard Voss. Does that help you remember why you were in Portland?"

Gorski smiled pleasantly. "I don't want to be rude, but I must decline to answer any of your questions until I have consulted my attorney."

"You do know that someone murdered Mr. and Mrs. Voss and burned down their house?"

Gorski kept smiling but said nothing.

"Take a good look at the date and time of this picture. It was shot from a traffic camera on the date that Mr. and Mrs. Voss were murdered and minutes after a neighbor saw flames coming from their house."

Gorski looked at the screen, then back at Anders.

"We know you were hired by Norcross to follow Leonard Voss in connection with his lawsuit. We know that Norcross wanted to bury the suit to avoid adverse publicity about its product. We also know that Tyler Harrison, the attorney who represented Norcross, and Frank Nylander, Mr. Voss's attorney, were both murdered."

Gorski smiled. He looked perfectly relaxed. "I couldn't have murdered Tyler Harrison," he said. "I was in Oregon when he was killed."

"Oh, so you know when Mr. Harrison was killed?"

Gorski stopped smiling. He realized he'd made a mistake.

Carrie waited a beat. Then she said, "You're probably thinking that this picture isn't enough to get a conviction, and you may be right. But it is enough to get an indictment, after which the Multnomah County district attorney will hold a press conference during which she will lay out everything she knows about the motive for the murder of Mr. and Mrs. Voss. That means that all your hard work to keep the public ignorant of the side effects of Norcross's drug will be for naught. If you have an alibi for Harrison, I guess we'll only be able to indict you for killing Mr. and Mrs. Voss. Either way, Norcross and you lose."

Gorski shrugged. "Do what you have to do."

"We will. But there is a way out for you. Even if you're acquitted, the publicity will ruin your reputation."

"You've taken up enough of my time," Gorski said. "Please leave. If you want to contact me again, do it through my attorney."

"No problem," Anders said. "Once we're gone, you can call Norcross and tell them what we have in store for them. But, if you do that, there's something you should think about. If someone at Norcross did order you to kill Leonard Voss to keep him quiet, don't you think they might hire someone to eliminate the only person who can incriminate the company? If you didn't kill Harrison, someone else on Norcross's payroll did."

Carrie paused to let what she'd said sink in.

"We know Norcross is behind the murders of Leonard and Rita Voss. Tell us who gave you your orders, and we might be able to deal."

"This is getting tedious, Detective." Gorski smiled. "If you don't leave, I'll have to call the police."

Anders laughed. "I'm glad to see you have a sense of humor. I wonder if your buddies at Norcross will be laughing when we tell them about our visit."

Anders and Jacobs stood up.

"See you around," Carrie said before she and Jacobs left.

"What do you think?" Jacobs asked when they were walking toward his car.

"I think that Ivar Gorski is one tough customer."

"Do you think he'll deal?"

"Honestly, no, but I intend to turn up the heat anyway."

PART SIX

THE ALUMNI ASSOCIATION

CHAPTER SIXTY

Private practice was often feast or famine. A few new cases had come in the door in the past few weeks, but none of them were very complex, so Robin had a lot of time on her hands. One afternoon she decided to organize the files in Doug Armstrong's case so they could be put in storage.

Around six, Robin's stomach began to growl and she decided to call it a day. She'd been going through the files Detective Jacobs had sent her from New York when he'd sent the questions he wanted Doug Armstrong to answer. She'd put the photographs of Tyler Harrison's law office in a neat stack and started to put a rubber band around them when something in the photograph on the top of the pile caught her eye. The photo showed Harrison's desk and the college and law school diplomas on the wall behind it.

Robin picked up the photo and studied it. Harrison had graduated from Columbia University, a prestigious Ivy League school, but he had continued his legal education at the Warren E. Burger School of Law at Sheffield University in Arkansas.

Robin frowned. Something about Sheffield University rang a bell, but she couldn't remember where she'd heard about the school before. Robin conducted a web search and learned that Sheffield was a small Christian college in a rural area of Arkansas.

Sheffield's law school was definitely third tier, and Robin couldn't understand why Harrison had gone there. A graduate of Columbia would be able to go to a better law school than the one at Sheffield even if he had terrible grades. And why Arkansas? And how had a graduate of Sheffield's law school landed a position at a prestigious New York firm that would do most of its hiring at top ten law schools?

Then Robin remembered where Sheffield had come up before. She felt light-headed. After taking a few deep breaths, Robin mulled over the implications of her discovery. When she was calm, Robin found the phone number for Greta Harrison, Tyler's widow.

It was nine at night in New York, still early enough to call.

"Mrs. Harrison?" Robin asked when a woman answered the phone.

"Yes."

"I'm sorry to call this late. My name is Robin Lockwood. I'm an attorney in Portland, Oregon."

"What is this about?" Greta asked in the tone Robin often used when she suspected that a caller was a solicitor.

"You know Detective Herschel Jacobs?"

"Yes," Greta answered warily.

"Frank Nylander was an attorney in Portland. He met with your husband in New York to negotiate a case during the week your husband was killed. Detective Jacobs called me a while ago to ask me to help him with your husband's case because I was representing an attorney in Oregon who was the partner of Frank Nylander."

"I still don't understand why you're calling."

"I ran across something odd that might help Detective Jacobs, and I have a strange question to ask you."

"What is it?"

"I was going through a file and I noticed a photograph of

Mr. Harrison's diplomas. I saw that he graduated from Columbia, which is a very prestigious university, but he went to a small law school in Arkansas. Can you tell me why your husband went to law school at Sheffield instead of a more prestigious institution?"

"How could that possibly be relevant to finding my husband's killer?"

"It may not be. I may be way off base."

There was dead air for a moment. Robin waited.

"The answer to your question is very simple. Tyler and I met at Columbia. Although I was in medical school and he was a freshman, we were almost the same age because Tyler had been in the army for several years before he went to college.

"The year Tyler graduated from Columbia, I decided to go to a rural county in Arkansas that was in dire need of a physician. Tyler had excellent grades and could have gone to law school anywhere, but we were in love and he insisted on applying to Sheffield's law school so we could be together. Tyler graduated number one in his class and edited the law review. Several people at his law firm knew him from Columbia. They told the partners about him when he applied. Is that what you wanted to know?"

"Thank you. That's very helpful. I have one more question: What year did your husband graduate from Sheffield?"

Mrs. Harrison told Robin. The sick feeling she'd experienced when she saw the photograph of Harrison's diploma returned.

"I still don't understand what this has to do with finding the person who murdered Tyler," Mrs. Harrison said.

"To be honest, I'm not certain it will help. If it does, you can count on me telling Detective Jacobs what I've discovered."

Robin said good night and hung up. She spun her chair around so she was looking out the window, but she wasn't seeing any of the sights. Doug Armstrong had gone to the Warren E. Burger School of Law at Sheffield around the same time as Tyler Harrison. He and Harrison were the only lawyers she'd heard of who had gone there. In fact, Robin had never heard of Sheffield or its law school, and she doubted that anyone who didn't live in Arkansas had heard of the school. Anyone, that is, but Frank Nylander. But what did that mean?

Robin let her imagination run wild. Frank is in Tyler Harrison's office negotiating the *Voss* case. He sees Harrison's diploma and he says, "What a coincidence. My law partner went to your law school at the same time you were there. His name is Doug Armstrong. Did you know him?"

What had Harrison answered? The class at Sheffield was small, so it would have been odd if Harrison didn't know Doug. Robin bolted upright in her chair. After a few minutes, she did a web search for the Warren E. Burger School of Law alumni association.

CHAPTER SIXTY-ONE

Robin was too distracted to work, so she went to the gym. An hour of exertion left her exhausted but did not bring her peace of mind. It had rained for most of the day, but the rain stopped by the time she started walking home. It was not uncommon for Robin to solve problems in her cases during a long walk, and she got a few ideas before she arrived at her apartment.

Jeff was interviewing witnesses for Mark Berman, her law partner, so Robin whipped up a quick dinner of leftover Thai food. She paid very little attention to her food because the implications of what she'd discovered kept tumbling around in her brain. She had brought a chopstick's worth of pad thai halfway to her mouth when she remembered the bullet. As Robin sat up, she forgot to grip the chopsticks, and the noodles dropped back onto her plate.

Detective Jacobs had told her that the bullet that killed Tyler Harrison and the bullet that killed Rex Kellerman had come from the same gun. That made no sense if Rex had nothing to do with the New York case, unless . . .

Robin grabbed her phone and punched in the number for Carrie Anders's cell phone.

"To what do I owe the pleasure?" Carrie asked.

"Do you have any suspects in Rex Kellerman's murder?"

"Why do you want to know?"

"Humor me, will you?"

"Remember our conversation on the division of labor between people who are paid to solve crimes and those people who are paid to represent people who are arrested for a crime?"

"Please, Carrie."

"If you know something, you should tell me."

"I don't *know* anything. I just have an idea. If I get anything concrete, I promise I'll let you know. So, do you have any suspects?"

"No one we can do anything about."

"What about Doug Armstrong? Do you know where he was when Rex was killed?"

There was silence on the line. When Carrie spoke, she was angry. "Do you know something that makes you think Armstrong killed Kellerman?"

"I don't have any evidence that Doug is guilty, but I might be able to help you if a few things pan out."

Robin heard Carrie let out a breath. "We talked to Marsha Armstrong. She said that she and Doug were home all night. When we talked to Doug, their stories matched."

"And you believe them?"

"Yes, but that's not because they can prove they were together. It's just their word."

"And there's nothing else. No one called Doug during the time Rex was killed and he didn't call anyone? They didn't have visitors?"

"Like I said, all I have is their word."

"Okay, thanks. One more thing: Do you know what kind of gun was used to murder Rex?"

"We think it was a Glock. Why?"

"Like I said, I have an idea."

"Robin, do not go off on your own on this."

"I won't. I promise. After Atlanta and what happened in the garage with Blaine, I don't need any more drama in my life."

"I'm glad you realize that."

"I do," Robin said before she disconnected, but she was lying.

Robin was still up when Jeff came home.

"Oh, hi. I thought you'd be in bed."

"I need you to check on something for me tomorrow."

"No kiss, no hug?"

Robin gave him a peck on the cheek. "Can you do this first thing tomorrow?"

"Do what?"

Robin told him, and Jeff looked puzzled. "We're not representing Armstrong anymore. Why do you need to look into this?"

Robin explained what she thought Jeff would find and what the implications were if she was right.

"Assuming your hunch pans out, what are you going to do with the information?"

Jeff looked shell-shocked by the time Robin finished explaining her plan. "Are you out of your fucking mind?!"

"It's the only way I can think of to get the evidence we need."

"*You* do not need evidence, because *you* are not a police officer. You need to explain what you know to Carrie Anders, a sworn officer of the law, and let her act on it."

"How? There's no way Carrie can get a search warrant based on guesses. And even if she did search, Doug isn't stupid. No one will be able to find it."

"I can't let you risk your life, Robin."

Robin glared at Jeff. "I make my own decisions. If you don't want to help, I'll find someone who will."

"Be reasonable."

"I have spent hours thinking this out. If you can come up with another way to get what we need, tell me and I'll back down. If not, I'm going ahead with my plan whether you like it or not."

CHAPTER SIXTY-TWO

Ivar Gorski watched Marvin Turnbull drive out of the Norcross garage. He waited until there were a few cars between him and Turnbull before pulling into traffic and following him. Ivar was certain he knew where the CEO was headed. Turnbull was married with two children who were in high school, but he had a mistress who lived in an apartment on Long Island. Turnbull changed up the days he visited her because he didn't want his wife to notice a pattern, but he got horny at least once a week.

Patience was one of Ivar's strong points, and the trait paid off when Turnbull passed the freeway entrance that would have taken him home and kept going to the entrance that would lead him to his love nest.

Three quarters of an hour later, Turnbull parked on a side street. When he got out of his car, he was wearing a Windbreaker with a hood to conceal his face. He hurried to the entrance to the garden apartment and let himself inside with a key. If Turnbull kept to his routine, he would be inside the apartment until eleven. Then he would drive home.

Ivar settled in and passed the time reading *War and Peace.* He had developed the habit of reading the Russian classics after assassinating a literature professor who had angered a Russian politician by publishing an essay that condemned corruption in his department. On the way out of the professor's apartment, he had seen Dostoevsky's *Crime and Punishment* in a bookshelf. The title amused him, so he'd taken the book and found it engrossing. Now that he had read all of Dostoevsky and Gogol, he was on to Tolstoy.

At ten to eleven, Turnbull reappeared. Ivar closed his book and slipped out of his car. Turnbull turned the corner and was enveloped in shadows. Ivar walked up behind Norcross's CEO and shot him with a silenced pistol. He was headed back to his car before Turnbull collapsed on the sidewalk. He was fairly certain that no nosy neighbor had seen him or his car, but he wasn't worried if he was in error. He had worn a disguise, and the car was stolen. He would leave it at the airport tonight before boarding a flight to Madrid using a ticket he had obtained under the false name that matched the name in his forged passport.

CHAPTER SIXTY-THREE

Doug Armstrong smiled when his secretary ushered Robin into his office a little before five in the afternoon. "Hi, Robin. What's up?"

"I haven't seen you in a while, and I wanted to see how you're feeling."

"Thanks for asking. I'm about ninety percent."

"Still having trouble remembering what happened on the evening Frank was murdered?"

Doug stopped smiling and shook his head. "That's still a blank. I keep trying, but . . ." He shook his head again.

"I might be able to help you fill in the blanks."

"Oh?"

"Yeah. I know who killed Frank."

"Really?"

Robin nodded.

"That's great! Who killed him?"

"We both know the answer to that question."

Doug looked puzzled, and Robin flashed a sad smile. "You can stop pretending. I know you murdered your best friend and I know why."

"What are you talking about?"

"You were always the most likely suspect. You were alone with Frank when he was killed, and your blood was under his fingernail. But everyone knew you and Frank were best friends, and you'd been in a great mood when you got back from Seattle, so everyone gave you a pass because no one could think of a motive so strong that you would kill Frank."

"That's because I would never kill Frank. I owed him everything."

"And he was going to take everything from you, wasn't he? Quite by accident, Frank had discovered a horrible secret— something you've been hiding for years, something that would destroy your world."

"I don't know where you're going with this, Robin. I don't have any deep, dark secrets."

"When did you graduate from law school, Doug?"

"Nineteen eighty-eight."

"That's not true, is it?"

"What do you mean?"

"Frank went to New York to negotiate the *Voss* case with Tyler Harrison. While he was in Harrison's office, he noticed that Harrison had graduated from Sheffield University's law school in 1988. You're the only other person Frank knew who had gone to Sheffield, so he told Harrison that his law partner, Doug Armstrong, had been a classmate. And that's when Harrison destroyed the myth you'd been promoting all these years. He told Frank the truth."

Armstrong looked directly at Robin, his mouth set in a grim line. "And what is the truth, Robin?"

"You flunked out of law school, Doug. I know that for a fact. I checked with the law school alumni association. Your diploma is a forgery. I'm guessing that you moved to Oregon because you believed that no one in this state would know anything about Sheffield University. You lied when you said you passed the Oregon Bar exam. I've looked for your name on every list of applicants who applied to take or passed the bar exam from 1988 on. Your name isn't on any of the lists. You never passed, because you never took it.

Doug stared at Robin in a way that made her recall the old cliché, "If looks could kill . . ."

"Aren't you going to tell me I'm mistaken?" Robin asked.

"This is your story, Robin. Go on. It sounds interesting."

"You know, it's amazing. Once you start practicing, everyone assumes that you graduated from a law school and passed the bar exam. No one ever challenges you or is even interested. There have been any number of cases over the years of people who falsely claimed to be attorneys and fooled everyone for years.

"Frank believed you when you told him your tale of woe in that tavern the first time you met, and once you started appearing in court, everyone assumed you were a lawyer. But you've been pretending all this time.

"Practicing law without a license is a criminal offense. I'm betting that's what Frank told you when you went to his office the night you returned from Seattle. I'm guessing that you begged him to keep your secret, but Frank is known for being very ethical and he must have told you that he couldn't do that. You knew your world would end once the cat was out of the bag, so you grabbed that sculpture, smashed Frank's head in, and killed your best friend."

"Even if what you say is true," Armstrong said. "I can never be prosecuted for Frank's murder. Thanks to you, the murder charges have been dismissed with prejudice."

"That's true, but you can still be charged with Tyler Harrison's murder."

"What makes you think I killed Harrison?"

"I couldn't figure out why you went through this charade of having amnesia. If you had gone to the party for your associate and said that Frank was coming later, you would never have been a suspect in Frank's murder. You would have had the perfect alibi. Then I realized that you had to disappear so you could drive to New York in Frank's car and kill Tyler Harrison."

"Why would I murder a New York attorney I'd never met?"

"Come on, Doug. Don't do this."

"No, Robin. I'm really curious."

"You knew that Harrison would hear about Frank's murder the next time he called him about the *Voss* case. Once that happened, there was a chance that he would tell the police that you never graduated from law school. That would reveal your motive to murder Frank, which no one could figure out otherwise. You couldn't take that chance.

"But, you had a problem: How would you get to New York without anyone knowing? You couldn't fly or take any other form of public transportation, because that would leave a paper trail. That's when you remembered that Frank's car was in the garage. Driving to New York and back would take days, and that presented another problem. How could you disappear for the time it took to drive to New York in Frank's car, murder Harrison, and drive back to Portland? Amnesia was the answer."

"Those are several clever deductions. Hercule Poirot would have been proud of you. Unfortunately, there's no way to prove I killed anyone in New York."

"Maybe, maybe not. Did you stop for gas? You must have. Did the gas station have a surveillance camera? You must have gotten food. Can a clerk identify you? This is the age of surveillance, Doug. There are eyes in the sky that see everything. And you'll still face criminal charges once I tell the authorities that you've never been an attorney, which will destroy you."

"Are you going to do that? You're my attorney."

"Was your attorney."

"So, you're going to go to the police?"

Robin shook her head. She looked sad. "I like you, Doug. Everyone likes you. So, I'm going to give you the opportunity to turn yourself in." Robin stood. "Get yourself a good attorney and have her negotiate a deal. Maybe she can even convince Vanessa to keep the fact that you've been lying about being a lawyer secret so you can keep your dignity."

"I'll give that suggestion serious thought."

"Don't think too long. If I haven't heard by tomorrow from you or your attorney that you've confessed, I'm going to the police with everything I know."

CHAPTER SIXTY-FOUR

The meeting with Doug Armstrong had drained Robin, and she was exhausted when she got home. She fixed supper, watched TV, and waited. At eleven, she turned off the set, turned out all the lights in her apartment, and went into the bedroom. At one in the morning, her doorbell rang.

Robin walked to the front door and looked through the peephole. When she saw who was at her door, she started to open it. As soon as the door began to open, Doug pulled out Frank Nylander's Glock.

"Freeze!" screamed Jeff, who had been hiding in the stairwell.

Doug swung toward Jeff, and Robin smashed her fist into Doug's gun hand, moving the barrel the inch she needed to force the bullet to go into the floor. Doug was turning back toward Robin when she buried her fist in his solar plexus. The blow drove the wind out of Armstrong. He dropped the Glock and collapsed in the hallway.

Robin kicked the gun away just as Jeff appeared beside her with his gun drawn. "Bag the Glock and call Carrie," Robin said as she knelt next to Armstrong. "You were going to kill me, weren't you,

Doug? Attempted murder is going to be easy to prove with two witnesses and one big fat motive."

Armstrong didn't say anything. When Jeff was satisfied that Armstrong had caught his breath, he pulled him to his feet and cuffed him. Doug stared at the floor as Robin and Jeff escorted him inside the apartment.

No one said anything until Carrie, Roger Dillon, Vanessa Cole, and two uniforms arrived twenty minutes later.

"Damn it, Robin," Carrie said after Robin explained what had happened, "Armstrong could have shot you."

"Unlike Blaine Hastings, Doug is soft and no athlete. I was counting on slow reflexes and a lack of conditioning. Plus, Jeff had the drop on him, and Jeff is a very good shot."

"It was still irresponsible."

Robin pulled up her sweatshirt to reveal a bulletproof vest. "I've been wearing this ever since I met with Doug at his office.

"What if he'd shot you in the head?"

"Then we wouldn't be having this conversation."

"You're an idiot."

"You would never have let me hold myself out as bait, but this was the only way to get Frank Nylander's Glock, the evidence you need to connect Armstrong to the murders of Tyler Harrison and Rex Kellerman. So, feel free to say thank you at any time."

"I agree with Carrie. You are an idiot," Vanessa said, "but thank you."

The officers escorted Doug Armstrong out of the apartment, and Vanessa and Carrie left shortly after. Robin shut the door and walked toward the bedroom. She didn't look happy.

"What's the matter?" Jeff asked.

"I know I shouldn't, but I feel awful. I really liked Doug, and I can't imagine what this will do to his wife."

"Tyler Harrison and Frank Nylander had wives, too."

Robin sighed. "You're right."

"Even though I agree with Carrie that you're an idiot, you've convinced me that you had to do what you did. Without the Glock, there's no case against Doug for killing Rex, and New York would never be able to prove Doug killed Tyler Harrison."

"I know. It's just that Doug had this great life, and so did Frank Nylander. Now everything is in ruins because of a one-in-a-million coincidence."

"He lied to everyone for years," Jeff said.

"But he was a good lawyer. He proved that over and over."

"There are rules, Robin. Our society depends on a respect for the law. We need to know that attorneys are educated and qualified. That's why we have a requirement that lawyers graduate from an accredited law school and pass the bar exam. We don't throw out all the rules because one phony lawyer does a good job."

"Do you know how many lawyers don't live up to the ethics of the profession and how many incompetents graduate from a law school and pass the bar? Doug did everything right, even if he didn't graduate from law school or pass the bar."

"Will remembering that Douglas Armstrong murdered Frank Nylander, Tyler Harrison, and Rex Kellerman, and was prepared to kill you, help you get over your post-arrest depression?" Jeff asked.

"Yeah, there is that."

"You liked Doug, and it made you feel good to save him when Rex went after him," Jeff said. "Now you know that Rex was right all along. You were duped, and it's hard for you to accept the fact that lovable Doug Armstrong is really a liar and a cold-blooded killer. Armstrong was wearing a mask all these years, and we're lucky you ripped it off."

"I guess."

"There's no guessing about it, so cheer up, and let's get some sleep. We're going to be spending a lot of time at the police station tomorrow, and I, for one, want to have a clear head when the cops grill us."

Robin wrapped her arms around Jeff. "I'm too wound up to sleep."

Jeff shook his head. "Does having someone try to shoot you always make you horny?"

"I'm two for two, so I'd say there's a good chance it does."

CHAPTER SIXTY-FIVE

"Hello, Herschel," Carrie Anders said. "I have good news for you."

"I have some news for you, too."

"Oh?"

"You first."

"Okay. We've solved the Tyler Harrison murder. An Oregon lawyer killed him, Frank Nylander, and Rex Kellerman. We have him in custody for the Portland murders."

"So, Norcross had nothing to do with Harrison's and Nylander's murders?"

"No."

"That's very interesting."

"Why?"

"I'll tell you after you tell me how you figured out who killed Harrison."

Detective Jacobs listened quietly while Carrie explained how Robin Lockwood figured out that Douglas Armstrong had killed Tyler Harrison.

"Has Armstrong confessed?" Jacobs asked.

"No. He lawyered up, but thanks to Robin, we have the Glock

that was used to kill Harrison and Kellerman, and we found a surveillance photo of Armstrong at a truck stop three-quarters of the way to Manhattan. So, we can give you everything you need to establish means, motive, and opportunity. I'll send everything to you as soon as you send me your paycheck for this month for doing all your work for you."

"The money should go to Robin Lockwood." Jacobs chuckled. "This is like one of those TV shows where the clueless cops are shown up by the brilliant amateur."

Carrie laughed. "I guess you're right. So, what's your news?"

"Ivar Gorski has disappeared. No one has seen him since our visit. And there's something else. I think you convinced Gorski that Norcross had Tyler Harrison murdered and was going to go after him, because someone shot and killed Marvin Turnbull, Norcross's CEO."

"Damn. Any leads on where Gorski's gone?"

"No. He hasn't used his passport, but we've done some digging, and he's got ties to the Russian Mafia—so he may be anywhere by now."

CHAPTER SIXTY-SIX

Robin was working on a brief in the Oregon Court of Appeals when her receptionist told her that Randi Stark wanted to see her.

"Good morning, Randi," Robin said when Stark was seated across from her in her office. "How are you feeling?"

"Really good."

"School's going well?"

"Yeah. I just got some grades back, and I aced three of my four tests."

"And you're sleeping well? No more nightmares?"

"Well, yeah, I'm still having trouble sleeping because of Blaine," Randi said.

"Are you seeing someone who can help with that, one of the therapists I suggested?"

"No. They're expensive. When the case is over, I'll try to get help if I'm still having problems."

"You'll definitely be able to afford it. So, why did you want to talk to me?"

"Annie told me what you said to her when you two met. She was really upset."

"What upset her?"

"You asked her if we faked the rape."

"I told her what Blaine's lawyer might argue."

"Why would he argue that?"

"You said that you found out about the party at the Oregon–PSU game from boys on the PSU team who played on your high school's team."

"That sounds right."

"They're the same boys who invited Blaine Hastings to the party. I know that because Jeff talked to them. They said they told you Blaine was going to be at the party."

"What if they did?"

"You told me that you didn't know Blaine would be at the party."

"I guess I forgot."

"When Blaine attacked me in the parking garage, he said the DNA evidence in his case had been rigged. I got the impression that he was implying that he got the idea for his scam from you."

"That's ridiculous. How would I know how to do something like that?"

"A nursing student would know all about DNA and what it can do. You're not stupid, Randi. You told me your GPA, remember. I think you're quite capable of coming up with a plan to frame Blaine."

Randi studied Robin for a moment. Then she leaned forward. "After Annie told me about your meeting, I researched the attorney–client privilege. It's pretty powerful. I even read about a case where a client told his lawyers that he'd murdered a person, and they couldn't tell anyone even though an innocent man was in prison for the murder. That was really awful." Randi looked directly at her attorney. "I definitely did not frame Blaine, but from what I read, if I did tell you I set him up, you and your investigator couldn't tell anyone that Blaine is innocent. Is that right?"

"That's correct."

"Even if I did frame Blaine—which I didn't—you shouldn't get upset. He deserves to be in jail."

"No one should be in jail for a crime they didn't commit."

"I agree. Ryan should never have been in jail. He wouldn't have been if Blaine hadn't framed him."

"Is this revenge for Ryan?"

"If I did frame Blaine, which I didn't, it would be justice for Ryan. But it would also be justice for me. Did anyone ever tell you why Ryan fought with Blaine?"

"Blaine insulted you and called you a slut."

"Yeah, he did after Ryan accused him of raping me."

"What?"

"I was pretty wild in high school. I had fake ID and I'd go to some pretty dicey bars. One night, I was with Ryan at one of them and we ran into Blaine. He came on to me and I blew him off. He couldn't take that, so he followed me into the parking lot when I went for a smoke."

Randi paused and looked at Robin. Her jaw quivered and her eyes teared up. She took a breath. "Have you ever been raped?"

"No."

"That's good, because you never forget it. Every time I have sex, I have to block out that bastard's face."

Randi took another breath. "He beat me and raped me in an alley. Ryan found me and took me home. The next day, he went after Blaine, and Blaine made sure Ryan went to jail to shut him up."

Again, Randi took a breath. "My conscience is clear. Blaine raped me and he's in prison for rape. And, by the way, I lied about the nightmares. Since the judge put that animal in a cage where he belongs, I've been sleeping like a baby.

"So, Robin, where do we go from here? Because, if you're not interested in representing me, I'm sure there are plenty of lawyers who would like a percentage of a multimillion-dollar verdict."

•   •   •

Robin was working the heavy bag with so much fury that she attracted Barry McGill's attention.

"Who you pounding on?" McGill asked.

Robin wrenched around, her fist cocked. "What?"

McGill nodded at the bag. "Who's that supposed to be?"

Robin dropped her fist. "Client trouble," she answered.

"Like the kind you had with Willis Goins?"

"Worse. There's someone in prison who might be serving time for something he didn't do."

"You sure the guy in prison is innocent?"

"He is and he isn't. It's complicated."

"Tell the DA."

"I can't. I'm forbidden by law to reveal anything a client tells me or anything I learn while I'm investigating the case. The attorney–client privilege has me handcuffed."

"That's got to weigh on you."

Robin's shoulders sagged. "Honestly, Barry, it's tearing me up."

McGill nodded at the heavy bag. "I can see that. Those bags are expensive."

Robin flashed a sad smile. "Sorry."

McGill shook his head. "I don't envy you. When I was boxing, I could take care of my problems with a left hook."

"The law isn't as simple as boxing."

"I get that. Well, I'll let you get back to work." He pointed at the bag. "Go easy on my friend."

As soon as McGill walked away, Robin squared up, but her anger had ebbed while she was talking with Barry and she didn't feel like working out anymore. After a few more halfhearted swings at the heavy bag, Robin headed for the locker room.

Robin didn't know what to do, but there was someone she knew who might. As soon as she was home, Robin checked the time in

Athens and called the hotel where Regina Barrister was staying. Stanley Cloud answered the phone.

"Hi, Judge, is Regina there?"

"Yeah. We're just getting ready to go out."

"I've got a problem at work and I hoped she could advise me on what to do. Do you think she's up for that?"

"Her meds have been working pretty well, so I think she'll be able to help you. Let me get her."

"How's Greece?" Robin asked a minute later when Regina took the call.

"We toured the islands. It was wonderful. Santorini is the most romantic spot on earth."

Robin laughed.

"Stanley says you have a problem at work."

"This is attorney–client stuff, so you can't discuss it with anyone, including Stanley."

"We're still law partners, and I still remember my ethics rules. So, shoot."

Robin told her about the *Hastings* case and Randi's confession that she had framed Hastings.

"But he did rape her in high school, and I believe that Hastings framed Ryan and coerced or paid his friends to lie. And that may have led to Ryan's death," Robin told Regina. "And he probably raped Julie Angstrom in eighth grade and other women we don't know about."

"You've got a very interesting dilemma, don't you?"

"You hit the nail directly on the head. What should I do?"

"Nothing. You can't disclose what Stark told you. And did she really tell you anything? She never admitted to framing Blaine, did she?"

Robin thought about that. "No," she said a few moments later. "She kept saying that she did not frame him."

"A bad person is in jail, where he belongs. I wouldn't lose any sleep over it."

"I can't keep representing Randi. Not now."

"Probably not."

Robin was quiet, and Regina let her think.

"You've been a big help. Go enjoy Athens and send more postcards."

CHAPTER SIXTY-SEVEN

Marsha took her seat on the other side of the glass from Doug. She hadn't slept well in weeks. The only way she could get any rest was if she took medication. And she'd lost weight. Doug stared at her for a few moments. Then he raised the receiver that was attached to the concrete wall on his side of the noncontact visiting room.

"I'm so sorry," Doug said. Tears trickled down his cheeks.

Marsha stared at them, at a loss for what to say.

"I did it for us, Marsha. I did it because I love you and I couldn't lose you."

"You . . . you killed three people," she said.

"I killed Rex Kellerman because of what he did to you and tried to do to me."

"What did Frank do? He was your best friend. How many times have you told me that you owed him everything?"

"Frank would have ruined our lives," Doug said. "I begged him to let it lie. I reminded him of everything we'd built together, but he said I had to go to the bar and tell them. I would have been disgraced and disbarred. We would have been sued by every client whose case we lost. We would have had to give up our home, all of our savings. And I could have gone to prison for pretending to be a lawyer. Worst of all, I would have lost you."

"I would never have deserted you, Doug. I love you. I would have stood by you."

"You say that now."

"I'm here for you now."

Doug looked down. "I don't want you to be here for me. I want you to file for divorce. I've thought about this a lot, Marsha. You're young, you're beautiful and smart. I don't want you wasting your life out of a misguided sense of loyalty."

Doug looked through the glass. Marsha had never seen anyone look as sad as Doug.

"This is our reality now," he said. "I'm never getting out of prison, not ever. I don't want you sitting by yourself in some cheap apartment for the rest of your life, waiting for the next visiting day at the Oregon State Penitentiary. You have to think of me as if I died, because it will be the same thing."

Doug choked up. "I ruined my life thirty years ago when I made my decision to lie about graduating from law school," Doug said when he regained his composure. "I couldn't admit that I'd failed, and I never imagined that there would be consequences. I fooled myself then, but I'm facing reality now, and you have to do the same thing."

Marsha looked sick.

"You have to leave me. If you don't, I'll find a way to kill myself. If I don't have the nerve to commit suicide, I'll get a prisoner to do it." Doug smiled. "Finding someone who'll kill me for a price shouldn't be hard where I'm going."

"Oh, Doug. Please don't say that."

"Then promise me that you'll never visit me again; that you'll get a divorce and find someone who is worthy of you. I've never been. You should be able to see that now." Doug pressed his hand to the glass.

Marsha started to raise her hand to cover his, but she stopped halfway. Then she looked into Doug's eyes, broke into tears, and ran away.

Doug watched her go until she disappeared from view. The phone Marsha had held dropped to the end of its cord. It swayed back and forth like a pendulum until the last evidence that the woman he'd loved and killed for had ever been on the other side of the bulletproof glass stopped moving.

Doug waited until he had regained his composure before he signaled for the guard. When the door to the cell block opened, Doug stood slowly, his shoulders slumped, bent slightly, walking like a much older man.

CHAPTER SIXTY-EIGHT

Being responsible for sending a client to prison should have had an adverse effect on a criminal lawyer's business, but Robin's caseload increased dramatically with every news story about the *Armstrong* case—proving the old adage that there is no such thing as bad publicity.

Robin was so busy that she rarely thought about Randi Stark or Blaine Hastings. She'd told Randi that she did not want to represent her anymore, and she'd given her the names of several excellent attorneys who could handle her suit against Blaine, so she didn't have to think about the case anymore.

Jeff was bound by the attorney–client privilege because he was an agent of the firm. She had told him why she dropped Randi as a client. He could see that she was troubled, and he tried to make Robin feel better by pointing out that Hastings deserved to be in prison, but Robin was still troubled.

Fall was starting to morph into winter on a dark November day when Robin's receptionist told her that Amanda Jaffe, a well-known Oregon criminal defense attorney, was in the waiting room. Jaffe was tall and athletic with high cheekbones, clear blue eyes, and black hair that tumbled over broad shoulders that were sculpted during years of high-level competitive swimming. Robin had gotten to know and respect Amanda when they'd represented clients in a monthlong federal drug conspiracy case.

"What's up?" Robin asked when Amanda was seated.

"I was just hired by a former client of yours, Randi Stark."

Robin stopped smiling. "Is this the civil suit against Blaine Hastings?"

"Yes."

"I'll have the files sent over to you."

"Can you tell me why you got off the case?"

"No."

Amanda waited for an explanation, then realized that none would be forthcoming. "Have you heard about Hastings's parents?"

"I've tuned out the case since I stopped representing Randi. What happened?"

"Senior entered a plea to obstruction of justice for his hand in the DNA scam. Vanessa dropped the case against Mrs. Hastings in exchange for the plea. Senior will go to jail, but he'll probably get an early parole. Junior hasn't been sentenced yet, because he was on the run—but he'll be back in court next week, and I expect Judge Redding is going to throw the book at him for the rape and for jumping bail."

Robin nodded but didn't say anything.

Amanda cocked her head. "What's troubling you? Is it something I need to know to represent Randi?"

Robin shook her head. "Go full bore for Randi. She deserves to be represented by a good lawyer. If you win, don't worry. Justice will be served."

CHAPTER SIXTY-NINE

Snow was a rare sight in the Willamette Valley, but the last days of December had brought three days of freezing temperatures accompanied by a light dusting of snow to downtown Portland. Robin had grown up in the Midwest, so the weather didn't bother her and was a pale reminder of the mountain-high snowdrifts and blustery winter storms of her youth.

Robin was on her way to the Pacific Northwest Bank building to negotiate a case. As she walked into the lobby, she remembered that this building had once housed the law firm of Nylander & Armstrong. Robin looked at her phone. She was early for her meeting. On a whim, she pressed the button for the eleventh floor. When she got out of the elevator, she saw someone walking out of the insurance company offices on one side of the corridor. When she looked in the other direction, she saw glass doors, but she did not see any writing on them that indicated that law had once been practiced behind them.

Robin peered through the glass. There was nothing to see: no serious associates hustling between the offices, no desks, chairs, or computers. What had once been the scene of merry chaos was now inhabited only by ghosts.

Robin stared for a moment more before taking a deep breath and walking back to the elevator.

ACKNOWLEDGMENTS

As usual, I had a lot of help in writing and researching this novel. I want to thank Earl S. Ward, for helping me understand the way probalistic genotyping is used in connection with DNA evidence and Dennis Balske, for providing me with cases that discussed a fascinating legal issue.

My editor, Keith Kahla, helped turn my initial flawed efforts into a finished product that I hope readers found entertaining. Thanks also for the fantastic support I received from Hector DeJean, Martin Quinn, Alice Pfeifer, Sally Richardson, Eliani Torres, Ken Silver, and David Rotstein at St. Martin's.

Thanks, as always, to my amazing agent, Jennifer Weltz, and everyone else at the Jean V. Naggar Literary Agency. You are the best.

Thanks, too, to the home team, Ami, Andy, Daniel, Amanda, Loots, Marissa, and my wife, Melanie Nelson, who helped me find happiness again.